D0338418

The Fourth Man

The Fourth Man

K. O. Dahl

Thomas Dunne Books
ST. MARTIN'S MINOTAUR
NEW YORK

This is a work of fiction. All of the characters, organizations, and events portrayed in this novel are either products of the author's imagination or are used fictitiously.

THOMAS DUNNE BOOKS.
An imprint of St. Martin's Press.

www.thomasdunnebooks.com
www.minotaurbooks.com

Library of Congress Cataloging-in-Publication Data

Dahl, Kjell Ola, 1958–
[Fjerde raneren. English]
The fourth man / K. O. Dahl.—1st U.S. ed.
p. cm.
ISBN-13: 978-0-312-37569-0
ISBN-10: 0-312-37569-7
I. Title.
PT8951.14.A443 F5413 2007b
839.82'38—dc22 2007042565

First published as *Fjerde raneren* in Norway by Kagge Forlag

First U.S. Edition: March 2008

10 9 8 7 6 5 4 3 2 1

There will be time to murder and create
And time for all the works and days of hands
That lift and drop a question on your plate;
Time for you and time for me,
And time yet for a hundred indecisions
And for a hundred visions and revisions,
Before the taking of a toast and tea.

In the room the women come and go
Talking of Michelangelo.

T. S. ELIOT
(from *The Love Song of J. Alfred Prufrock*)

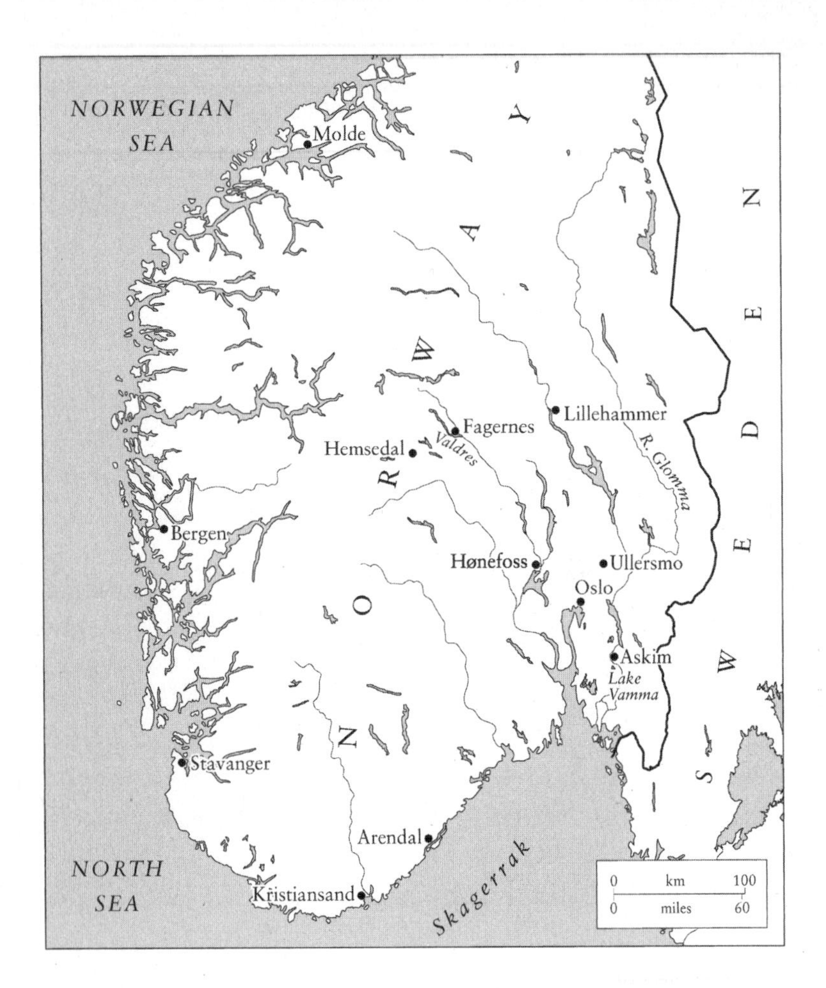

NORWEGIAN SEA
NORTH SEA
Skagerrak
NORWAY
SWEDEN
Molde
Lillehammer
Fagernes
Hemsedal
Valdres
R. Glomma
Bergen
Hønefoss
Ullersmo
Oslo
Askim
Lake Vamma
Stavanger
Arendal
Kristiansand
0 km 100
0 miles 60

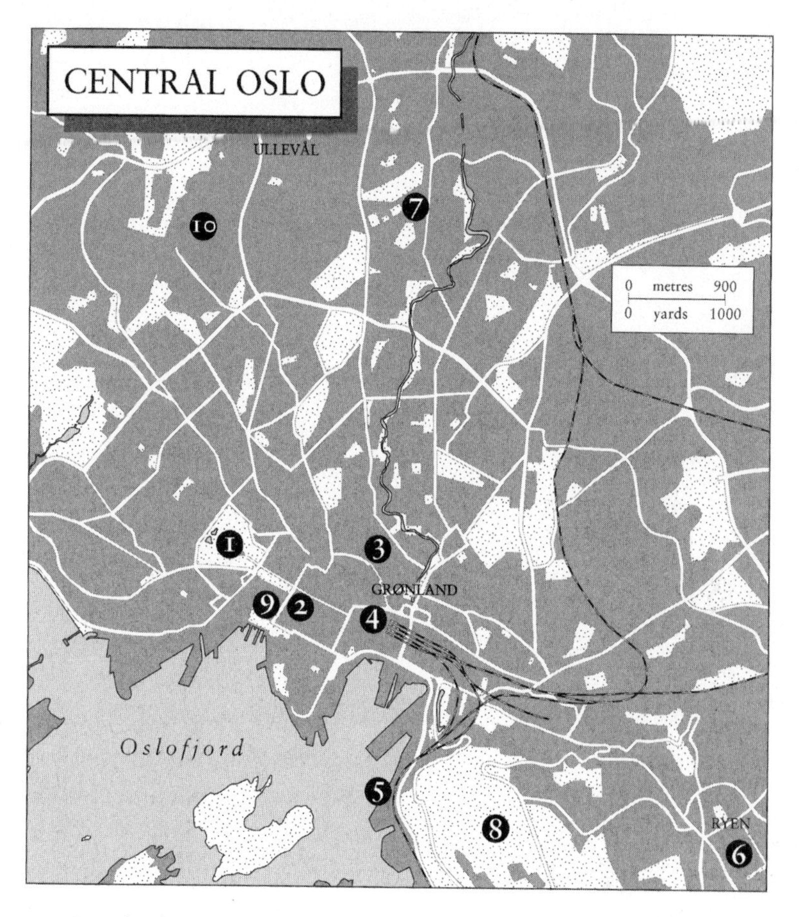

1 Royal Palace and Gardens
2 Stortinget (Parliament)
3 Badir's shop in Torggata
4 Oslo Central Station
5 Lohavna (where the first body is found)
6 Havreveien (home address of Frank Frølich)
7 Bergensgata (home address of Gunnarstranda)
8 Ekeberg Ridge
9 City Hall
10 Blinden University

PART ONE

Pas de Deux

I

Two men had stopped outside the gate. Time to check them out. Frank Frølich skipped down the last two steps, went through the gateway, past the two men and out into the street. They didn't react. He thought: *They should have reacted. Why didn't they react?* He shoved his hands deep into his jacket pockets and with lowered eyes continued walking. In the window of the fishmonger's, a man was shovelling ice into a polystyrene box. He shot a quick glance back over his shoulder. Neither of the men was taking any notice. They were still fidgeting with their rosary beads. One of them said something and both burst into laughter.

A rusty cycle stand creaked. A woman was pushing her bicycle into it. She walked past the boxes of vegetables on display. She opened the door to Badir's shop. The bell over the door jingled. The door closed behind her.

Frank Frølich felt as though some wild beast were gnawing at his stomach: a customer in the shop? Uh-oh. That wasn't supposed to happen at all.

He leapt into the road. A car braked sharply. The car behind hooted its horn and almost crashed into it. Frank Frølich ran up the pavement. He passed the bicycle, the boxes of mushrooms, grapes, lettuce and peppers – went through the door into the shop, which smelt like a rotten-apple cellar with the added sickly-sweet odour of oil.

The woman was alone in the shop. She had a shopping basket hung over her arm and was walking slowly between two lines of food shelves. There was no one else in sight. No one was sitting by the cash till. The curtain in the doorway behind the cash machine flapped gently.

The woman was short in stature. Her black hair was gathered at the back of her head. She was wearing jeans and a cut-off jacket. A small rucksack swung from her shoulder. Black gloves on her hands, fingers clutching a tin can. She was reading the label.

Frank Frølich was two metres away when it happened. He glanced to his left. Through the shop window he saw the police car on the other side of the street. They had started.

Suddenly he launched himself at her and dragged her down with him. Half a second later there was a screech of brakes. The man who sprang across the counter was one of the two with the rosary beads. Now he was holding a gun. A shot was fired. There was a jangle of broken glass. The display case containing tobacco and cigarettes tipped over. Another shot was fired. And then chaos. Sirens. Barking voices. Clattering heels. The noise of a door and glass breaking, shattering in a never-ending stream. The woman lay still beneath him. Cigarette packets showered down onto them. She was probably around thirty years of age, smelling of perfume. Her blue eyes glinted like sapphires. Finally Frank Frølich managed to tear his eyes away. Then he discovered her hands. Fascinated, he lay watching them industriously working away. Long fingers clad in leather, small hands automatically stuffing packets of cigarettes into her rucksack, which had come loose in the fall. Then he became aware of the silence. There was a draught from the door and window.

'Frølich?' The voice came from a megaphone.

'Here!'

'Is the woman all right?'

'Yes.'

'You're a policeman,' the woman whispered. She cleared her throat to speak.

He nodded and finally let her go.

'Wouldn't be a smart idea to pinch anything then?'

He shook his head, fascinated yet again by how efficiently the small hands took the cigarettes out of the rucksack. He rose to his knees.

They stood there looking at each other. She was attractive in a vulnerable sort of way; there was something about her mouth.

'Sorry,' he mumbled. 'This shouldn't have happened. Someone should have stopped you. Long before you came into the shop.'

She continued to stare.

'There was a foul-up somewhere.'

She nodded.

'Are you all right?'

She nodded again, put her arms to her sides. As yet he hadn't looked around him, gained an overview of the situation. He heard the cold sound of flexi-cuffs being tightened around wrists and the curses from one of the men arrested. *That's what it's come to*, he thought. *I rely on others.*

'May I take your name?' he asked in an unemotional voice.

'Have I done something wrong?'

'No, but you were here. Now you're a witness.'

The autumn days passed. A gloom pervaded the daylight hours and time crystallized into work: larceny – petty and grand, murders, suicides, robberies and domestic violence; everyday life – a series of incidents, some of which make an impression, while most are soon forgotten. Your consciousness is trained to repress. You crave a holiday, two weeks on a Greek island in the summer or, slightly shorter-term, a long weekend on the ferry to Denmark. Drinking, shouting, laughing, homing in on a woman with just the right kind of husky laugh, who has warm eyes and thinks pointed shoes are absolutely great. But until that happens: days like photographic slides – images which flicker for a few seconds before disappearing, some easier to remember than others, but then those disappear too. Not that he thought any more about her. Or perhaps he did? Perhaps he occasionally remembered the sapphire blue eyes, or the feeling of her body pressed against his – there on the floor of Badir's shop. Or the man who was now slowly but surely being dragged through the mill of penal indictment, soon to be convicted of the organized smuggling of meat and cigarettes, then resisting arrest, threatening behaviour, illegal possession of a weapon and so on.

Soon to swell the ranks of those waiting for an available cell to serve their term. Despite such thoughts crossing his mind, there was one thing Frank Frølich was pretty sure about, and that was he would never see her again.

It happened one rainy afternoon in late October. Darkness was drawing in; a cold wind was blowing up Grensen in Oslo city centre. The wind caught hold of people's clothing, replicating Munch's paintings: shadows of figures ducking away from the driving rain, huddling up, using their umbrellas as shields or – if they didn't have an umbrella – thrusting their hands into their pockets and sprinting through the rain in search of a protective ledge or awning. The wet tarmac stole the last of the daylight, and the water trickling into the tramlines reflected the neon glare. Frank Frølich had finished work and was feeling hungry. Accordingly, he made for Kafé Norrøna. The room smelt of hot chocolate with cream. He immediately wanted some and queued up. In front of the cash till, he changed his mind and asked what the soup of the day was.

'Italian. Minestrone.' The serving lady was the impatient kind, sour expression and limp posture.

He took his tray of hot soup, a roll and a glass of water. Found a place by the window, eased himself onto the stool and stared out at the people hurrying down Grensen with upturned collars. A woman rested her chin on the lapels of her jacket to keep it closed. The rain worsened. The reflections of car lights and flashing neon signs swept across house walls. People in the street resembled cowering children, hiding from a booming voice somewhere above.

'Hello.'

Frank Frølich put down his spoon and turned round. There was something familiar about her face. About thirty years of age, he thought. She had black hair, partly covered by a woolly hat, held in place like a beret. Her complexion was pale, her lips were bright red and her eyebrows formed sharp angles, two inverted Vs high on her forehead.

Classy, he thought. It struck him that she wouldn't have been out of place in a black-and-white still from a forties film. She was wearing a long, clinging woollen skirt and short jacket. Her outfit emphasized her figure – hips, waist and shoulders.

'Torggata,' she said, tilting her head, becoming a little impatient at his slow-wittedness. 'Marlboro, Prince, cigarettes.'

Then he remembered: the eyes and especially her mouth. Which lent her an air of vulnerability. But the small wrinkles around her mouth told him she was older than he had at first believed. Instinctively, he searched for the blue of her eyes – without being able to find it immediately. Must be the light, he thought, must be the harsh neon light which deadened the blue. The lightbulbs in Badir's shop must have been the regular variety.

'You let me go.'

He suddenly felt uneasy and looked for ways out. Not much was left of the soup and he had paid. Something about this encounter put him on edge; the situation activated a slumbering sensation at the back of his mind. He would have to rebuff her approach, but he was slightly reluctant. She was standing quite close to him, looking into his eyes. It would be unpleasant turning his back on her. He said: 'My pleasure. You hadn't done anything wrong.'

'You don't think so?'

'Excuse me?'

'I took three packets of Marlboro and a Snickers bar.'

He pushed his bowl away. 'So you're a thief, then.'

'You saw, didn't you?'

'Saw what?' He put on his jacket and patted his pocket to check he had his wallet.

'You saw me.'

For a brief moment, the words unsettled him. *You saw me.* She could have expressed herself differently, but this was a message which he could not misunderstand. It was an attempt to present herself not just as an object for his attention, but to suggest she owed him a favour because he had done something for her, something that would have to remain a secret.

'I have to go,' he announced. 'All the best . . .' He reflected. Her name. She had told him her name. He had even made a mental note of it. In the nick of time the name emerged in his consciousness. He said: '. . . Have a nice evening, Elisabeth.'

He stood still for a few seconds as the glass door slid to behind him. The wind had dropped a little, but the rain was still pouring down. Buttoning his jacket, he shook himself, as if to rid himself of the discomfiture of the incident. He took the few metres to the underpass leading to the Metro at a brisk pace. Here, he went into his usual Metro trance to the accompaniment of the smell of refuse, used air, wet woollens, autumn and influenza; elderly women ran gloved fingers under their noses; men raised their eyes to God in a quiet prayer to be spared another bout of angina, here in this tight scrum of humanity in which everyone was blind to each other's existence. He squeezed back against the glass wall of the Metro carriage, touched the condensation on the glass; only to wake from the trance when the doors shut at Manglerud and the creature of habit in him liberated itself from its corner to step closer to the doors as the train braked on its approach to Ryen station. The doors were two metal lips which opened, ready to spit him out. At this altitude, the rain had turned into the autumn's first sleet showers. Car headlights shone on the tarmac of the ring road and were devoured by the blackness. He trudged up the hill as cars sped by.

Something must have caught his attention, a sound or a shadow behaving differently, as he approached the entrance to his flat. He stopped and turned. The street light by the petrol station was directly behind her, outlining her silhouette in yellow light. She stood still. He stood still. They were alert to each other's every move. Her hands deep in the pockets of the short jacket and her facial expression in shadow. Her hair cascaded down onto her shoulders, with the light from the street lamp like an aura above the woolly hat, the tight jacket and the skirt covering her knees.

It was just the two of them – in the dark. No one else around. The remote drone of the traffic. A street lamp buzzed. He walked towards her with determined steps. She didn't move. He walked into the road and then around her, forcing her to follow him with her eyes and turn towards the light so that he could see her face.

They were staring into each other's eyes throughout this whole carousel movement. He detected something in her gaze: an energy, something he couldn't define in words, something it was difficult to confront without speaking. 'Are you following me?'

'You'd rather I didn't?'

The response took his breath away – again.

Finally she lowered her gaze. 'You saw me,' she said.

Those three words again. 'And?' he said.

They stood close to each other. He had gone right up to her but she hadn't budged. He could feel the warmth of her breath on his cheek.

She took his hands in hers.

His mind froze. He cleared his throat, but didn't move. She had heavy eyelids and long, curly eyelashes. At the end of each lash a tiny drop of condensation had gathered. Her breath streamed like mist from between the half-open lips, caressing his cheeks before it dissipated. As she spoke, the words nestled against his cheeks.

'What did you say?' was as much as his voice could manage. His mouth was only a few centimetres from hers as she softly whispered: 'I forget no one if I kiss you.'

Then he released his hands and clasped her slender face between them.

Before leaving, she stood for a long time in the shower. He lay on his back in bed listening to the murmur of the water.

When she closed the front door behind her, it was four o'clock in the morning. Then he got up and went into the bathroom. He stood with his forehead against the tiled wall as the water stroked his shoulders. His mind was on the hours that had passed. The way his body towered over hers. The way she had held his gaze as he breathed in again and again, then let it out loudly, breathing in again and again, letting it out loudly again and again. The beads of sweat between her breasts, reflecting thousands of facets. The way her soft breasts rose and fell to the rhythm of her breathing before he thrust the breath out of her. The desire raw, untamed, hungry – the kind that leaves in its wake guilt, shame, abortions, fatherless children, HIV. He could still feel the pressure of her fingers as she grabbed him hard around the waist, ten nails digging into him. She wanted more, yet had less breath because she could see the countdown flicker behind his eyelids.

Afterwards, alone, his head pressed against the tiles: Frank Frølich twists the tap to red and allows himself to be scalded by boiling-hot water – recalling the strange tattoo on her hip as she straddles him backwards. He cannot picture this without becoming aroused yet again, feeling the urge to do it once more, knowing that if she had walked in through the door at that moment, he would have thrown her down on the bathroom floor, or in there, over the desk – and he would have been unstoppable.

Such thoughts are a virus. In the end they disappear, but it takes time. Eventually everything passes. Three days, possibly four, a week – then the thoughts release their grip. In the end your body is left numb and begins to function normally, glad that it is over.

Six days went by. He was back in shape. But then the mobile phone on his desk bleeped. One message. He read it. A single word: *Come!*

He automatically tapped in the sender's number and sent it off to enquiries. His phone bleeped again. Another message. This time with the sender's name and address: *Elisabeth Faremo.*

Frank Frølich sat down. His body was tingling. He lifted his hand. It wasn't shaking. Nevertheless, this woman had thrown a switch. He had assumed he was symptom-free and unaffected, assumed he had come to terms with the intoxication. But no. Bang. Feverish. Unable to think. A bundle of pent-up energy. He was charged up. As a result of one solitary word!

He sat looking at the small phone with its illuminated display. It began to vibrate in his hand. The phone rang. The same number.

'Hi, Elisabeth,' he said and was surprised at the clarity of his voice.

Two seconds of silence. Long enough for him to think: *Now she knows I have looked up her telephone number. She knows the effect she has on me, she knows she can throw a switch and raise my temperature to fever pitch by keying in a message.* But then came the gentle voice he had not heard for several days: 'Where are you?'

'At work.'

'Where?'

'Police HQ, Grønland.'

'Oh.'

It was his turn to speak. He cleared his throat, but he had hardly drawn breath before she interrupted: 'Don't you have a break soon?'

'What's the time?' he asked, looking at the place where the clock had been that had hung over the door until a few weeks ago but was no longer there. Just two wires protruding from the wall.

'No idea. Around lunchtime.'

'Where shall I pick you up?'

'Are you driving?'

'Yes.'

'I'll be at Lisa Kristoffersens plass, near Voldsløkka.'

'In ten minutes.'

He couldn't think. No room in his head for anything but images: the curve of her back, the roundness of her hips, the black hair flowing across the pillow – the sapphire-blue stare.

He threw on his jacket and left. Down the stairs and into the street. He started the car and drove off. What was the time? He didn't have a clue. He didn't give a shit about anything in the world, concentrated simply on not hitting pedestrians. Accelerated. As he was driving down Stavangergata she appeared from nowhere, came walking towards him on the pavement. With her came the scent of late autumn, perfume and throat lozenges. She took a seat without uttering a word.

He fixed his eyes on the wing mirror. Breathing normally, despite her sweet fragrance. Cold, controlled check of the mirror.

He waited until the road was clear, then signalled and drove off – conscious of her constant gaze, directed at his impassive profile. She wriggled out of her lined brown leather jacket.

Finally, after passing the turn-off for Nydalen, she broke the silence: 'Aren't you happy to see me?'

He stole a furtive glance at her. She was feline. Two huge blue eyes with large pupils, the look of a cat. He could feel his pulse racing. Temples pounding. But he maintained his mask. 'Of course I am.'

'You don't say anything.'

Her hand over his, on the gear stick. He glanced down at the hand – the fingers, glanced at her again. 'Hi. Nice to see you again.' The words stuck in his throat. He was driving towards Kjelsås, Brekke and Maridalen.

What am I doing?

Lips stroking his cheek. The hand that slipped off his and under his jacket. It was as if she had filled a recently tuned engine with high-octane fuel and pressed START. His heart was beating so fast and so hard that the blood in his ears was thumping. Trees on both sides. He slowed down, drove into the lay-by, over to the copse, away from the road. Came to a halt. Put the car in neutral and let the engine idle. As he snatched another sidelong glimpse, she covered his lips with hers.

When she spoke, it was the first time for an hour: 'Would you mind driving me somewhere?'

'Where?'

'Blindern.'

'What are you going to do there?'

Wrong question. Her eyes narrowed.

The atmosphere melted away.

He breathed in and stared at the trees outside – collected himself to look at her again. The daggers in her eyes had changed into a kind of preoccupied sheen – she regarded him from inside a private room where she did not want to share anything with him. The voice from a cool, smiling mouth: 'I'm going to look for a job.'

He pulled into the kerb and dropped her off in Moltke Moes vei. He sat watching her. A tiny amount of snow had fallen overnight; he noticed it now for the first time. The snow had melted into a slush in which her footsteps left large puddles. The woman who until a short time ago had been a very part of him was now reduced to a slight figure lifting her feet much like a cat not wanting to get its paws wet. Is it possible? *Is this small stooped figure, a mere nobody wrapped in cotton, wool and skin, is this the creature who has me totally in her power, who makes my heart pound so hard that I feel my chest will explode?*

Drive! Far away! After a couple of weeks she will be forgotten, airbrushed out. But as the slender form disappeared into the Niels Henrik Abel building he switched off the engine, opened the car door and got out. He followed her. *Why I am doing this?*

Because I want to know more about her.

She had continued through the building to the other side. He followed fifty metres behind her. A mini-tractor came across the snow-covered flagstones. He moved to the side and walked past students conversing in low voices in twos and threes. She went into the Sophus Bugge building. He stopped a good way behind her, observing her through the high windows as she disappeared into an auditorium.

If she was a student, what was she studying? He entered the building through the heavy doors.

He walked towards the broad door leading into the auditorium. Reidun Vestli's name dominated the timetable. It was she who was now giving the lecture.

He took a seat outside and picked up a newspaper lying there. He was plagued by doubt. What would he do if she came out and saw him?

He closed his eyes. *I'll tell her straight. I'll tell her it isn't enough to have casual sex in a parked car – I want to know who she is, what is going on in her mind, why she does what she does . . .*

Do you yourself know why you do what you do?

Frank Frølich sat staring blindly at the front page of the newspaper. A photograph of a military vehicle. Civilians murdered.

An incident which engaged people's attention all over the world. *Dagsavisen* had given it front-page status believing that he would care, would be lured into immersing himself in all the verbiage they managed to spawn about this incident. But he didn't care. Nothing at all was of any significance now, nothing, except for Elisabeth, this – from where he stood – completely anonymous and rather delicate woman with the pale face, red lips and eyes of a blue he had never seen before. Her existence meant something, meant a great deal. He had no idea why. He only knew that she did something to him – physically, but also mentally, something which aroused a craving in him he had only read about, heard about, something he had never given credence to – and now he was spying on her.

He had met her three times.

That phone message: *Come!* His brain was immediately empty of all other images except those of her body – her lips, her eyes. And barely half an hour later they were caught up in a sexual intensity he had seldom experienced the like of before. *The word – did she know what she had set in motion? Was she doing it on purpose?*

At last the door opened. Out streamed a faceless mass of students. Most wearing their outdoor clothes. He looked at his watch. It was four o'clock. The lecture was over. He had butterflies in his stomach. *What if she sees me?*

There were fewer and fewer students emerging now. Soon there wouldn't be any more. Had she passed him?

Slowly Frank Frølich stood up. He walked warily towards the door and opened it.

He was at the top end of the auditorium, behind the rows of chairs looking down on the lectern. There were two people down there. Elisabeth was one of them. The other woman was talking to her in a soft voice. She was in her fifties with black hair in a kind of page-boy cut, wearing a long black dress.

They were standing very close to each other. They may have been very good friends. They could have been mother and daughter. But mothers don't caress their daughters like that.

He was spotted.

The two women looked up at him. Both very calm, as if they were politely waiting for him to retreat. He searched for something in Elisabeth's eyes, but he found no signs of recognition, no suggestion of guilt, no shame, nothing.

They stood like that for several seconds, three pairs of eyes meeting across rows of chairs, until he backed out and left.

2

From time to time he tried to see himself from the outside. Focus on the subject – which caused his cheeks to burn with anger and shame. His brain dominated by one single desire: to rewind and edit out everything, to escape such an embarrassing, abject condition. So, Elisabeth was no more than a student involved with a lecturer – who, furthermore, was a woman. Frank Frølich made up his mind: never again. Never go near her again.

But the rational voice inside him protested. Why? Because she is dangerous? Bisexual? Mysterious? Because she had pretended not to know him? Because he had been snubbed in such an ignominious way?

No, thought the scorned voice, not to be silenced. It was because she had put him in a fever. Because she had rendered him incapable of action, and weak – turned him to jelly.

When she rang him next time he didn't answer. He sat there with the mobile phone in his hand. It vibrated as if a little heart was beating inside it. Her name glowed in the display. But he didn't stir. Ignored it every time.

Soon she began to ring him at home.

It was a farce. Running to the phone and reading the name in the display. Not answering it if it was her. Definitely not touching the phone if it was an anonymous number. Thus he sat at home late one evening letting the phone ring and ring. He didn't get up because it was her calling. That was how much power she had over him – even when he was alone, he struggled to extricate himself.

A week went by. Frank Frølich felt that the fever had almost run its course. It was Thursday afternoon now. He had finished work, endured the mind-numbing journey on the Metro as usual and strolled up to the front door. One of the elderly ladies living on the seventh floor of his block was going through her post box in the entrance hall. Frølich was still in his Metro state. He held open the lift door for the stooped woman, who was no different from all the other stooped women he occasionally met in the lift. As the door closed he pressed the button. He stared vacantly in front of him at the floor dividers on his way up.

He got out of the lift.

He heard the bump as it continued on its way upwards while he fumbled in his pocket for his keys.

He froze.

A tiny detail about the front door stopped him in his tracks. The peep hole in the door glowed yellow. It was usually dark. Had he forgotten to switch off the light in the hall this morning?

Finally, he slipped the key into the lock, hesitated, then turned it. The door opened without a sound. He sidled in. Closed the door quietly behind him. Held his breath. The lights in the hall, that was one thing, but the door to the living room ajar – that was quite another.

This moment was to imprint itself on his consciousness ever after.

Someone was in his flat.

He stood still, mulling the notion over and over again as his body slowly went numb, his mouth dried and he lost sensation in his hands. Without considering what he was doing, he noiselessly glided two metres across the floor to the living room door. He was no longer in control. It was as if he was watching himself from the outside: he saw himself lift one hand and cautiously place it on the door and push it open.

Sharp intake of breath. His body still numb, as though from shock.

She was sitting with her back to him. On the floor. Undressed, wearing only turquoise underwear. The delicate back bent forwards. Two prominent birthmarks beside her spine. From a distance her tattoo looked like a long, dark pen stroke. She was sitting cross-legged in front of the record player and stereo unit. She couldn't hear him. Over her ears she wore his new headphones. The music in the room sounded like wind rustling dried leaves. She seemed very much at home. She had intruded into his space and then encapsulated herself in her own world. CDs and LPs were strewn across the floor.

His emotions formed a knot in his stomach: tension, fury, curiosity. She had forced her way into his flat – his mind raced. One thing was the physical intrusion – the practical side, her 'actually doing it'. The other was the mental intrusion, forcing her way into his innermost sanctuary, his home – simply performing this act without asking him, usurping the right. He was unable to break the spell. A flood of emotions had him in thrall.

Perhaps it was the draught from the door, perhaps a glint in the glass door of the cabinet, but suddenly she gave a start, ripped off the headset and jumped up.

'My God, you gave me a fright!'

The next moment she was close to him. 'Hi.'

'Hi to you, too.'

She looked up, sensed the agitation, the well of conflicting feelings besetting him.

'Aren't you just a tiny bit . . . happy?'

'How did you get in?'

'I borrowed a key.'

'Borrowed a key?'

'When I was here last.'

'So you're a thief?'

An echo of an earlier conversation. Utterly composed, she looked into his eyes and said: 'You knew, didn't you?' Provocatively at first, but then she lowered her gaze – as if ashamed.

As if, he thought repeatedly: *As if*!

'I borrowed it. From the bowl in the kitchen.'

'Borrowed the key?'

'Are you annoyed?'

'Did you take the key from my kitchen last time you were here – without mentioning it to me?'

'You're annoyed.'

'Far from it.'

'You don't like this kind of surprise?'

'I'm not sure if "like" is the right word.'

'I meant well, though.'

'Why aren't you wearing more clothes?'

Her voice darkened. 'So you can see me better.' She feigned a giggle when he didn't respond.

There was an inherent vulnerability in her awkwardness. But she sensed that he noticed, and smothered this mental nakedness in a tighter embrace, quickly adding: 'No, it wasn't that. I took a shower. I was so cold.' She tugged at his body and stiffened slightly when she felt his reluctance. 'I know it was wrong. Borrowing the key without asking. Sorry.'

She let go of him and marched through the room, towards the kitchen.

Her jacket was on the chair under the window. She bent down for it, keeping her legs straight – a living pose from a glossy men's mag. She looked through the pockets and showed him the key, flicking back her dark hair. The pearl in her navel glinted and then she was back close again. 'I won't ever do it again.' Then she marched into the kitchen. He heard the key clink against the foreign coins and the odds and ends in the bowl. She straightened up, rested her head against the door frame and studied him. He had to swallow. When she moved towards him, it was as though she was walking on a catwalk, one foot in front of the other. She held his eyes the whole way. Her lips said: 'I thought you would be happy. Probably because I like surprises myself.' Her hand groped and she glanced up at him. 'You *are* happy. Your body is happy.'

'But how did you manage to find the right key?'

She loosened his belt, pulled his shirt loose; her fingers undid the button on his trouser waistband. The cool fingers gliding down his stomach. She stood there with her eyes closed and lowered her voice. 'Why do you always have to talk about dreary things, Mr Grumpy?'

He relented and kissed her.

'She's my mentor,' she said simply.

'Who is what?'

'Reidun, the lecturer at Blindern university, she's my mentor.'

'Now you're talking about dreary things. Anyway, you appeared to be totally immersed in each other.'

'She is.'

'She is what?'

'She's in love with me.' She faltered, then looked up. 'And neither you nor I can do anything about that, can we?'

He didn't say anything.

'I had to listen to her. She was telling me something important. Anyway, it wasn't very nice of you to follow me, was it?'

He held his tongue. Wasn't sure whether it was nice or not. All the blood in his body was drawn down to her cool hand. Her lips curled into a smile as his erection grew. A smile with closed eyes; some make-up on her eyelids had dried into clumps.

She sank onto one knee. He closed his eyes and breathed in sharply. He ran his fingers through her hair. She glanced up. The rustling sound from the headset on the floor returned. He asked her: 'Shall we go into the bedroom?'

'Are you frightened someone will see us?'

'I want all of you.'

He lifted her, carried her slender body, which weighed nothing at all, threw her laughing onto the bed, ripped off her underwear and grabbed her ankles. The gold ring on her big toe shone in the light of the afternoon sun coming through the window. He held her tight. She liked that, being held tight.

That night he followed her. It was almost three o'clock when she crept out. He gave her three minutes before sneaking after her. His brain was in turmoil. Part of his consciousness stretched out like a cat in the sun, remembering how she had taken what she wanted but had also given so much back. Another part of his brain sat behind a bush, suspicious, jealous, fearful that the performance was a deception. This is what drove him out into the cold autumn rain, what made him skulk along the street a hundred metres behind her, hiding in the shadows. *You're doing this because she already had a secret plan to break into the flat when she first went there. She stole a key! She took the fucking key! And she lets herself in – as if she lived there. She speaks in codes, never talks about herself, doesn't say what she does and avoids openness even when you ask. She plays down her relationship with the lecturer and makes up some pretext. She's full of lies!*

She walked ahead of him with long bouncing strides. Suddenly there was a vibration in his pocket. His mobile phone. He took it and looked at the display while trying to keep in the shadow of the trees shielding him from the street lights. He read: 'Hi Frank, Thank you for a wonderful evening. Sweet dreams, kiss, Elisabeth.' Involuntarily, he stopped. He observed the slim back well ahead of him. From a distance she seemed so delicate, so well meaning. What am I up to? Following a woman who has given me the night of my life! You know where she lives. She's on her way home.

Standing there in the dripping rain, mobile in hand, he came to. He looked up. She was gone. He jogged down Ryenbergveien. At the bottom he caught sight of her figure again. A taxi with an illuminated light on the roof passed him. It was on its way towards her. He hid as she turned towards the taxi. It slowed down but continued on past her as she made no move to flag it down. So she was telling the truth. She had felt like walking, not getting home quickly.

He was taken aback when he saw the complex of flats where she lived. Even more taken aback when he read the names by the door-bells. More than taken aback. He was stunned. *Elisabeth and Jonny Faremo.*

3

He was in a new phase of convalescence.

First day: fever.

Second day: fever.

Third day 07.30–12.00: no fever; prospects of recovery looking good.

12.03: SMS: Come!

12.03: fever returns!

12.06: mobile rings. It is her number.

He let it ring. He stood in the canteen queue with the phone ringing in his hand. People turned to face him. He ignored their looks. Sweated. Clenched his fists and looked in a different direction. The rest of the day passed in a haze.

On the fourth day, the first thing he did was to check criminal records. The search came up with one hit: *Jonny Faremo*. History: three convictions for GBH and one for armed robbery, one for breaking into a car and stealing. Total time behind bars: thirty-eight months of a five-year sentence. Time served in Ila, Sarpsborg and Mysen prisons.

The sweat ran down his back. He blinked twice but was alert enough to print out the page. Then a new search: *Elisabeth Faremo*, no hits. An unblemished record.

But if Elisabeth was married to Jonny Faremo, she could have taken his name. Perhaps she was registered under another one?

He felt queasy. He could see her face in front of him. No, not the face, just the body. His hand tightly grasping her ankle, her feet and the contours of her figure on the bed beneath them. He blinked again. *What trap have I walked right into?*

The door opened. Yttergjerde stomped in. Yttergjerde with the *snus* lip – the plug of tobacco under his top lip made him look like an overgrown rabbit with a deformed set of teeth – with the unshaven chin but shaven skull.

Yttergjerde: 'Hi there!'

Frølich felt his head nodding in response. He wasn't in a mood to talk now, wasn't in a mood to grin at Yttergjerde's stale jokes, angling anecdotes or tales of flings with women.

The odour of gentlemen's cologne filled the room. Yttergjerde always smelt like the taste of chewing gum. Frølich had no idea how the man could stand it.

'Well, I never.'

He looked up. Yttergjerde was standing in front of the printer. In his hand he was holding a printout about Jonny Faremo. Frølich could feel the sweat breaking out again – all over his body this time. He blinked. His eyes were dry, absolutely dry. He felt like throwing up.

'I know *this* one,' Yttergjerde mumbled.

'Which one do you know?'

'Faremo, Jonny. What has he been up to now?'

Frølich cleared his throat: 'I'm just checking out a few names. Let's hear it.'

'Hear what?'

'What you know about Jonny Faremo. For me he's a beefcake who wears caps and sun glasses.'

'Well, there are three in the gang. Armed robbery, same type of guys as the Stavanger mob – commando style, automatic weapons, balaclava and overalls. I can remember an armoured van job about five–six years ago. It says here the van went from Østfold to Oslo. He's a hard nut. Hit first and ask questions afterwards. I'm one of very few to have had the pleasure of smacking him in the face a couple of times. I was in the party when we arrested them for robbing the armoured van.'

'He did his stint a long time ago. Do you know any more?'

Yttergjerde turned to face him.

Frølich automatically went on: 'I know he lives in quite a flashy area. Terraced apartments on Ekeberg Ridge.'

'You know what it's like. These guys drive fast cars and drink Hennessy when they're not inside, that's why they end up inside.'

'So the flat is just show?'

'No, I believe they inherited it. The place is theirs. I remember it was an incontrovertible fact at that time – during the trial.'

'*They* inherited? Who are *they*?'

'Him and his sister. He lives with his sister. Used to at any rate – then.'

Yes! She isn't married! It's her brother!

Frølich, stony-faced: 'And her?'

'Her?'

'Is she implicated too?'

'Don't think so. Seems more like his mother in fact. Although she's younger. But I don't know. Where there's shit, there's usually a lot more to wallow in, as my uncle used to say. He was a farmer.'

A lot more to wallow in. He blinked. 'How do you mean "like his mother"?'

Yttergjerde shook his head and shrugged his shoulders. 'Just something I said. No idea. Why are you so curious?'

'Eh?' He could feel the sweat breaking out again.

'Faremo,' Yttergjerde said impatiently. 'Why are you so curious about Faremo?'

'A tip-off. Someone said I should take note of the name.'

Yttergjerde turned round, his eyebrows raised. His powerful hands wrenched the top off a Coke bottle.

Frølich blinked. *Get this conversation over with before it stinks to high heaven!*

Yttergjerde, pensive, ears pricked up: 'A tip-off?'

'Forget it. I only needed to know who we were talking about. And how are things otherwise? Still with the Thai patootie you were checking out?'

'Gentlemen prefer blondes!'

'So she finished it?'

Yttergjerde used his forefinger to scrape out the plug of tobacco. He grinned, showing his brown-stained teeth. 'Hey, at the station it's me who finishes relationships!'

Frank Frølich went to the toilet to be alone and think. He was alarmed by his own reaction, the boundless joy he had felt when he found out that Elisabeth was Jonny Faremo's sister and not his wife. But the brother's being a criminal was a problem. What was the right way to behave now?

He looked at his reflection. He told himself aloud: 'The right thing would be to confront her, to talk about her brother. *No, you must cut the connection.*'

He sat down on the toilet seat and chewed his knuckles. *What is the right thing to do? Break all contact over the phone? Stammer out: You know I can't have a relationship with the sister of a criminal! Only to get the obvious response: Frank, is it me you're interested in, or my brother?*

He ran the back of his hand across his forehead. Was this actually so unusual? Others must have been in this situation too. He tried to console himself by finding examples. The head of Inland Revenue discovers one day that his wife is fiddling taxi bills and deducting them from tax. *No. Irrelevant. This is about relationships.* There are socialist party members who go to bed with right-wingers and vice versa. Women prison officers who start relationships with inmates.

This last analogy makes him sweat even more.

A male priest, who is against women becoming priests, woos a woman priest. A militant neo-Nazi goes to the wrong pub and realizes he is homosexual. *Fatuous examples. Use your head!* The chairman of a local right-wing extremist party finds out his daughter has got engaged to a black man who, in fact, is a great guy.

Frank Frølich shook his head at himself. Is that why I'm getting anxious, because it's about me this time? Is this panic caused by my paranoia, or is the fact that her brother has done time the real problem?

He imagined the conversation again: *You have to understand, Elisabeth. I'm a cop! Your brother is a member of a gang. These are not people who are open to the general blather about individually tailored safeguards and fresh starts in life with roses and violins. Jonny and his pals are hardened criminals. We're talking about organized crime!*

He shook his head at himself. As if she didn't already know these things!

Well, isn't that the heart of the problem?

Yes, the problem is that she has kept her mouth shut. She knows I'm a policeman, has always known that. We first met because I was a policeman. So she should have said something about her brother a long time ago!

The brutal truth of this conclusion unnerved him at first. Afterwards it was like emerging from the water after holding your breath too long. The conclusion would be his platform. She had kept her mouth shut, she had manipulated him, kept things quiet, had played with him.

Straightaway he took a decision.

He washed his face with cold, clean water, dried it with a paper towel and went out, back to his office.

Gunnarstranda had arrived. He said: 'You look pale, Frølich. Tired?'

Frølich took his jacket, threw it over his shoulder and walked towards the door. 'No, just bloody sick of paperwork.'

Gunnarstranda peered over his glasses. 'Take it easy. Soon be Christmas. Then, on Christmas Eve, some jealous young brat is bound to exact his murderous revenge for being cuckolded.'

Gunnarstranda's wheezing laughter followed him out into the corridor.

When she next rang he answered the phone. All his unease was instantly swept away by her gentle, veiled voice.

She wanted to go to the cinema.

He said yes.

They met outside the Saga cinema. First of all, they went to Burger King. He had a baconburger and she wanted a milkshake. A vanilla milkshake.

'I only eat burgers at McDonald's,' she said as they sat down by the window facing the street. There were almost no customers on the first floor. Apart from a father with two daughters who were making a mess and smearing ketchup all over their clothes.

'Shall we go to McDonald's instead?'

'No. Now I want to have a milkshake. When you come to visit me I'll make you a banana milkshake. You'll like it.'

'Have you thought about inviting me home?'

She, glancing up: 'Why shouldn't I?'

'No, why shouldn't you indeed?'

Silence – uneasy silence. And then – as if she had read something in his facial expression, as if a light had gone out somewhere: 'What's the matter?'

'Hmm?'

'I can see there's something wrong. Tell me what it's about.'

He took another bite. The burger tasted of cardboard. But it was better to stuff cardboard in your mouth than fly off the handle. Besides he didn't know how to express himself. Immediately he became hot and flustered. He didn't like the place: the stench of frying oil, the stuffy air, cold walls and the harsh light that turned your skin an unhealthy shade of pale and your eyes colourless. 'There's something I have to talk to you about,' he said quickly.

'Wait,' she said.

'Right,' he said.

'First of all, there's something I have to say to you. It's about my brother.'

He held his breath. *Can she read my mind?*

'My brother, Jonny. He . . .' She went off into a dream and fidgeted with her serviette. The slim fingers folded the serviette, then again, as she gazed pensively out of the window.

'What about your brother?' he heard his own voice say as she chewed her lower lip.

'We live together.'

'And?'

She tore the serviette slowly into two pieces. 'Jonny . . . he's . . . he's done time.'

She stared at him now. He stared at her. The toxin was gone; the narcosis that made him feel as if he was fumbling in her presence, incapable of action in a deadened cotton-wool world, had worn off. His body felt as if it had been squeezed out of a cocoon. An unpleasant, clammy straitjacket had been removed. He breathed more easily, his heart wasn't beating like a drum any more, his ears weren't rushing like gushing blood. The person on the other side of the table was a fragile creature with dry lips whose sapphire-blue eyes avoided him, the same as prisoners who lower their gaze as they frantically search for fragments of a story they can fabricate, revealing dry lips with tiny flakes of skin hanging off, which sting but which they feel an irresistible urge to moisten.

This is what I am waiting for, for her to moisten her lips and serve up the first lie. What is going on inside my head?

'Jonny has always been a little wild and crazy, but there's only him and me. He's four years older than me and he's the only brother I have – let's put it like that – my big brother, my . . . what can I say? . . . he's the fixed point in my universe. But you're a policeman. I do realize that I have to tell you that he's been inside. He's done more than three years altogether. Jonny can walk down the street and be nicked by plainclothes men at any time simply because he's Jonny – an old acquaintance of the police, as they say on TV. But that doesn't change the fact that he's my brother, do you understand? I can't love my brother less because he's been to prison. He's all I can call family. It's always been us two. Do you understand that?'

'Elisabeth, what are you trying to say?'

Look up. Let me see you.

'I'm trying to say that maybe you won't like my brother. But that doesn't mean I feel any less for you. Your being a policeman doesn't have to make any difference. Jonny is looking for a new job. He's going straight.'

'Does Jonny know about me?'

'Hm?'

She doesn't know what to say. She's trying to gain time.

A noise broke the tension and gave them some respite.

Footsteps clattered on the spiral staircase by the end wall. He looked over. Someone was on their way up. It was someone he knew: Lena Stigersand, a police colleague, Lena and her racist friend/lover, coming up the staircase, each with a tray of food. The staircase was five metres away. Soon Lena would be level with them and exit the stairs facing this way. She would see him with Elisabeth.

'Your brother, does he know about us?'

'I don't think so.'

At that moment Lena turned to look for somewhere to sit. She was only seconds away from spotting Frank Frølich out on the town with a new lady friend; he was seconds away from a rumour about him being spawned.

Elisabeth smiled disarmingly.

As he refrained from answering the smile, she became earnest and looked down. Fidgety fingers. 'Does it matter?'

'Does what matter?'

'About Jonny. Does it matter?'

Lena Stigersand shouted: 'Hi, Frank!'

Game over.

Frølich peered up and pretended to be surprised: 'Hi, Lena!'

Elisabeth remained absolutely silent.

Lena Stigersand came over to him with a smile, accompanied by her idiot of a partner/undercover policeman, who was bound to know about Jonny Faremo and probably even knew that Jonny had a sister. Both were now waiting beside the table where he was sitting with Elisabeth, who was concentrating on sucking her straw.

Frølich cleared his throat. 'Lena, meet Elisabeth.'

It enveloped them, the slightly reserved atmosphere that arises when you exchange names.

Smiling, Lena said, 'We've met before, Elisabeth.'

'Oh?' Elisabeth replied, puzzled.

Frølich remembered before Lena could say anything. So he interceded in and told her himself. 'In Torggata, Badir's shop. Lena was leading the operation.'

Elisabeth's face cracked into a smile. 'That was where Frank and I first met.'

Lena Stigersand's face was a transparent pane of glass. He was able to see the wires connecting up in her head. The look she gave him. The detective now, the policewoman making connections, not the nice woman friend meeting a good colleague in town.

Lena and her partner moved off and were soon out of hearing. They scraped their chairs at the far side of the room. Frank Frølich pushed the half-eaten burger away. He was unable to think about food. 'Elisabeth . . .'

'Yes?'

'I asked if your brother knew about us.'

'I don't know.'

He took a deep breath. 'If you have talked to him about me, he knows.'

'I don't think he knows about you.'

'You haven't said a single word about me to your brother?'

'Relax, calm down.' Elisabeth had tears in her eyes now.

'It's you I'm interested in,' Frølich said reassuringly. 'I've never considered starting a relationship with your brother.'

Her face all smiles and gleaming eyes again. But why was she relieved? He reflected and knew the answer: she was relieved because the conversation was over.

4

Frølich was at work, sitting at his desk. He gave a start. Momentarily, he had been absent, his mind elsewhere – with her.

He gave another start as Yttergjerde repeated: 'Go on, Frankie.'

He sat staring at Yttergjerde. For those blanked-out seconds he had no idea what they were talking about.

This is me. I start a conversation and switch off. What is going on?

His memory returned. He resumed the theme he had initiated: 'I was just saying we were on a course learning about those blind dogs.'

'They're called guide dogs.'

'Yes, that's it. We were learning about how to recognize particular signs in dogs, ones which might be suitable for the job, about their natures . . .' Frølich stared at Yttergjerde's face, almost switching off again as his mind went in a different direction. But he focused firmly on the task in hand and continued: 'And the eyes, the body language, right? It's the same with drugs dogs. Some are suitable, some aren't.'

Yttergjerde nodded enthusiastically. He sensed a witticism coming.

'So, there I was, looking at these dogs, using what I had learned, right, and convinced that the Alsatian in the middle, that Alsatian was guide dog numero uno, right . . .'

'Yes?' Yttergjerde had a broad grin on his face, ready. He was already laughing at an as yet undelivered punch line. A grin was straining, held in by tensed cheek muscles.

And I'm sitting here, he thought, as the tip of Yttergjerde's chin impatiently bobbed up and down, waiting for the gag, for the twist, the final quip which would justify the release of his laughter. *What am I doing?*

'And the course director says we have to show what we have learned and there I am, sitting there, having sussed out the top guide dog in all of Norway, right, and I put out my hand, don't I . . .'

'Yes?' More laughter, more bobbing chin.

'And I get up . . .'

'Yes?'

'Go over to the dogs, the dog, the Alsatian in the middle . . .'

'Yes?'

'Stick out my hand . . .'

'Yes?' Yttergjerde's laughter was on its way up his throat, it was already in the man's mouth.

'Then the dog snaps at my hand and I topple over backwards!'

He sat watching Yttergjerde, who had released his laughter.

Is this what I want? Is this what is known as social competence? Is this what defines me as a successful person? Is this the moment I might jeopardize by making a false move? Is this the moment I'm risking? A moment I'm not even sure I enjoy.

Yttergjerde wiped the tears of laughter from the corners of his eyes. 'Oh shit,' he sighed. 'That's so bloody typical, oh shit . . .'

'The rumour's true,' Frølich said abruptly.

Yttergjerde, who didn't know what he was talking about, said: 'What rumour?'

'About me and this woman, Jonny Faremo's sister.'

Yttergjerde's face was in flux, a laughing mask stiffening into a gentle gape. Yttergjerde was shaken, as they say in boxing circles. He was at that stage when the shock has had its physical effect, but he still hasn't begun to comprehend that he has been struck.

'So now you know,' said Frølich grimly. 'Everything the lads say is true. I've got together with Jonny Faremo's sister – the same Jonny Faremo who served three years for armed robbery.'

He grabbed hold of his jacket and left.

5

Simple Minds were on the stereo. The voice was singing 'You Turned Me On' and a little later 'Alive and Kicking'. As soon as the voice finished, the CD player went back to the beginning and a song called 'Hypnotized'.

She wanted to have music on when they made love. She wanted precisely this music. But that was fine by him. There were two of them now; he was in her and she was in him. Her eyes betrayed no uncertainty, no pretence, no dissimulation. So the noise around them was of no significance; the music simply completed the picture, in the same way that on-shore breezes emphasize that air is something you breathe, that moisture states that water is matter in which you can swim. But he wasn't listening to the words of the songs, he didn't hear the drum rolls, or the backing vocals; his body was simply dancing with hers, he was focused on two lights quite close and at the same time far away, her blue eyes.

When he came in from the bathroom, she was lying on the bed reading. 'Is that the same book?' he asked.

'The same?'

'You always seem to be reading the same book.'

She put it down on the bedside table. 'Have you ever heard anyone say that you can never go into the same river twice?'

'Greek philosophy?'

She shrugged. 'Maybe. But I don't believe it's possible to read the same book twice.'

She made room for him under the duvet.

A little later she asked him: 'Why did you become a cop?'

'I just did.'

'You don't even believe that yourself.'

He turned his head and looked into her face. Smiled instead of answering.

'Are we in a private domain?' she asked. 'Keep off! Danger! Beware of the dog?'

'I applied to Police College when I finished studying law and I got in.'

'After law? You could have started in a solicitor's office. You could have been a practising solicitor and earned millions. Instead of that, you run around snooping into other people's business.'

'Snooping into other people's business?'

The intonation. It had been the tiniest bit sharp. But it was too late to moderate it after it was said. He cast her a glance. She was resting her head on his chest while the fingers of his left hand were following the pattern of the wallpaper. He stroked her hair with the other hand, knowing that she was trying to appraise the atmosphere.

'It does happen, doesn't it? You do snoop?'

He didn't answer.

'Are you annoyed?'

'No.'

'At least you aren't a judge, that's good.'

'What's the matter with judges?'

'I have a few problems with judges, either because of the job they do or because they're just so – judgemental.'

They lay in silence. Her head on his stomach. He lay there, playing with a lock of her black hair.

She said: 'What are you thinking?'

'That actually I could have become a judge. Perhaps from a career point of view I should have done.' He was still playing with her hair. She was lying still. He said: 'I like my job.'

She raised her head: 'But why?'

'I meet people. I met you.'

'But there must have been something that made you consider becoming a cop. At some point, you must have wanted to become one, a long time ago.'

'But why do you want to know?'

'I like secrets.'

'I guessed that.'

Her head went down again.

'There was a policeman living in our street,' he said. 'The father of a nice girl in my class, Beate. He drove a Ford Cortina. The old model with the round rear lights – in the sixties.'

'I have no idea what car you're talking about,' she said, 'but it doesn't matter.'

'In the flat above me there was a girl called Vivian who went on the game, even though she was only eighteen or nineteen.'

'How old were you?'

'Ten maybe. I didn't have a clue what a prostitute was. Didn't have a clue about sex. The other boys talked about Vivian and showed me pornographic magazines with women baring their sexual parts. I thought the pictures were revolting.'

'Were there pictures of her, of Vivian?'

'No, but the boys wanted me to see what she did, or it gave them a hard-on, who knows? I was a late developer in this area. When I was ten, I was only interested in fishing, my bike and things like that. I remember Vivian as a rather drained, dark-haired girl with lots of thin, blue blood vessels on her legs. And her legs were always quite pale. She often sat on the steps smoking. Anyway, one day two men came along. One was wearing a coat and had slick, greasy hair. The other one, with a fringe, wore glasses and a short leather jacket. His face kept twitching. I was playing rounders with the other boys in the street and Vivian was sitting in her hot pants on the steps, smoking. When the two men came, she got up and went inside. Just sloped off.'

Frølich went quiet when the telephone rang.

She peered up at him. 'Don't tell me you're going to answer the phone now.'

'Maybe not,' he said and watched the telephone without moving a muscle.

They lay listening to the ring tones until they stopped.

'Go on,' she said.

'Where was I?'

'Two men and Vivian went off.'

'One of the boys was called Yngve. He had a Tomahawk bicycle, one of those with a long saddle. Yngve picked up a stone and threw it at the two men. And we joined in immediately. The two men were the enemy, sort of. Then we picked up a couple of stones too.'

'Two ten-year-olds?'

'There were probably five or six of us. Yngve was the oldest, he was fourteen. My friends were thirteen and twelve. I was the youngest and I remember I was shit scared. I'd never been so frightened. The man with the twitch went for Yngve and he lay on the road bleeding. He had to go in the ambulance afterwards. I remember I ran behind the block of flats, panic-stricken. I hid between the rubbish bins and was sick, I was so scared.'

He looked down at his chest and met her eyes. He grinned.

She whispered: 'Go on.'

'Beate's father sorted everything out. He was the undisputed king, he didn't say a word, he didn't flash police ID or a badge, he wasn't in uniform, he just came and put the world back to rights. I suppose it all started there. His character – a symbol.'

'Bruce Willis,' she grinned.

'He wasn't a particularly nice man.'

'Bruce Willis?'

'Beate's father.'

'What did he do?'

He shrugged his shoulders. 'Beate became a heroin addict and died a few years ago. At the class reunion she was the only one who didn't turn up and all the girls talked about how she had been mistreated, screwed by her father for years.' He stretched. 'Illusions fade and die,' he said drily.

She didn't say anything.

'It's inherent in the word. Illusion, something which isn't real.'

'You're telling me.'

'What do I like?' He lay on his back thinking. 'I like playing air guitar to 'LA Woman' by The Doors.'

'You're so boring. Come on. Say what you like doing.'

He stretched under the duvet and said: 'I like looking out of the window when I wake up in bed in the morning.'

'More,' she said.

'More what?'

'More of what you like.'

'You first.'

'I like lying on the grass in the summer and seeing what images the clouds form.'

'More.'

'Cycling down a mountain on a mild summer's evening.'

'More.'

'Now it's your turn.'

'I like copying down the titles of my records and organizing them alphabetically.'

'Is that true?'

'Yes.'

'Right.' She snuggled down under the duvet. 'It's your turn,' she whispered.

'I like being on my own in a special place.'

'So do I.'

She lifted her head from his chest and looked up. 'A beach,' she said. 'In the evening when I sit there, eventually all I can hear is the lapping of the waves on the shore. If anyone comes and talks, you don't hear it.'

'Water's like that,' he said. 'I have the same experience when I go fishing, by rivers or streams with rapids.'

'I don't believe that.'

He looked at her again. She seemed slightly offended. 'OK, I give in. It's not like that.'

'When you say things like that I don't feel like saying any more,' she said.

'You!' He sat up until they had eye contact again. 'Don't be cross.'

'I'm not cross.'

'So what's the name of your beach?'

She smiled. 'Hvar.'

'What's that?'

'The name. Hvar.'

'Of the beach?'

'It's an island.'

'Where is it?'

She rested her head without answering.

He caressed her hair and yawned. Soon he would be asleep, he could sense that and he was happy. 'By the way,' he mumbled and yawned again. 'I like the smell of bonfires in spring.'

At one point during the night he opened his eyes and the weight of her head was gone. He heard a soft voice speaking. She was sitting on the chair by the window with her mobile phone to her ear. 'Aren't you asleep?' he asked. 'What's the time?'

'I'm coming now,' she whispered. 'Just go to sleep.'

His eyes were closed and he felt her crawl in under the duvet. Before drifting off again he looked at her black hair cascading over the pillow.

PART TWO

The Fourth Man

6

'We have a customer.'

'Murder?'

'A man. Cold and stiff as a Christmas anchovy,' Gunnarstranda went on. 'In Loenga.'

The line was cut. There was nothing to discuss. There was never anything to discuss. Frank Frølich turned over in bed. 'I have to be off,' he whispered with a croak and stopped short.

She wasn't there. The duvet she had wrapped herself in a few hours ago was half on the floor. He sat up in bed, massaged his cheeks and cautiously called out: 'Elisabeth?'

Not a sound.

He looked at his watch. It was half past four. It was night. He got up and sauntered into the living room. Dark and quiet. The kitchen – dark. The bathroom – dark and empty. He switched on the light, splashed water over his face and met his tired eyes in the mirror. Why does she do this? Why does she run away? When did she go? Why?

Exactly six minutes later, he was sitting in his car and driving down Ryenberg mountain. It had turned colder. A sliver of a moon shone in a starry sky. The temperature gauge in the car showed –5 °C. And he thought about Elisabeth in her skin-tight skirt and skimpy underwear walking down the road in this cold. Out of bed, out of the house, gone. Inside the car, he was so cold that he was hunched over the wheel, holding it with both hands. The studded tyres made a metallic sound on the tarmac and the bends in the road were frozen. Mist steamed over the water in the harbour basin. The right atmosphere for a murder, he thought, as he swung into Gamlebyen.

A patrol car stood outside the fence with its blue light flashing. Gunnarstranda's Skoda Octavia was parked across the pavement. And behind the wire fence a small circle of people was standing around a shape on the ground.

Frølich closed the car door behind him and went through the gate with his hands thrust deep into his trouser pockets. He was frozen and pangs of hunger for breakfast were stabbing at his stomach. The figure of Gunnarstranda came towards him. With the shirt under his autumn coat buttoned up wrong. An unlit cigarette bobbed up and down in his mouth.

'Guard for Securitas. Found at 3.43 by a workmate. Obvious signs of an attempt to break into containers.' Gunnarstranda pointed. The doors of a green metal container gaped wide open. 'The container is owned by something called A. S. Jupro. It's not clear what they took – but presumably it was some kind of electronic equipment.'

From a distance the dead man resembled an unconscious slalom skier. He was lying in a so-called stable lateral position. Wearing a boiler suit. Frank Frølich winced when he saw the man's disfigured head and all the blood.

'Pathologists call it "injuries inflicted by a blunt weapon",' Gunnarstranda said formally. 'The back of his head has been stoved in. Finding the cause of death shouldn't be the most difficult task on earth for the boys. Most probably that's the murder weapon.' He pointed towards a blood-stained plastic bag beside the corpse. 'Baseball bat, aluminium.'

A sudden crackle came from one of the uniformed policemen's short-wave radios. The man passed it to Gunnarstranda, who barked formally into it.

Frølich was unable to decode the message which came crackling back. But a grinning Gunnarstranda could. 'Lock them up.'

He turned and checked his watch. 'We've got them and now we can grab a bit more shut-eye. Sorry to wake you at such an ungodly hour, but that's the job, isn't it? No two cases are the same. I'll catch another couple of hours myself,' Gunnarstranda added. 'Then we'll do the interrogation at a more godly time. It'll be wonderful to hit the sack.'

'Who have we got?' Frølich asked, bewildered.

'A gang of bruisers,' Gunnarstranda said. 'A tip-off. Not worth a great deal perhaps, but on the other hand there is a clear sequence of events.' He pointed to the open container. 'These boys were breaking in when the security guard arrived in his car.' He pointed to a small Ford van a few metres away. The security company's logo was printed on the side. 'The guard saw something, stopped and went to check.' Gunnarstranda pointed to an object next to the open container. 'His torch – a Maglite – is over there. The men were caught red-handed, and a struggle ensued. One of them has a baseball bat and wallop. The guard falls there. Unfortunately for these three, he's dead now.'

'And we know who did it?' Frank Frølich said with a yawn.

Gunnarstranda nodded. 'As I said, a tip-off, and I would be very surprised if it wasn't spot on.' Gunnarstranda took a scrap of paper out of his coat pocket and read aloud: 'Jim Rognstad, Vidar Ballo and . . .' Gunnarstranda held the scrap up to the light. 'Sometimes I can't read my own writing . . . Jim Rognstad, Vidar Ballo and . . . can you read the name of the third man?' he asked, straightening his glasses.

Frølich read it first to himself before reading out aloud: 'It says Jonny Faremo.'

7

Frølich had felt the beast gnawing at his stomach all morning and decided to find out what had happened at the court hearing. However, as he was running down the steps between the court and Kafé Gabler he felt a growing reluctance to go on. So he retreated to Kristian Augusts gate to stand and wait on the pavement. Soon a group of people gathered in front of the court entrance. A little later the door opened. Elisabeth came out. He followed her movements. She left alone, taking small quick steps, without looking to the left or the right. He stood watching her slender back until she had rounded the corner and was gone.

The moment Gunnarstranda came through the wide doors, Frølich showed himself and stepped out onto the tramlines to cross the street. Gunnarstranda detached himself from the crowd on the steps, strode down to the pavement and also crossed the tramlines. Frølich joined him.

Gunnarstranda, uncommunicative, continued along the pavement at a brisk pace.

Frølich cleared his throat: 'How did it go?'

'How did what go?'

'The hearing.'

'Shit.'

'Which means?'

Gunnarstranda stopped, let his glasses glide down over the bridge of his nose and scowled sharply over the top. 'Are you wondering whether her brother will have to go to prison? Or whether all of them will have to go? Or are you wondering about your own future prospects?'

'Just say how it went.'

'Elvis has left the building.'

'Eh?'

'Jonny Faremo gave me the finger and walked out a free man. Because his sister, the little bit of fluff you've fallen for, alleges she was with her brother and the others in the flat at the time Arnfinn Haga was killed.' The last word was delivered with a yell to drown the tram as it rumbled past.

Frølich waited for the din to subside. 'She said she was in the flat with her brother and two others – after she was with me?'

'Yes.'

'She sneaks out of my flat while I'm asleep, wanders off in the middle of the night, to her place where her brother, Rognstad and this Ballo are, then they party until dawn?'

'Don't you two talk to each other, Frølich?'

Frølich didn't know what to say.

Gunnarstranda continued: 'Jonny Faremo, Jim Rognstad and Vidar Ballo and your ... *sweetheart* ... were playing poker in their flat. She also mentioned your name.'

Frølich felt his face go numb. 'Me?'

'She went into juicy detail about her night with you – prior to this round of poker.'

Frølich could still hear an echo in his head of his pathetic 'Me?'

The silence between them grew. People passed them in both directions. A taxi trundled slowly by. The driver looked up at them questioningly.

Frølich said: 'You don't buy the story about the poker game?'

'Of course not.'

'Why wasn't I called in as a witness?'

'Would you have been able to say when she left?' Gunnarstranda's tone was acid.

'Listen,' Frølich said, annoyed. 'I don't like this any more than you do.'

'I doubt that.'

'I don't understand why the judge accepted her testimony. It seems bloody unlikely.'

'Could you have refuted it?'

'No.'

'So why should I have called you as a witness? I have no idea whether the judge believed her. The point is that her testimony denies us a reasonable cause for suspicion and hence their release is a clear sign to me: before the next round, produce more evidence against the Faremo gang or undermine Elisabeth Faremo's testimony.'

'What time of night are we actually talking about?'

Gunnarstranda took a deep breath.

'What's up?'

'Pull yourself together, Frølich.'

'Eh?'

'You're the one having a relationship with this woman! You're the one who has been to bed with her. And you stand there like a donkey asking me about times. I don't recognize you. Have a break. Go on holiday, take time off. You've been – excuse my French – humping the sister of a hardened criminal . . . for how long? For weeks? As far as I know, it might be all love and sweet music, but you're a policeman for Christ's sake. It might be a set-up. If you can't see that, it's my job to point out the possibility. Soon the whole force will see it. And then you'll be suspended. And you can imagine how they will formulate the suspension, can't you? That route is no good for you or me or the force. So, move out of the way of the elephants coming thundering around the bend. If you don't move, you'll be trampled underfoot. And whatever happens, you could do with a holiday. You're a fucking shadow of yourself, man!'

Frank Frølich looked the other man in the eye. 'What are you talking about? A set-up?'

'The woman must have had something going right from the off.'

'Why's that?'

'You told me you protected her – in Badir's shop – got her out of the way when the police went into action?'

'No one knew about the operation. Her going into the shop was a glitch. Chance.'

'Fine, she entered the shop quite by chance. But then – during the shooting and while the crazy guys were being nicked – you say she was stuffing cigarettes into her rucksack? She must have been doing that to get you interested.'

'I haven't the slightest idea why she was doing that.'

'Remember, she doesn't have a record. But when the bullets fly and she is lying underneath a cop on the shop floor, she starts pinching stuff – isn't that a bit odd?'

Frølich was sweating. 'It might be odd, I don't know.'

'Just use your head. You're in deep shit.'

'But if this is all calculated and planned, I don't understand why. Was she supposed to go around selling her body for months, making the wildest plans with me, in order to give her brother an alibi for killing a security guard in the harbour? My God, Arnfinn Haga, a twenty-two-year-old student working as a guard to earn some money on the side. Can't you see that a conspiracy theory is completely absurd!'

'So you think she's in love with you and the business with her brother is pure chance, do you?'

'Yes, in fact I do.'

'Frølich, how long have we worked together now?'

'A lot too long.'

'Yes, probably, but we've muddled our way through quite a few cases. And even if no two cases are alike, a number of things about this one stink.'

'Right!' Frølich cut in. 'But it's also possible!'

'What's possible?'

'It's possible she had honourable intentions!'

'Frølich! Stop being so bloody naïve! There's something not quite kosher about this bit of skirt. It doesn't matter which way you look at every single bit of what you've told me, it all boils down to a con.'

Gunnarstranda moved off. He strode briskly along the pavement. Frølich caught up with him and said, 'OK, let's say you're right. She did have something going. If you're so damned sure, what was she after, then? What was she planning on the shop floor? If this is not about the murder of the Securitas guard, what is it about then? Is it about getting me into deep water? There must be easier ways of causing me trouble than to start killing people. You must be able to see that. The only thing she has achieved is to put me in a spot of bother with some colleagues who are wondering now about my judgement – and what would be the point of that? Well? Can you tell me?'

'No.'

'So, why the hassle?'

Gunnarstranda stopped again. He glared at the other man with ice-cold eyes. 'I'm not hassling anyone. I never do. You're the one following me. You're the one doing the hassling. We both know that the main suspects left court free men and your name was used in the trial to achieve that outcome. That means – if you have to have it spelt out for you – you cannot continue with this investigation. I'll investigate the murder of Arnfinn Haga now without your help. If I were you, I would do two things: first, take a week off to avoid a blemish on your record. Next, I would have a chat with the girl. You owe that to yourself and your future, and not least the girl herself – if she really does have honourable intentions. And now you'll have to excuse me. I have a job to do.'

Frank Frølich watched him go. Gunnarstranda's open coat flapped like a cape in his wake.

Time off? Suspension? The words ricocheted through his brain. The blood in his ears pounded. He put his hand in his pocket and pulled out a mobile phone.

He rang Elisabeth Faremo's number. There was no answer.

He stood looking at the phone. Nothing. Because she didn't answer. That had never happened before. He tried again. Again no answer. He tried a third time. Her phone was switched off.

8

Three hours later he had treated himself to a week off and was sitting in his car on the road up to Ekeberg Ridge. He drove onto the roof which formed the car park for the flats beneath. A staircase led downwards, beside the building complex. One landing for every floor. Every landing led to two entrances. He found the door to Jonny and Elisabeth Faremo's flat. Rang the bell but nothing happened. He listened. No padding feet could be heard behind the door. Everything was dead, dark and still. The only thing to be heard was the engine of a crane which barely drowned the usual drone of traffic in the streets below. The icy air, which until now had wrapped itself around his body like a cool skin, suddenly penetrated his clothes and made him shiver.

He rang again. The skin on his forefinger went white as he pressed the bell.

He stamped his feet to keep warm, went to the side to find a window to look through.

'Are you looking for someone?'

An elderly man with a stoop, stick and beret was standing on the staircase landing staring at him.

'Faremo,' Frølich said.

The man took out a bunch of keys and tried to find the correct one. 'Him or the lady?'

'Both actually.'

The man put the key in the lock of the neighbouring flat. 'She went off about half an hour ago. Probably going on holiday. Had a rucksack and suitcase with her. I haven't seen Jonny for several days.' The man opened the door.

'Did she take a taxi?'

'No, she just went down there.' The man pointed with his stick. 'Took the bus, I suppose.'

'Did you see her get on the bus?'

'No. Why are you so interested?'

Frølich was about to show his ID, but refrained. 'We were meant to meet,' he said, looking at his watch. 'Pretty important. That was half an hour ago.'

'Oh yes,' the man said, moving to go indoors.

Frølich waited.

The man kept mumbling, 'Oh yes, oh yes,' then finally closed the door.

Frølich plodded slowly back up the stairs to his car. As he was about to get in, a silver-grey Saab 95 rolled up and parked in one of the reserved spaces. He put the key in his pocket and observed the other car. The driver was taking his time. Finally the door opened. A man got out: white, about 1 metre 90 tall, strong – either from intensive training or anabolic steroids – wearing green military trousers, Gore-Tex mountain climbing boots, a short leather jacket, brown leather gloves, sunglasses and a black cap. Frølich had never seen him in real life, but he knew instantly who he was and walked over towards him.

They were the same height, but Frølich probably couldn't lift as much in the bench press as this action-hero clone. Nevertheless, when Faremo took off his sunglasses he immediately recognized Elisabeth's features: the nose, the forehead and the eyes.

He said: 'I'm looking for your sister.' He thought: *Big mistake. I should have introduced myself, been coldly courteous, not brazen like a little kid.*

The man took off his gloves with an effort and stretched out his hand. 'Jonny.'

'Frank.'

'So you're a friend of Elisabeth's?'

'Yes. Earlier today you were in court and got off because your sister talked about a man called Frank. You may remember?'

Faremo grinned. 'Elisabeth and I have occasionally discussed the fact that you were a policeman.'

Frølich could feel the words sinking in: *Elisabeth and I have occasionally discussed . . .*

Faremo went on: 'She has always maintained that *you* weren't an asshole, that you were . . .' Jonny Faremo gave a cool, ironic smile as he prepared for the sarcasm: '. . . that you were different.'

Frølich controlled himself and refrained from giving a riposte. 'Do you know where she is now?'

'No.'

'A neighbour claims she left half an hour ago with a rucksack and another bag.'

'Then she must have done.'

'But you must know if she was going anywhere.'

'Why's that?'

Frølich thought: *Because she's your alibi, asshole!* He said: 'So you don't know?'

'You should drop the Gestapo style when talking to members of her family.'

'I apologize if I've been offensive, but it's important for me to get into contact with her.'

'Really?'

'Yes. Really. Is that so strange?'

'A little.'

'Oh yes?'

'From what I have understood from my sister, she was the one who had to take the initiative in your relationship.' Faremo smacked a glove against his palm. 'But now I'm in trouble, you've turned into a bloodhound and come running round here.'

Frølich said: 'If you see her, please ask her to ring me.' He turned to go. The packed snow on the concrete roof was slippery. He almost fell, but he didn't look back. *She has told her brother everything*. That was the only thing he thought. Jonny Faremo knew God-knows-what all the time he had been asking her about her brother. She had been sitting and shielding her cards like a child caught cheating.

When he joined the main road Faremo was still standing in the same place, watching him closely.

Frølich glanced at his watch. It was lunchtime, but he couldn't swallow a bite. He pulled into the verge and stopped before he had driven fifty metres. What would be the best course of action? Find out where Elisabeth had gone or focus on the brother? How would he find out where she had gone? He hardly knew anything about her.

He wove his hands round the wheel. Perhaps do nothing? Go home and sleep maybe? After all, he was off work.

He didn't have long to think. Faremo's Saab drove past. Frølich switched on the ignition and followed him.

9

It was late afternoon when he parked alongside a picket fence near the tram stop at Forskningsparken. From here he made his way to the part of the university complex housing the history and philosophy faculty. The thought of this visit was distasteful. The thought of searching for the Elisabeth he didn't know was distasteful. However, the distaste he felt for this side of her seemed less important as long as he was unable to get in touch with her, to find her. He wanted to hear what she said about the poker game, the alibi – all the things he couldn't grasp. So he ignored the beast gnawing at his stomach, went into the Niels Treschow building and took the lift up the tall structure. He haphazardly roamed the corridors, took the stairs and wandered further afield as he read the names on the doors. The door to Reidun Vestli's office was ajar. He knocked and pushed the door open. A young woman with blonde hair and an unusually powerful jaw looked up from the computer. 'Sorry,' Frank Frølich said. 'I'm looking for Reidun Vestli.'

'She's gone home.' The young woman looked at her wristwatch. 'A couple of hours ago.'

'Home?'

'She wasn't well. So she went home.' The powerful jaw split into a big white smile. 'On the Master's course we're allowed to use her office. She's great like that.'

'Was it serious?'

'Haven't a clue. No, I don't think so. Reidun is rarely ill.'

Reidun Vestli had packed up and gone off a couple of hours ago. Elisabeth packed up and went off a couple of hours ago.

Frølich said: 'I really need to talk to her. We had an appointment.'

Reidun Vestli's office was tidy; the only object to disturb the impression of meticulous order was the quilted anorak the student had slung over the table in the corner. The woman behind the computer looked as if she belonged to the office.

'You can try her home phone number, if it's important.'

'Yes, of course. You don't have the number by any chance?'

The student had a ponder. 'Reidun is one of the few professors who has a business card,' she said, pulling out a drawer in the desk. 'I know she usually has a few lying around. Here we are.' The powerful chin broke into another smile as she passed him the card.

He studied the business card on the way down in the lift. Reidun Vestli lived in Lysejordet.

He called her home number as soon as he was back in his car. It rang five times. No one answered. Then the little pause which indicated that you were being transferred. So she wasn't at home. It rang twice more before she answered.

'This is Reidun.' The voice was clear; in the background, a low whistle. Frølich knew what that meant. It meant that she was in a car.

'This is Frank Frølich. I would like to talk to you.'

Silence.

'It's about Elisabeth Faremo.'

The conversation was broken off.

He stared down at the display. This was a conversation he had dreaded, but for Reidun Vestli it must have been worse. The panic-stricken refusal to speak made him ring again, instantly. The number rang and rang. Then the answer service took over.

He was fed up. Pissed off. Right now the situation seemed totally ridiculous. He could hear Gunnarstranda's voice in his head as he drove home. *A set-up! Of course it is, Frølich!*

He had opted to take a whole load of accumulated time off because . . . why had he, actually? Because Elisabeth Faremo was covering up for her brother? Or was he doing it to hide, to bury his head in shame?

A young man had been killed. But Elisabeth *could* have been telling the truth. Why couldn't what she said have been true? Elisabeth had always sneaked out of his flat at night. What might have happened was this: Elisabeth had gone home. She had sat up for a few hours with her brother and then all of a sudden the police ring at her door. *Except for the tip-off.* The problem was that he knew nothing about the tip-off. Who had tipped off the police and what was their motive?

He automatically steered a course homewards. It was a dark winter afternoon and rush hour. He had taken time off. Nothing to do. What does a Norwegian man do when he has nothing to do? He has a drink – or five. Frank Frølich headed for the shopping centre in Manglerud.

10

He set out on his pub crawl. Had a couple of lagers at a bar registered under the name of Olympen Restaurant and known locally as the Lompa, the Rose of Grønland. The place was half full. Most of the customers were of the jaded variety, who lived nearby and went to the Lompa to have profound conversations with their beer glasses. Frank Frølich sat alone at a table watching the people around him. Lean men, most so rigid from years of hard drinking that they looked as if they were balancing on stilts when they walked into the toilet. When he moved on, it was to find a bar to prop himself up on. He went to Oslo main station, to platform two in the old Østbanehalle. The place was packed. Travellers. Commuters on their way home waiting for the next train. Men and women from Moss and Ski with their suitcases, warming up with a beer before catching the ferry to Denmark. The loudspeakers were playing the Hollies' 'He Ain't Heavy, He's My Brother' and a group of women dressed in track suits were singing along. Frølich studied himself in the mirror and felt like a Martian on Pluto. He drank his third and fourth beers while witnessing two old acquaintances of the police selling dope to some teenage girls. Frølich raised his glass. He was off duty for fuck's sake. None of his business. But old acquaintances are as alert as wild mink. They immediately sensed Frølich's passive state and were ready to misinterpret it. Frølich drank his beer and moved on, up Karl Johans gate. He paused at the intersection with Dronningensgate and the row of obscure bars. But then another old acquaintance limped out of the shadows by Kirkeristen: 'Frankie, fancy a beer?'

Frølich shook his head and walked back towards Jernbanetorget. Is it possible to sink any lower than being bought a beer by someone you have arrested countless times? He thought: the safest place to go on a bender seems to be further west. He caught the first tram, hung onto the strap as the tram swayed up Prinsens gate, got off at the lower end of Kontraskjæret, crossed to Fridtjof Nansens plass and decided to start on the corner and work his way along all the watering holes around the City Hall. It was a strenuous job. But he didn't feel drunk; he just needed to keep emptying his bladder. A couple of hours later he wobbled into the lounge of the Hotel Continental. This was the place where original Munch paintings used to hang on the wall, where the male guests are the type of men who look forward to the weekend to try out their new golfing trousers and where the wallflowers are cultivated women with a nose for port wine. This was where an unshaven, furloughed cop could walk around incognito too, he thought, and fell over a sofa in the middle of the room. He ordered a whisky. After drinking another, knocking over a glass of beer and attempting to wipe up the mess with the table cloth from the neighbouring table, he was politely asked to leave. Things are improving, he thought. If I play my cards right now I will be taken to the drunk cells before the night is out. 'I'm not drunk,' he said to the girl who had been given the unenviable task. 'I'm just suffering from a few synchronization problems.' He stood up, impressed that he had managed to pronounce such a long, tricky word.

He tottered out and almost collided with Emil Yttergjerde. Yttergjerde must have been in the middle of his own pub crawl because there was a red, almost purple, glow to his face and he had to hold onto the lamppost as they stood contemplating each other. Together, they staggered around the corner and into Universitetsgata. Several bars there. And he still had some money left.

It was evening, maybe night, at any rate many hours later, when he and Yttergjerde were sitting at a table in Café Fiasco. No, he concluded, it had to be night. He was drinking his beer and struggling not to slide off his stool while concentrating on Yttergjerde's mouth. The music was hammering away and he was shouting to be heard through the din.

'She was from Argentina,' Yttergjerde bellowed.

Frølich put his half-litre down on the table, wishing Yttergjerde would shut up and stop his awful shouting.

'But I didn't find that out until later,' Yttergjerde shouted.

'What was that?' Frølich shouted back.

'The woman from Argentina. She was broke, you see, and I kept her going with cigarettes and some food. I was arseholed when I got into this bus, it was four in the morning and I was going to Milan. Anyway, I sat down in the bus and then she came and sat down beside me. She'd spent all her money on rented cars and expensive hotels in Paris and Rome. She needed somewhere to live because there were still two weeks to go before her return flight left from Paris to cross the Atlantic.'

Yttergjerde paused for breath and took a drink from his glass of beer.

'What are you talking about?' Frølich asked.

'My holiday,' Yttergjerde said. 'Keep up, will you?'

Frølich raised his head. It was impossible to hear yourself think. There was a break in the music. But not for long. Someone put on some Springsteen. One chord, one riff: 'Born in the USA'.

Frølich was about to say something. Just to prove that he wasn't going to collapse. Instead he had to battle not to fall off his stool. He clung to his beer glass and said: 'I guess I'll have to be off now.'

Yttergjerde didn't hear. He put down his glass, wiped his mouth with the back of his hand and roared through the music: 'I couldn't talk to her about Swedes, you see. This woman had been with a Swede and he'd been knocking her about for a long time. And she was whingeing and nagging me – that was probably why it finished – always asking me if I was all right and telling me in the morning I looked extremely aggressive. I have no idea what I look like in the morning actually, but I was sick of the nagging, really sick of it. I mean, I've never heard that I look aggressive before. Anyway, in the end, I lost my temper and told her in my Oxford English I wasn't angry. But, I said, if you don't stop asking me if I'm angry, I'll lose my temper. Perhaps I was a bit rough. I mean, it's not so easy to catch the nuances using Oxford English. Anyway, she legged it and that was the last I saw of her. Just as well maybe. I mean, it was a hopeless business. I was on holiday. I put the woman up and kept her in cigarettes for four days – while she was doing the best she could to pay in kind. That's no healthy basis for a lasting relationship.'

Frølich stood up. The room swayed. He was plastered. He said it out loud: 'I'm plastered.'

'What I mean to say is,' Yttergjerde unflaggingly pointed out, 'the world is full of women, Frankie. I mean people like me, divorced, can relax. What about people like you who have never worn the ball and chain? I've got a pal, thirty-something, he's up to his eyeballs in women. Single mothers, Frankie, trips on the ferry to Denmark, dances. You don't have to get fucking depressed because of this woman.'

'I know you mean well,' Frank Frølich said. 'But the only thing I need now is a taxi and a bed to lie in.'

'Yeah, go on home, Frankie. Sleep it off, have a lie-in, forget the bloody woman. Last time I felt like that I went to the whorehouse in Munkedamsveien, I mean, just to release some of the pressure. But the one who got the job was one of those sneaky pusses. I'm sure she was married or engaged, and what's the point of being a whore then, eh? If you think the whole thing is revolting. Eh? She was a looker but she refused to do anything but missionary, so I got angry, didn't I? I don't mean to be difficult, I said to the madame in reception, but I'm paying a lot of wonga, so these women of yours should be able to manage a bit of customer service, shouldn't they, I said, and then I was given a voucher. What about that, Frankie?' Yttergjerde sobbed with laughter. 'You know, that's how it should be in marriage too. You just get vouchers!'

11

When the telephone rang, he tried to lie still, not to disturb his comatose body. Judging by the light, it was afternoon. He had been sleeping like a sunken log on the sofa for several hours, stiff, heavy and torpid. He turned his head and contemplated the phone. The movement brought on a headache, dizziness and nausea. The pain from his liver stabbed at his side like a fakir's bed of nails – from the inside. My liver is a ball of pain, he thought, and the air a nail, no, the ring tone is like a drill pounding against my temples. He sat up and felt dizzy again. Stood up, dizzy, holding onto the doorframe and grasping the telephone receiver.

'So you're at home.'

'What did you imagine?'

'You never know.'

Frank Frølich sank back on the sofa. When I die, he thought, the angel coming to collect me will have the same voice as Gunnarstranda. The man is a spook. The spikes continued to attack his liver. He was incapable of thinking; he said: 'So you're ringing. Is it anything to do with the job or are you just missing me?'

'Jonny Faremo is dead.'

'Dead?'

'Yes, dead. Drowned.'

Frank Frølich had never felt a greater need for a glass of water. The words constricted themselves in his throat, his head. He managed to say: 'Where?'

'Some kilometres outside the city boundary, in Askim. He drowned in the Glomma and was picked up by some people working at the Vamma power station. His body was caught in a net.'

'A net?'

'Does that mean you know where the Vamma power station is?'

Shit. The intonation. 'No idea. Where is Vamma power station?'

'I told you, didn't I? Fifty kilometres east of the city boundary.'

'Oh.'

'Power stations are susceptible to getting logs and other junk caught in the turbines. That's why they have a net to pick up the stuff. It picked up Faremo last night.'

'Accident?'

'If it was an accident we ought to have a heap of circumstantial evidence. In this case we don't have anything.'

'Suicide?'

'Well, he certainly drowned.'

'What's your view?'

Gunnarstranda chuckled into the receiver. 'My view? I had a call from Krimpolitisentralen, Kripos, about ten minutes ago. But, well, I suppose I did run the man in and I did have him appear at a hearing on suspicion of killing the security man in Loenga. He gets off – on an alibi as thin as a pussy hair. Two days go by and then he's found floating with his lungs full of water in the dam by a power station. Perhaps he was depressed and threw himself in? But why should he be depressed? Because you'd taken up with his sister? And if he was and drove off to kill himself, where's the car? Where's the suicide note?'

'He drives a silver-grey Saab 95.'

'How do you know that?'

The intonation, the suspicion. 'I have, as you yourself pointed out, some knowledge of the family.'

'If he was thrown into the river, he wouldn't have had much of a chance. It's late autumn. There's a strong current. Water temperature, maximum four to five degrees.'

'Faremo's well built. All muscle.'

'The body was in a bad way. The doctor who wrote the death certificate has, it seems, used a local phenomenon to explain why. There's a place called Vrangfoss just above the power station. It's a narrow ravine and right there the river bends. This means that a few hundred metres above the power station all the water flowing serenely along in the Glomma is compressed and channelled through the ravine. A horizontal waterfall in other words, a kind of inferno of water and currents. If Faremo ended up in the river above the ravine his body would have been whirled around and thrown against the cliff face for a good long time before he emerged a few hundred metres further down. Most of the bones in Faremo's body were simply smashed to pulp.'

Frank Frølich saw in his mind's eye the man of 1 metre 90, dressed like a commando with the same expression as his sister.

'Is it known where he fell?'

'Fell, you say?'

'Or was shoved. Do you know anything about the crime scene?'

'This power station – Vamma – is the last of three power stations in a row. The highest one is called Solbergfoss, a little lower down there is one called Kykkelsrud and right at the bottom Vamma, where Faremo was fished out of a kind of collecting net. So you can imagine. He was found in front of the last dam. The stretch between Kykkelsrud power station and Vamma is the interesting bit. Frølich?'

'Yes?'

'Aren't you wondering why I'm ringing?'

'Haven't thought that far ahead.'

'It's not my case. Follo police district is dealing with it, helped by Kripos. You will have to be able to account for your movements over the last twenty-four hours.'

Finally the cat is out of the bag. 'And why's that?'

'You know why.'

'No, Gunnarstranda, I don't know why!'

'You don't need to take that tone with me. We both know that Faremo may have died as the result of an accident. He could have been arguing with someone who pushed him in – maybe with premeditation, maybe in the heat of the moment. And you've already been seen in what was termed a heated discussion outside his home.'

'Are you having me followed?'

'No, but I am investigating a murder. You have a lot of good friends here, Frølich, but no one can or will disguise the facts. Until last night Jonny Faremo was among the group of men suspected of murdering Arnfinn Haga. We've been watching Faremo's place. Your discussion with Faremo in the car park has been duly documented.'

'OK, but will you believe me if I say it cannot have been me who threw Faremo in the river?'

'Try me.'

'What you say is correct. I was outside their flat. When Faremo and his gang were released after the hearing, I did as you said. I took a week off. Then I went straight to the Faremo flat. I talked to him, but my voice was never raised and there was no heated discussion.'

'The question is: what did you do afterwards?'

Frank Frølich stared vacantly at the wall. He had been outside Faremo's flat last night – for some reason he had taken a taxi up there and puked in a ditch. *Why did I go there? What the hell was I trying to do?*

'Are you there?'

'Yes.'

'Others, apart from me, are going to ask you, Frølich. I'm just giving you a little head start.'

He didn't feel nauseous any more, just thirsty. Lethargically, he got onto his feet and staggered into the kitchen. Nothing in the fridge apart from two cans of lager. No. He closed the door and drank water straight from the tap.

He lurched towards the bathroom. In the shower, he soaped himself down thinking about Elisabeth and how she had testified on behalf of her brother and two others. He could see her in front of him as she strode out of the court towards Grensen without a look to either side. *Why didn't I stop her? Why didn't I talk to her?*

He scalded his body with hot water while conjuring up the sight of her hurrying home as fast as her legs could carry her. That delicate frame of hers nervously rushing around her flat, opening drawers, slamming them shut, throwing clothes and other things into a rucksack and bag. A phone to her ear. *She had done a runner, but where – and why?*

His brain churned slowly, all too slowly. When he got to her flat, she had already disappeared. Then her brother came. *Had she done a runner from her brother? And if so, why? She had already given him an alibi for the murder.*

He remembered his own trembling fingers as he tapped in Reidun Vestli's phone number: the clear sound of being transferred, the muffled sound of a mobile phone. The conversation that was broken off as soon as he introduced himself.

Suddenly it became important to ring Elisabeth. *Everything that has happened is the result of a silly misunderstanding. If I ring now, she will pick up the phone and give me a convincing explanation of the whole thing.* He turned off the water and walked into the living room without drying himself. His feet left big damp patches on the lino. Found his mobile phone and rang Elisabeth. But her phone was switched off. He rang Reidun Vestli. No answer. He stood naked, looking at his reflection. Never seen anything so pathetic.

At that moment the doorbell rang.

He staggered into the bedroom, found a clean pair of trousers and a T-shirt and went to open the door.

A man stood on the mat. Frølich had never seen him before: lean, 1 metre 80, light brown hair and brown eyes.

The man said: 'Frank Frølich?'

'That's right.'

'Sten Inge Lystad, Kripos.'

The man's face was dominated by a crooked mouth which lent it a twisted appearance. The slanting smile divided his face into two in a peculiar, but engaging, way. Lystad's face was one you remembered. Frølich ransacked his memory. *Lystad* . . . the name was familiar, but not the face.

'It's about Jonny Faremo.'

Frank Frølich nodded. 'Tragic.'

'So you know about it already?'

Another nod

'Who told you?'

'As I'm sure you know, I work for the police. We're colleagues.'

'But who told you?'

'Gunnarstranda.'

Lystad smiled coyly.

Frank Frølich thought: *He doesn't like this turn of events. The conversation hasn't taken the direction he anticipated.*

The ensuing silence was a clear sign that Lystad wanted to be invited in. But Frank Frølich didn't want anyone in and so observed Lystad in silence.

'Have you been to Faremo's house recently?'

On the positive side: no beating about the bush. Negative: his method is to keep a distance, be cool.

'You mean Jonny Faremo?'

'Yes, I mean Jonny Faremo.'

'I've been there, that is to say, outside. I rang the doorbell, a couple of days ago, the same day he was released from custody. I was supposed to meet his sister, Elisabeth. I don't know if you know the background here?'

'I'd prefer to know as little as possible, apart from what happened between you and Jonny Faremo when you saw him last.'

'OK,' Frank Frølich said, thinking: *high arsehole factor.*

'Was his sister at home when you rang?'

'Elisabeth? Does the question mean that your interest goes beyond my dealings with her brother after all?'

A shadow crossed Lystad's face.

He doesn't like the direction the conversation is taking – positive.

'Frølich, listen.'

'No, you listen. I've been a policeman for many years. I can see you're aware you're making a mess of this. I'm also the first person to understand that you don't like the job, but you don't need to kick people in the balls even if they're standing conveniently close by. You say the background doesn't concern you. Well, it concerns me to a very considerable extent. I've taken a load of time off because of the background. That's what has led to this conversation between you and me. Well, if the background doesn't concern you, don't ask about it. Either you don't care or you do.'

Lystad didn't say anything and Frølich continued.

'My version is that I started a relationship with a lady who has the wrong connections. The same lady's brother is dead now. But be absolutely clear about one thing: I've never ever been interested in Jonny Faremo, neither when I met him two days ago, nor at any other time. When I showed up at his place – after Faremo was released from custody – that was the first time I'd ever met the guy. I'd never seen him before. But I went there to meet her, to talk to her, and I did that because a situation had arisen in our relationship: she had used my name in her testimony to give her brother an alibi at the hearing.'

Lystad nodded gravely. 'Go on,' he said.

'When I got there, I parked in the visitors' car park. There are stairs leading from there to the flats. I went down and rang the doorbell. I assume your witness is an elderly man – the neighbour with whom I spoke when no one answered the door. I exchanged a few words with the man. Then I went back to the car and was about to drive off when Jonny Faremo appeared. He was driving a silver Saab. I'd never seen the man before, but I realized who he was and I approached him to ask where his sister was. He didn't know. At least he claimed he didn't know. Then I got back into my car and left.'

'Where did you go?'

'Two hundred metres further down Ekebergveien.'

'Why did you stop there?'

'To think.'

'What happened then?'

'Jonny Faremo came down the hill in his car.'

Lystad stared at him with interest.

Frølich made him wait.

'What happened?'

'I followed him in my car.'

Lystad had to wait again.

'It was lunchtime. It was half past one.'

'But what happened?'

'He must have spotted me. I lost him ten minutes later. Somewhere between Gamlebyen and the main station. The whole idea was stupid, so I wasn't particularly bothered when he disappeared.'

'What did you do then?'

'I drove home and had a bite to eat.'

'And then?'

'Then I drove to Blindern University where I tried to meet a lady who works there. Reidun Vestli.'

'Why was that?'

'She has a close relationship with Elisabeth.' Frølich searched for words before continuing: 'They have, or have had, a relationship. I assumed this woman might be able to tell me where Elisabeth is.'

'And could she?'

'I didn't meet her. She's off sick.'

'What did you do then?'

'I tried to ring the lady at home, but only got the answer machine. Then I drove home.'

They stood looking at each other. Lystad cleared his throat. 'Anyone able to confirm you were at Blindern?'

'I would presume so.'

'Presume?'

'There was a student. I was trying to find Reidun Vestli's office. She was an MA student, borrowing Reidun Vestli's office, and it was she who told me Vestli was off sick.'

'And what did you do when you got home?'

'Watched a film, looked at the walls, had a few beers.'

'And the day after?'

'Nothing. Looked at the walls. Got sick of that and went on the town in the evening.'

'And can anyone confirm that?'

'Yes.'

'When did you get home last night?'

'Don't remember.'

'What time did you get to Blindern the day before yesterday?'

'I don't remember, but it was in the afternoon.'

'Well, Frølich . . .'

The same smile, a touch patronizing, sympathetic.

'I'll find out and let you know.'

'Were you in Ekebergveien last night?'

'Possibly. I have no idea.'

'And what do you think I'm supposed to make of that answer?'

'I don't think anything.'

'You were seen in Ekebergveien last night.'

'Well, then, I must have been there.'

Lystad waited for more.

Frank Frølich breathed in. 'I was drunk. It wasn't meant to happen, but I became sentimental. The last thing I can remember is that I was talking to a colleague in Café Fiasco. It's by the main station – they sell cheap beer. Met a colleague there, Emil Yttergjerde. He and I stayed there drinking and chatting about this and that. At some point in the night I got into a taxi. The cabs are, as you know, parked just around the corner between Oslo Spektrum and Radisson Hotel. I don't remember much about the drive, but I didn't go all the way home because I was feeling ill. I got off in Gamlebyen because I had drunk too much and needed to throw up. And I began to walk to freshen up a little. I walked up and down the streets all night. I got into my own bed at eight o'clock this morning. I'd been wandering the streets for several hours, along Ekebergveien too, I'm sure.'

'Did you try to get in touch with Faremo or his sister during the night?'

'No.'

'And you're absolutely positive?'

'Yes.'

'One of Faremo's neighbours thought he saw a powerfully built man sneaking around outside their door.'

'I don't sneak.'

'What time was it when you got home?'

'As I said, at eight. Came right in and straight to bed.'

Lystad shoved his hands in his pockets and gave a crooked smile. 'We'll have to come back to this story, Frølich.'

'I wouldn't have expected anything else.'

The silence hung in the air for a few seconds. The lift shaft hummed.

Then stopped. The door opened. A woman with a stoop came out. She peered up at them. 'Hello,' Frølich said.

The woman stared at him, then at Lystad, then turned her back on them and rang the neighbour's bell.

Lystad said: 'You haven't seen anything of his sister – since she vanished?'

'No.'

'If you see her, tell her to get into contact with us.'

Frank Frølich nodded. The antipathy he had felt towards Lystad was gradually dissipating.

After closing the door he stood motionless staring, first at the door, then at the floor. His mind was a blank. Finally he went to the fridge. His liver should have something to do, but only a little bit. A tiny little bit.

12

Next morning it was cold, but there was no frost. It was a day for the last yellow leaves to exhibit themselves, another attempt to clothe the grey-green countryside in colour. Reidun Vestli's house lay to the west, on the slope over the river Lysaker, roughly midway between Røa and the Kolsås Metro bridge – an affluent, modern estate. Here there are lines of terraced houses between apartment buildings, each house with its own patch of lawn, each drive its own BMW. Frank Frølich passed a man wearing suit trousers and rubber boots washing his car with a small high-pressure cleaner. He passed two more drives, two more BMWs and one more man in suit trousers, rubber boots and a high-pressure sprinkler over the roof of his car. A clone, he thought, or maybe just a déjà-vu experience. Anyway, neither of the two men had seen him. No one sees anything, no one remembers anything. Only in police interviews do they see and remember much more than you could imagine.

Her doorplate was made of brass. He stood in front of the door and rang. Above the brass plate was a bronze lion's head with the doorknocker hanging from its jaws. He banged the doorknocker. One single knock. The door was opened.

He hardly recognized the woman at the door. That time, in the lecture hall, she had given the impression of being strong. Then, she would have typified the profile of the terraced house, fitted the row of house fronts – decorated in cleverly devised earthen colours, brown and dark red shades which matched her skin, her hair with the henna tint and her brown eyes. The Reidun Vestli standing in the doorway now was a shadow of herself. Her face was harrowed through lack of sleep; her lower lip had unhealthy coffee stains. She was wearing an unbecoming track suit, which emphasized the impression of decline. The smell of unventilated smoke wafted through the front door. 'You,' she said in a rusty voice. 'I know who you are.'

He cleared his throat. 'May I come in?'

'Why?'

Frølich didn't answer.

Finally she took a decision and stepped aside.

The room smelt of smoke and full ashtrays. Reidun Vestli stood in front of an enormous coffee table overflowing with loose sheets of paper and old newspapers. There were a few unframed canvases hanging on the walls.

Frølich guessed one had been painted by Kjell Nupen, another, a darker motif, by Ørnulf Opdal. He didn't dare hazard a guess at the last. But there was something clean and tidy about the two walls. They reminded him of her meticulously tidy office and dominated the room like immovable pillars. On the floor, empty wine bottles and crisp packets, a half-open pizza carton and empty packets of cigarettes. A mini stereo balanced precariously on a mass of loose cables beside a makeshift unmade bed which looked like a divan. A large number of CDs were scattered around the floor. A dusty, greasy, rusty tea maker had pride of place on the window sill, surrounded by dead flies.

This is what Elisabeth was drawn to! He took care not to step on any CDs. *To this woman with metallic-coloured teeth from the previous day's red wine, smelling of nicotine, coffee, lack of sleep and dust. Her longings brought her here.*

The woman lit a cigarette from the stub of the one she'd just finished. Her hand shook. When she stood like that, concentrated and bent forwards, she also revealed the pouches of fat on her hips and thighs, a network of wrinkles between cheek and chin, a head wreathed by lifeless, unwashed hair, in turn wreathed by blue cigarette smoke. She was the crowning glory of a total work of art: the materialized essence of litter, blaring radio, mess and an aura of liberated indifference. The hoarse voice said: 'What do you want?'

'I rang you a couple of days ago. But you broke off the conversation and switched off your phone.'

'Have you come here to have that confirmed?'

'You were driving a car.'

'You really are a detective. No wonder you work for the police.'

'You were suddenly taken ill.'

'The detective is correct. I'm still ill.'

'It happened at the same time as Elisabeth chose to disappear.'

'Really? Has she disappeared?'

'You know very well she has.'

'Your imagination is running away with you. You should stick to the facts, Sherlock.'

'Tell me them.'

'What would you like to know?'

'Everything.'

'Everything?' She went closer and pulled her lips into a venomous grimace.

Frølich sensed a feeling growing inside him: irritation at everything she stood for, the snobbish arrogance, academia, all the mess in this room, all the secrets she had hoarded in this nest of hers. 'Everything,' he repeated in a thick voice.

Reidun Vestli went in closer. 'But can you take it?'

'Take what?'

'The truth.'

'I think I can, so long as you spare me bullshit like this.'

He ran his eye along a row of books against the wall and stopped when he saw titles like *The Story of* O and *Catherine M* – erotica, the term used in academic circles for what others call pornography.

'Are you capable of understanding that someone can develop a deeper insight into, for instance . . .?' Reidun Vestli hesitated as Frølich took the top book from the pile and held it up.

'What, for instance?'

She looked at the book he was holding in his hands. 'My God, don't be so banal.'

They exchanged looks and he turned away. 'You disappoint me,' she said.

'Banal?' he asked.

'You're just so damned predictable and tedious.' She put the cigarette between her sore lips and inhaled deeply. Her fingers were still trembling. 'I really thought you were a rather interesting person,' she said. 'According to Elisabeth, you are.'

'Perhaps she's mistaken,' he said. 'Perhaps I'm completely predictable and tedious, but I didn't come here to talk about me. I want you to tell me where she is.'

'I've no idea what you're talking about.'

'Now it's you who disappoint me,' he said, toe-punting a book. 'I knew Elisabeth was studying. Is she into books like this?'

'Don't you know? I had expected you to know, you being a detective and all that.'

'I just want to find her.'

'Why?'

'That has nothing to do with you.'

'What will you do if you find her?'

'That has nothing to do with you, either.'

'Well, I know how men and women spend their time. You don't need to give me your version.' She pulled a scornful face. 'Not surprising you're jealous, you poor thing. Of course you know nothing about her mind. Has she never told you?'

'About what? About you?'

Reidun Vestli smiled disdainfully. 'Not about me,' she whispered. 'Not a single word about me, while I know most things about you. So she hasn't talked to you about what she and I have in common? Does that make you a little jealous?'

Jealous. Am I? And if this obsessive unease I feel is jealousy, what triggered this jealousy? Elisabeth's and Reidun's physical or intellectual intimacy? Or both? Or the fear of being kept as an onlooker to whatever it is they share?

'What should I be jealous of?'

'For instance, our common sense of wonder.'

'Wonder.' He articulated the word with derision.

'Yes,' she went on. 'Elisabeth is, for example, captivated by language. She even has her own theory about the power inherent in words, where there is no place for emotions, how words can fill out and add extra dimensions when perceptions and the physical stop short.'

Frank Frølich watched her mouth. She enjoyed saying these things. She enjoyed telling him she had a nearness with Elisabeth which he had never had. She had pronounced the word *physical* with disgust. *This is what you are*, he thought: *you're an ageing lesbo who cannot stand the thought that I entered and satisfied the woman you desire. You cannot bear the thought that as a man I am capable of giving her something you cannot.* He whispered: 'You should be able to accept . . .'

'You going to bed together?' Reidun Vestli interrupted with a malicious smile. 'What do you think of me, actually – or of her? Do you imagine I would get involved with another person if it wasn't about emotion? Do you think you're something special or unique because you've got a dick?'

The aggression that came with the words was numbing. He managed to force out: 'Vulgarity doesn't become you.'

'I'm not vulgar. I'm defending myself against you. You think you can come here and enter my home, driven by a pathetic longing to possess and dominate the woman I love. You enter this house asserting that your gender gives you extenuating characteristics which are supposed to make you special in my eyes. You don't have an inkling about Elisabeth; you don't know who she is. You know nothing about a single thought or dream she and I have shared. Have you and Elisabeth ever talked? Have you discussed anything? Have you and Elisabeth ever taken your minds off your genitalia to explore whether you can share the pleasure of anything intellectual?'

It was his turn to jeer at her. 'Share the pleasure of something intellectual, my arse!'

She drew in her breath sharply. 'Quite honestly, I cannot fathom what she sees in you at all. In addition to being simple, you're not even particularly good-looking.' She looked away and added casually: 'Has it ever occurred to you she's trying to escape from you?'

'That idea is totally irrational.'

She sent him an oblique glance. 'Are you frightened I know something you don't?'

Her facial expression, the malicious glee following the question caused him to swallow hard.

She noticed and laughed. It was a bright resonant laugh, a spiteful laugh. 'You pathetic little man, what do you take me for? I love her and she loves me. Apart from sharing a bed, we share something else, something with a soul, a mind and self-respect!'

Frølich was sweating. This intense creature who crushed him with her words, the tense atmosphere in this stuffy flat, the unmade bed where she and Elisabeth had made love. 'The great love affair of yours seems to have faded,' he said deliberately. 'Or perhaps you're ill for other reasons?'

Reidun Vestli lit another cigarette, folded her arms across her chest and smoked with trembling hands.

'Say what you want or get out.'

'Did I touch a sore point perhaps?'

'As I said, get out if you have . . .'

'I want to know where she is.'

'I have no idea where she is!'

'I think you're lying.'

'Your word against mine.'

He stood up. 'It would be to Elisabeth's benefit if you told the truth.'

'Are you threatening me?'

'Not at all. In my pathetic masculine way I'm taking care of her. I'm searching for her because I wish her well. I respect her decision to be with you, or on her own or with someone else. But I happen to know that she is in hiding and because I work for the police, I know she's being stupid to hide in this way – after all, a murder has been committed. Whether she likes it or not, she's part of this case. You may be able to satisfy her physically and intellectually, and your high-flown intellectual love may be worth more than mine, but I know one thing you cannot distort with your prattle: hiding will do her no good.'

'You don't know everything.'

'If she's hiding, I assume she's afraid of something. And this is where she's made a miscalculation.'

'You don't understand that it's you she's hiding from?'

'I think Elisabeth intended to go on her travels when she supplied the alibi for her brother and his gang at the hearing. I think she contacted you to help her find somewhere to hide. I think your so-called illness started when she contacted you. And I think you and she were together in the car when I phoned you a few days ago. I'm certain you know where she is.'

Reidun Vestli slowly raised her head. The look she gave him was red-rimmed, but thoughtful at the same time.

Frølich was unsure whether he should tell her or not, but decided he would. He said: 'Elisabeth's brother is dead, in all probability murdered.'

Her eyes clouded over now, still thoughtful though, almost calculating.

'It's important you tell us where she is!'

'Do you imagine I'm completely stupid?' Reidun Vestli hissed. 'Do you imagine you can come here with no other authority than your physical bulk and order me about? Will you leave! Off you go! Out!' She shoved him towards the door. 'Out!' she repeated.

He sighed heavily and obeyed. She slammed the door with a bang. He stood on the step, heard her steps dying away. Reidun Vestli's reaction told him he was right. But so what? He hadn't got anywhere.

He stood listening. Silence at first. Afterwards the sound of a voice. Reidun Vestli was talking to someone on the phone. Who else could it be but Elisabeth?

He was gaping at the door, but collected himself, turned and walked back slowly, past the car-washer clones, the BMWs, the fence posts and the spiraea hedges. Had he known, he would have spared himself this confrontation. On the other hand, some things had been confirmed. She knew. He was sure.

13

That evening he sat at home with a cold beer in front of the television. But he couldn't concentrate. He zapped. A man and a woman were under a duvet murmuring into each other's ears. Reality TV. He continued to zap. A cheetah running in slow motion. The animal was an explosion of muscular power and concentration. The cheetah's eyes and body seemed to be living separate lives. Two lives merged into one, an engine which ran automatically. A body hinged at the hip joint. The cheetah launched itself at a Thomson's gazelle, forced the poor beast to the ground and killed it with one bite to the throat. Afterwards the cheetah guarded its prey, breathless. The TV voice delivered its spiel about how this was the most critical moment for the cheetah. It was too tired to eat, but if it didn't start soon, a lion or a hyena would come along and steal its prey. The commentator had hardly finished speaking when an extraordinarily ugly-looking hunched creature roared and frightened off the cheetah. The hyena bolted down the food while the poor exhausted cheetah sat some distance away watching its own lunch disappear. Several more hyenas arrived. They sank their jaws in the gazelle's stomach, peered up and bared their blood-stained teeth.

He switched off the television.

Hesitantly, he reached for the telephone. He dialled Gunnarstranda's number and for some strange reason felt guilty about doing it. It wasn't quite ten o'clock in the evening. Most probably the old codger was in the office. But he wasn't: Gunnarstranda's hoarse voice carried into the room: 'Please be brief.'

'I've been talking to Reidun Vestli,' Frølich said, promptly regretting he had called.

'And who is Reidun Vestli?'

'Elisabeth Faremo's lover.'

Silence on the line.

'I suspect she knows where Elisabeth Faremo is.'

'And?'

'Just a tip. You could perhaps have a chat with her.'

'Thank you for that.'

Frølich didn't know what to say.

Gunnarstranda cleared his throat. 'I take it you spoke to her in a private capacity.'

'Naturally.'

'My advice to you is to stop doing this too. You're on leave, Frølich. Keep out of it, go on holiday.'

With that, the line went dead.

He sat there with the receiver in his hand. If he hadn't felt stupid before, he did now. On top of that, Gunnarstranda's coldness. But it was part of him. The problem was that he had never felt it before, not in this way.

That night he had confused dreams about Elisabeth and her brother. The two of them had the same look. One moment black with desire, the next mortally afraid. But which were her brother's eyes and which were hers?

During the night all the clouds had dispersed and once again the cold had slipped in – setting the scene for a freezing cold late November morning. The air was as keen as a razor blade. The sub-zero temperatures had glued the night mist to the ice on the tarmac. He got into the car, drove out of town and headed east. Transparent mist steamed off the black ploughed fields as he approached Hobøl and Elvestad. Beyond the margins of the forest, in the distance, the globe of the sun resembled the red-hot bald dome of a creator poking his head over the crest to release a little more light for the people in the north. Soon the rays were so bright that Frank Frølich had to flip down the sun shield.

He paid at the toll gate in Fossum, turned into the Shell garage by Fossum bridge and filled the tank. The Glomma was flowing quietly but robustly under the bridge. He thought about Jonny Faremo. About swimming against the current in icy water.

After paying he got back in his car and studied the map. He was lower than Solbergfoss power station, but still above Kykkelsrud power station.

He sat thinking for a while before starting the engine and then drove behind the petrol station. There was a narrow, winding side road leading to a footbridge further along. He parked, got out and leaned against the stone barrier by the river. The water coiled as it followed the slow-moving current.

He stood watching the eddies in the brown-black water. If he fell in here his body would be carried far away in seconds. The cold water would paralyse him. His wet clothes would make it difficult to move. They would become heavy and sap his strength as he was dragged under. The river bank was inhospitable, only slippery rocks. To crawl ashore would be almost impossible. The strong current and the cold would make time a vital factor. How long could he survive?

He strolled along the path by the river. From here paths ran up to the ridge, between the old wartime bunkers. The picnic area on the opposite side of the river was less protected from prying eyes, but you could get rid of a body here relatively easily as well. Nevertheless, there was one fact that suggested that Jonny Faremo had not been thrown in here: the river was closed off further down by Kykkelsrud power station. Faremo had been found in a net further down.

He thought: *Perhaps it's wisest to start there – in Kykkelsrud.*

Frank Frølich crossed the footbridge. On the other side there was a commemorative monument – 'The Battle of Fossum Bridge'. Here the Germans had met determined Norwegian resistance before their safe passage through to Oslo in April 1940. The full names of the fallen Norwegians were carved in stone.

Frølich went back to his car and drove on, over Fossum bridge, up the hills towards Askim. He passed a couple of automatic radar traps at such a slow speed that they didn't flash.

A road sign indicated the turn-off to the next power station. He took it. They were building a new motorway here; he passed a few of the roadworks and machines. He accelerated down towards the local waterworks and bore left, towards the power station. The car continued downwards, approaching the river again.

He passed a few isolated old-style wooden houses – probably the homes of the power-station workers. Another turning. Shortly afterwards, a road sign: HAFSLUND ENERGI. The stone building was modern with large windows. Behind it the bank of the river towered up on the opposite side of the reservoir. He let the car roll down towards the power station and the dam.

There was a bleached, though still blue, parking sign by some fenced-in sheds to the left of the road. A relatively new Skoda Octavia estate was parked there. He recognized the car and was not at all pleased, but he parked next to it.

This wasn't a good moment to meet Gunnarstranda. Frølich didn't have a plausible explanation for why he was here. But did he have to have one? Did every step he took have to have a rational motivation? He scanned the area. Gunnarstranda was nowhere to be seen. He couldn't see anyone. There was no discernible activity from the houses scattered across the mountainside. Even the Hafslund Energi offices appeared dead. The frost made the tarmac smooth and slippery. He walked cautiously, stiff-legged, towards the dam. On his way down to the power station he passed three enormous discarded turbines which had been left for viewing on the frosty grass. To the right lay the reservoir, dammed up and black like a huge troll's mirror. A tiny island close to shore stood out. The trees on the mountain slopes in front of the power station were reflected in the black surface of the water. The rate of discharge was low and revealed the whole stone construction forming the dam. On the left-hand side there was a fifty-metre-long dry concrete structure – a sluiceway without any water. It was a long way down to the bottom of the sluice. He felt an attack of vertigo as he peered down over the edge. Between the dam and the far sluice wall there were two large brick grids. A clammy stench of stagnant water came from an undisturbed muddy bed below. He walked out onto the dam and passed over what must have been the water inlet. The dam trembled slightly – a huge grumbling pulse. Water streamed down beneath him. And to the right, up to the wall, the surface water coiled slowly into eddies and currents. Here water was at work. In front, the waterfall was stemmed by a wall consisting of three large sluice gates.

He could positively feel the force of the water pressing against the wall as he stared at the course of the river a few hundred metres lower down. At that moment the sweet smell of a freshly lit Petterøe prickled his nose. Without turning his head, he said, 'Gunnarstranda, are you still smoking?'

'I've smoked for over forty years,' Gunnarstranda said and went over to him. Gunnarstranda had his hands in his pockets as his cheeks greedily sucked the smoke into his mouth and down into his lungs.

'But you really should give it up. You're ill.'

'I had thought about stopping, but then the doctor wanted me to chew gum with nicotine in. But that's still nicotine, isn't it? What's the difference then? May as well continue smoking.'

Frølich smiled to himself.

'What are you laughing at?' Gunnarstranda asked grumpily.

'I heard this joke about a man who was intent on giving up smoking. He met a friend who had succeeded. "How did you manage to stop smoking?" the man asked. "Well," said the other man. "Giving up smoking is the easiest thing in the world. You buy a packet of cigarettes as usual, but whenever you want to light up, you first of all stick a cigarette up your arse."

'"Up your arse?" asked his friend. "Yes, up your arse. There's no better way to tell yourself smoking is shit. You would never dream of putting the cigarette you had up your arse in your mouth afterwards," the man said.

'Well, the two men met a couple of months later. "Hi," his friend shouts. "How did it go? Did you manage to stop smoking?"

'"Of course," the first man says. "Giving up smoking was easy. But actually it didn't help very much."

'"It didn't help very much?"

'"The problem now is I can't stop sticking cigarettes up my arse!"' Frølich slapped his thighs and gasped with laughter.

Gunnarstranda glowered at him just as grumpily as before. 'And there was me thinking the rumours about you were just bollocks,' he said.

Frølich assumed a serious face again. 'I was looking for you after I saw your car,' he said.

'You're beginning to get on my nerves,' Gunnarstranda said.

'Oh?'

'Just the fact that you come out here when you're off work. At some point, if you continue to get under my feet, I'll be forced to report you.'

'And?'

'Perhaps you can't see your own stupidity, but everyone else can.'

'Relax,' Frølich said. 'You won't have to report me. Do you reckon Faremo was thrown in here?'

'No, there isn't enough water in the river.' Gunnarstranda nodded in the direction of the exposed rocks in the river bed beneath them. 'The waterfall is almost dry. It must have happened further down.' He pointed. 'On the promontory down there, perhaps. Perfect place for a crime. There's a gravel path down to the river from it. Unfortunately, however, there's a barrier closing it off. Padlocked.'

'Has anyone got a spare key?'

'Hardly. A man I met in there.' Gunnarstranda tossed his head towards the turbine building. 'He told me he lives in one of the houses on the slope. Reckons he would have noticed if anyone had passed through the barrier.'

They looked across the wide river valley in silence.

'This station is not being used,' Gunnarstranda said finally. 'I was given a long introduction into energy and its history over there. Vamma, further down, and Solbergfoss, higher up, are the ones which produce the energy. This power station is only used when the water level in the Glomma is particularly high.'

'But what do you think happened to Faremo? Was he pushed in? Or did he lose his footing on a slippery rock?'

'Hard to say.'

'They may not have driven down to the river. It could have been one person, or two, going for a walk.'

'Could have been. And if there have been any sightings, I'll soon find out.'

Frølich interpreted Gunnarstranda's answer as an indication that this topic of conversation was not taboo. He said: 'It's absolutely crazy that Faremo should have died right now, isn't it?'

'Not everyone is permitted to choose the time of their death, Frølich.'

'I've had a look at the map. There's a road nearer to Askim looping down towards the river. From a logical point of view, a murderer could have driven along the road, got as close as possible to the river and found somewhere to offload Faremo. And he doesn't need to be familiar with the locality.'

'Why not?'

'Well, if he had been local he would have known about Vamma power station; he would have known that the river is closed off with a net which sifts the water and picks up debris. If he had driven a bit further and thrown Faremo in the river under Vamma, the body could have drifted several kilometres before it turned up in Sarpsborg – it's quite a distance from Vamma to the net before Sarp waterfall.

'Sounds logical – apart from one thing.'

'What's that?'

'You're talking as if Faremo was killed first. But he had water in his lungs. He drowned. If it was murder, and the murder was *not* premeditated, Faremo may have ended up in the river as a result of a row, a fight, and that is the most likely scenario. So most of the investigation will be taken up with searching for someone with a score to settle with Faremo.'

Frank Frølich pretended he hadn't heard the veiled reference to himself and said: 'There's a lot of footwork in a case like this. Are you going to go around asking questions?'

'I told you the Jonny Faremo case is in the hands of Kripos. Didn't I?'

'I've had the pleasure of speaking to them. A young lad – Lystad.'

'He's good.'

'What conclusion did he come to – murder or accident?'

'No idea.' Gunnarstranda took the cigarette out of his mouth and stared at it grimly. 'Do you know that this mess between you and the Faremo woman has made me smoke more than I should?'

'So, what are you doing here?'

'It's Sunday,' Gunnarstranda said. 'I'm free.'

Frølich grinned. 'And you can stand there and threaten to report me? It's not in your jurisdiction.'

'Anyway, it's not a good idea for you to wander around asking people questions. It's better if you ring me. I'm always kept up to date.'

'The area of interest is a stretch of river about a kilometre in length,' Frølich said, unruffled. 'And Faremo is certain to have come here by car. If he didn't fall off the promontory over there, Faremo or the murderer must have taken the right-hand turning just before Askim. On my map there are two narrow gravelled paths or cart tracks leading to the river. And I'll give you odds of nine to one that there are witnesses. At any rate, someone must have noticed the car.'

They ambled slowly back. Gunnarstranda cleared his throat and said: 'As a matter of form, Frølich . . .'

'Yes?'

'Are you putting in a report, perhaps? Describing the last few days, what you've done and who can confirm it, etc?'

'So I haven't been cleared of suspicion of murder?'

'Which murder?'

They looked each other in the eye. Frølich had never been able to read what went on in the other man's head. And he didn't want to try now, either.

'Strange business, this, Frølich. There's only a tip-off connecting Jonny Faremo to the murder of the security man in Loenga, and let's be honest, that tip-off isn't worth a lot.'

Frølich squinted up at the sky. The day wasn't many hours old, yet the sun had already set up a flamboyant farewell spectacle behind the mountain ridge. Vermilion tongues of cloud licked between ochre-yellow flames above the azure-blue aura over the trees. He asked: 'How little is the tip-off actually worth?'

Gunnarstranda took his time to answer. 'Private initiatives from you are likely to be misunderstood. If you don't take it easy, you'll be suspended.'

'Tell me about the tip-off,' Frølich persisted obstinately.

'A woman, twenty-nine years old, a freelance model who gets most of her jobs working as a waitress in a so-called Go-Go bar.'

'Prostitute?'

'Doubt it. She calls herself a model and appears in *Aftenposten* in lingerie adverts and that sort of thing. On top of that, she's the girlfriend of one of the boys in the gang we banged up.'

'Whose girlfriend?'

Gunnarstranda hesitated.

'Which one of them?' Frølich repeated.

'Jonny Faremo.'

'What's her name?'

'Forget it, Frølich.'

'The only thing I'm interested in is her name. It's ridiculous that you won't tell me.'

'Merethe Sandmo.'

'Is she a suspect?'

'No idea. This case is being dealt with by Kripos, not me.'

'Why would Faremo's woman blow the whistle on him?'

'No idea. But the relationship must have been stormy. The tip-off reeks of revenge, which makes her statement worth very little. It wouldn't take much to break the link between these boys and the murdered security man. If it does break, we'll have to look elsewhere for someone with a score to settle with Faremo. And, obviously, one of those people is you.'

'The woman whose name you just mentioned, who shopped them, she could have given him a shove from behind.' Frølich stood admiring the sky.

'By the way . . .' he said finally.

'By the way what?'

'Do you think I'm a few bricks short of a load?'

'I don't think you're a few bricks short of a load, no. But I don't think anything about anyone in an investigation. And you know that very well.'

'But that means you would bust me if there was enough evidence to support such a hypothesis?'

Gunnarstranda smiled mirthlessly. 'Would you blame me?'

Frølich sighed. 'Probably not.'

'Why do you want me to talk to this academic, Reidun Vestli?' Gunnarstranda said in a gentler tone.

'Because, for some reason or other, Elisabeth Faremo has gone into hiding. Lying low. She must have panicked. At any rate, she packed a rucksack on the same day her brother and his pals were set free at the hearing. I haven't a clue where she went or why she disappeared. She hasn't turned up again now that her brother is dead and that's a little strange, isn't it? On top of that, Reidun Vestli went off sick at the same time as Elisabeth packed her rucksack and went on the run. And Reidun Vestli wasn't at home when I rang her a few hours later. She was driving somewhere. When I did eventually get hold of her, I was left with the impression she knew where Elisabeth was. I somehow feel the two of them are complicit.'

'Perhaps Elisabeth Faremo has run away from you?'

Now it was Frølich's turn to sigh heavily. 'Her brother's dead. She's still in hiding.'

The silence hung in the air between them. Gunnarstranda broke it: 'Why would Elisabeth Faremo ally herself with Reidun Vestli?'

'She and Elisabeth are, or have been, an item. This Reidun Vestli sees me as a masculine avenger from the heterosexual world. And the woman can't see anything wrong with Elisabeth disappearing, despite the fact that Elisabeth has a key role in this murder case and her brother is dead. The woman cannot connect her relationship with reality. I feel she's Elisabeth's willing collaborator right now.'

'What would your interest in this be – if I talk to Vestli?'

'Mine?' Frølich shrugged his shoulders. 'As you can see, I'm in a bit of a cleft stick. Obviously, it would be fascinating to know what Reidun Vestli has to say when you flash your police badge and take a hard line with her.'

14

After Gunnarstranda had got into his car and driven off, Frank Frølich waited for a while and looked at the weather. He thought about physical intimacy on dark autumn evenings, when car headlamps struggle to penetrate the mist, when frost quivers like a circular rainbow for a brief instant in the light of street lamps. He thought about knitted gloves and intertwined fingers.

He tore himself away, went back to his car and drove until he came to the afore-mentioned side road just before Askim. There he turned and followed the winding gravel road, searching for a tractor track leading to the river and imagining how natural it would have been to park. In the end, he gave up and pulled over onto the gravel verge just before a copse. On the right-hand side of the road, there was a large field with straw stubble in neat rows protruding through the hoar frost. The field ended in a dark hillside overlooking the river. He wandered across the field. The frost crunched beneath his shoes. He reached the trees and stopped in front of a birch. The branches were covered with tiny ice-thorns; each bough resembled a carefully designed decoration. He looked down and ran his shoe along a branch of a raspberry bush; the ice-thorns came off with a dry rasping sound. The ice covering the spruce trees transformed the mountain ridge into a matt light-green surface. Further into the wood, there was the same formation of ice on withered stems, dead fern leaves and cranberry heath. Every cranberry leaf was wreathed in small ball-shaped ice crystals. A birch caught by the sun had been forced to relinquish its ice costume, which lay like granular snow on the forest floor.

He went on, across the blueberry heath and moss blanket, down towards the river. Soon he could hear the water. The noise increased in volume and became an impenetrable roar. He walked out onto a crag and stared down into the foaming water. This had to be the horizontal waterfall Gunnarstranda had been talking about. The water in the ravine coiled into a green-grey spume, smashed against the mountainside with enormous power, was hurled back and thundered on. Further down, the heavy mass of water pitched around like the backbone of a ferocious animal, laying bare fierce, capricious back eddies, which flowed away and swept lazily along a river bank of rocks and protruding branches snagged on ice-encased, tangled roots. He could see that a body would not stand a chance in this inferno. He felt giddy and sat down on the roots of a fallen tree. The rock ledge, which was a protection against the ravages of the water, was covered with ice and seemed perilously smooth. Anyone could slip on this if they were unlucky. But that begged the question: what would anyone be doing on this icy river bank on a cold November day?

He sat on a tree trunk in the dusk thinking that Elisabeth would be sitting somewhere too, and if she wasn't terribly busy, perhaps she was thinking about him. Once again Frølich took his mobile phone and called her number. The signal didn't get through. No ring tone, nothing. Pathetic creature, he thought contemptuously about himself. It was beginning to get dark. He rose and went back to his car.

15

When Gunnarstranda drove into Oslo, he turned off as usual at the raised intersection known as the Traffic Machine, continued up to Bispelokket to cross the bridge over Grønland and then took Maridalsveien, heading for Tåsen. Waiting for green at the traffic lights in Hausmannsgate, he caught sight of a familiar figure in the doorway to Café Sara. Vidar Ballo was holding the door open for a young woman – he recognized her too: their tip-off. Merethe Sandmo.

Gunnarstranda pulled over, half onto the pavement. He sat watching them. They crossed Hausmannsgate and headed for Ankerbrua. Walking side by side. There was a peaceful quality about the couple: the suspect and the woman who had betrayed him. Gunnarstranda mused on the significance of Merethe Sandmo and Vidar Ballo looking like a pair of lovers on a shopping trip.

He got out of his car and followed them at a brisk pace towards Ankerbrua. They heard his rapid footsteps and stopped. Ballo put down the large travelling bag he had been carrying over his shoulder.

'Going somewhere?' the policeman asked, out of breath.

'What do you want?' Vidar Ballo said.

Gunnarstranda observed Merethe Sandmo. She was slightly taller than Ballo, slim, almost skinny, with unusually beautiful chestnut-brown hair reaching down to the middle of her back. Gunnarstranda had always wondered what made unappealing louts among the criminal fraternity attractive to a certain type of bimbo. Merethe Sandmo was a woman who tried to enhance her sensuality through her choice of clothes, heels and meticulously applied make-up – probably, he thought, to draw attention away from the frown lines around her mouth. The last time they had spoken he had promised her complete anonymity. He decided to keep his promise. 'I don't believe we've met,' he said and offered his hand to the attractive woman. They held eye contact until she understood the pretence and took his hand.

'Merethe,' she said and curtseyed like a little girl.

'What do you want?' Ballo repeated brusquely.

'To find out what you were doing last night and the night before that,' Gunnarstranda said without taking his eyes off the woman. 'What's your other name, Merethe?' he asked in a friendly tone.

'Sandmo.'

'Then we already know each other.'

Something died in Merethe Sandmo's eyes.

Ballo sensed it immediately. 'You two know each other?'

Gunnarstranda turned to Ballo and said: 'Perhaps you were forgetting you were at the court hearing?'

'Are you still going on about that business?'

'A twenty-two-year-old student, doing part-time security work at the harbour to earn a bit on the side, was murdered. He's sorely missed by his parents, a sister, a girlfriend and others. He was beaten to death with a baseball bat. Something tells me you have something to do with it. Perhaps you should take it easy?'

'You seem to be the one who has forgotten what happened,' Ballo answered with a measured tone. 'The judge ruled that you were mistaken.'

He took the woman's hand and said: 'Shall we go?'

Gunnarstranda said: 'You don't know, then?'

Ballo straightened up. The woman let go of his hand and cast concerned glances at both of them.

Ballo, expectant: 'Know what?'

'Jonny Faremo is no longer with us.'

Merethe Sandmo blanched. She supported herself on the wall. Ballo stared at Gunnarstranda through blurred eyes. The silence lingered. Merethe Sandmo fidgeted until she found something to hold onto. She ended up playing with a lock of her long hair.

'I said Jonny . . .'

'We heard what you said!'

Gunnarstranda caught Merethe Sandmo's hand and prevented her from falling. 'May I offer my condolences?' he said and when he saw how pale she was, went on: 'Shall we find somewhere you can sit down for a few moments?'

Ballo gave him the sort of look he would have given a maggot. 'You reckon you're invulnerable working for the bloody police, don't you?' he mumbled.

Gunnarstranda turned away from the woman and focused on Ballo again. 'And you aren't curious enough to ask me how he died?'

'You could do me the favour and tell me.'

'There are a couple of formalities first. What were you doing the night before last?'

'He was with me!' It was the woman who answered. Ballo hadn't changed expression or moved a muscle.

'Have I misunderstood?' Gunnarstranda asked hesitantly. 'A little bird told me you and Jonny were an item?'

'That was a long time ago,' she stammered.

'Who finished it?' Gunnarstranda asked gently.

Merethe Sandmo started crying.

'You're a fucking gent, you are,' Ballo muttered.

'Answer the question,' Gunnarstranda said to her before turning to face Ballo: 'Where were you the night before last?'

'You heard. I was with her.'

'When?'

'Night before last and last night.'

'When did you go there and when did you leave?'

'Merethe lives in Etterstad and I haven't the faintest what time it was. I don't look at my watch when I visit people.'

Gunnarstranda glanced over at the woman, who was nodding. 'Do you remember when he arrived?'

'Four o'clock in the morning. He picked me up from work and then we drove back to my place.' She added: 'I finished with Jonny.'

'Where do you work?'

The policeman already knew the answer. Nevertheless, the question was still worth asking so that the woman would realize he wouldn't tell anyone it was her who had tipped them off about the murder of the security man. Merethe Sandmo did realize. She lowered her eyes as if embarrassed at playing this little comedy in front of her boyfriend. She said:

'Bliss.'

'The club, Bliss?'

She nodded again.

He looked across to Ballo. 'Funny you couldn't remember that.'

'Lots of funny things in the world.'

'But you drove there? Drove your own car when you picked . . . Merethe, you said your name was?'

The woman nodded, reassured.

Ballo said: 'Yes.'

'Do you remember where you'd been before picking Merethe up at this club?'

'I was at home. I had stayed up and watched a couple of films.'

'Anyone able to confirm that?'

'No one comes to mind off the top of my head.'

'But I'm sure you wouldn't object to us asking the neighbours?'

'*I* don't. *They* might. The police have been around asking quite a lot of questions already.'

Gunnarstranda smiled. 'Then they'll be used to us. And you'll be dealing with other people.'

'Thank Old Nick for that.'

'You'll have to wait to thank him,' Gunnarstranda said jovially. 'At least until you know what you're thanking him for.'

'And what do you mean by that?'

'There's bound to be another round in court. I'm still investigating the murder of Arnfinn Haga, in case you've forgotten. The death of your good friend Jonny is thought to be suspicious at best and the Follo police will be investigating it with help from Kripos. We'll be all over you, Ballo. The devil's little messengers. Best wait for a while before you send us a thank-you letter.'

Ballo was keen to go.

'You wanted to know how Jonny died, didn't you?'

He had their attention.

'I'll expect to see you tomorrow at the police station,' Gunnarstranda said. 'You're required to be there at nine sharp to confirm your statements. Then we'll talk a bit more about Jonny.'

'Come on,' Vidar Ballo said to the woman and dragged her away.

Gunnarstranda stood watching them. Eventually, he turned and walked back to his car.

As he was getting in, his mobile phone rang.

It was Yttergjerde.

'Jonny Faremo had a woman friend, didn't he?' Gunnarstranda asked.

'Merethe Sandmo,' Yttergjerde said.

'That's what I thought. Just checking,' Gunnarstranda said. 'Now she's Ballo's woman friend.'

'What?'

'The king is dead; long live the king,' Gunnarstranda said. 'Why did you ring?'

Yttergjerde said: 'We've got a witness.'

'To what?'

'The murder of the security man – Arnfinn Haga.'

16

He was sitting in his armchair, staring apathetically at the chaos in his flat when there was a ring at the door. Frølich got up with some difficulty and shuffled into the hall. He pulled open the door with surprising energy.

Who had he been expecting? Elisabeth?

The person on the doormat was as far from this fantasy as you could imagine. Police Inspector Gunnarstranda was standing there with both hands in his coat pockets, regarding him with a look he had only seen his boss give suspected criminals.

'You've never been here before,' Frølich said and felt silly saying it.

Gunnarstranda shook his head.

'And we've worked together for over ten years.'

'Shall we chat inside or should I invite you out for a beer down town?'

'Come in.' For some unknown reason Frølich was embarrassed. He kicked a pair of worn shoes to the side and started tidying the table on their way in.

'Don't worry about that,' Gunnarstranda said. 'Don't do anything, and you don't need to offer me anything either.'

'I've only got beer.'

'Then I'll have a beer.'

Frølich hurried off into the kitchen. Damn. No clean glasses. He took a couple of tumblers from the dishwasher and rinsed them in tap water. 'Why have you come?' he shouted through the living-room door.

'Because work has finished for today.'

Frølich carried in two bottles and two glasses.

'And because those I have to work with are not very talkative.' Gunnarstranda cleared the table, produced a map and spread it out. Large scale. The Glomma snaked its way across the map like a twist of blue wool. 'I've had meetings with Kripos, amongst others, and I thought I could share some of the information with you – off the record.'

Frølich, who was filling the glasses, glanced up.

'You can't go too far wrong, then.'

'That was a generous thought.'

The response and the intonation, both were ignored.

'Faremo was found here – in Lake Vamma.' The blue line on the map expanded into a bubble: the water behind the dam was called Lake Vamma. Gunnarstranda ran his finger tip across until it indicated a small square beside the river. 'This is Oraug farm.' His index finger stopped at the square beside it. 'And this is Skjolden farm. Kripos have a witness who says there was a car parked right next to this farm. A car stops on the gravel road. Two people – in all probability the same two as were sitting in the car – had strolled down a tractor track to the river.' Gunnarstranda's finger moved to a red line on the map. 'This tractor track. The two of them had been walking, no signs of an argument. It was afternoon, the sun was low – the witness was out taking photographs. You know, autumn afternoon, good time for colours. Red maple leaves, yellow-brown birch leaves, all that sort of thing. The man claims the air was almost orange and perfect for photos – so the sun must have been very low. Kripos reckons it must have been three in the afternoon, maybe half past. I remember the day myself. It was a beautiful sky with hazy clouds gleaning colour from the sunset.'

'Two people – what gender?'

Gunnarstranda nodded. 'Not clear. But we assume they were men.'

'Did he take any pictures of them?'

'No. But he says they didn't seem like the usual walkers.'

'What did he mean by that?'

'No idea. He says they seemed rather too *urban*.'

'And Jonny Faremo was one of the two?'

'It might have been Faremo. One of them had been wearing a black cap. Faremo wore a black cap to the hearing.'

'And he was wearing one when I met him in the car park a little later.'

'And that's the only sighting we have. The tractor track leads down to the river between Kykkelsrud and Vamma power stations. And the time could be about right. This is most probably the last time anyone, apart from the murderer, saw Jonny Faremo alive.'

'When was this?'

'The same afternoon Faremo walked out of court a free man.'

'Two people walking, no arguing or fighting?'

'Right.'

'Did anyone see the car start up again and leave?'

'No one, as yet.'

'But the car?'

'Gone.'

'Why would two people go for a stroll in such a godforsaken place down by the Glomma on a frosty November day?'

'Why do Norwegians go walking in general?'

'To get some exercise, fight the flab . . .'

'There's one reason you haven't mentioned.'

'What?'

'When my wife was alive and we went on walks, it was always to talk about things.'

'Clearing the air – a dialogue, face to face, ending in a row and . . .'

'That would be a hypothesis.'

'Who did Faremo need to have a chat with – if it wasn't the woman, Merethe Sandmo?'

'Vidar Ballo. He's the one occupying Merethe Sandmo's bed now. But there's one thing that suggests it wasn't Ballo.'

'What's that?'

'These three, Faremo, Rognstad and Ballo, are best friends and partners. They've done several jobs together and shared the loot without falling out. It's nigh-on inconceivable that Jim Rognstad or Vidar Ballo would have any motive whatsoever to kill Faremo. The only thing we have is that Merethe Sandmo *possibly* swapped beds and bed-pals – from Jonny Faremo to Vidar Ballo.'

'Possibly?'

'Looks like that. But we don't know for certain. On the other hand, these boys have swapped women before – without any spats. So, Merethe Sandmo's pussy is not necessarily a motive here.'

'Are you positive Merethe Sandmo and Vidar Ballo are a couple?'

'If they aren't, they certainly give the impression they are.' Gunnarstranda took a swig of his beer.

'Nevertheless. Merethe Sandmo – she's the one who tipped us off about the Loenga murder, isn't she? If Jonny Faremo was murdered, he was – statistically speaking – murdered by someone close to him. Here we have a woman who swaps beds. Next she rings the police. Finally, the first bed-pal is found dead.'

'Of course you've got a point,' Gunnarstranda said, putting down his glass.

'At least it's more likely than an accident.'

Gunnarstranda shook his head. 'We're dealing with a gang under pressure. There's a lot of evidence to suggest the gang was going separate ways. However, one of the mysteries remains: why did Merethe turn snitch?'

They sit looking at each other.

Gunnarstranda pulled out his tobacco and his roll-up machine: 'Vidar Ballo and Merethe Sandmo have flown.'

'How do you know?'

Gunnarstranda picked at the superfluous flakes of tobacco on his roll-up. 'I've had men out to bring them in. You see, I bumped into Ballo and Merethe Sandmo yesterday and instructed them to come in for questioning today. They didn't show up.'

'But could it be so obvious? Faremo on his own against Ballo and the ex?'

'Maybe.'

'It's happened all the way through history. The French have their own term for it: *cherchez la femme . . .*'

Gunnarstranda pulled a sceptical face. 'I would go for that hypothesis if I knew of other conflicts between Ballo and Faremo. With both of them in a fix, thanks to her tip-off, I don't understand how the woman was intending to play them off against each other.'

'Assuming she isn't the object of attraction they're both competing for. That's more than enough material for conflict.'

Gunnarstranda reflected for a moment, then said: 'Then there's your role in all this. Someone will ask you if *you* were walking by the Glomma with Faremo.'

'It wasn't me.'

They looked each other in the eye.

'Someone will ask you what you were doing during these hours. You've already admitted you were trying to tail Faremo – a few hours before the witness's sighting.'

'But I was driving my car to Blindern. I was searching for Reidun Vestli when this happened.'

'Lystad told Kripos that was what you said, but he also said the timing was blurred. You might have been in Askim during daylight, then you drove like fuck to Blindern to give yourself an alibi.'

Frank Frølich sighed heavily. 'That's ridiculous of course.'

Gunnarstranda lit his roll-up. 'Have you got an ashtray?'

Frank Frølich motioned with his head towards an empty peanut bowl on the table. 'Use that.' He straightened up and looked at the map again. He cleared his throat and said: 'What make was the car parked in Skjoldenveien?'

'We don't know. Lystad says it was a saloon, silver-grey. Could be anything from a Saab to any Japanese car. But we know that Faremo had a silver-grey Saab.'

'And I have a silver-grey Toyota Avensis – saloon.'

'Exactly,' Gunnarstranda said laconically. 'And when we were up at Kykkelsrud power station you talked all the time about this road here.' He tapped the map with his finger.

'And, naturally, you said that to Lystad?'

'Naturally.'

Frank Frølich gave a wry smile and said: 'This Vrangfoss place is quite special. There's a spit protruding into the river so the water has to flow around it in an extremely narrow channel.'

'You seem to know the place well.'

'I went there after we'd talked by the dam.'

'OK.'

'What's the real reason you came here?' Frølich suddenly asked.

Gunnarstranda raised his head, a crooked smile playing around his lips. He coughed. 'A witness has turned up in the Loenga case.'

Frank Frølich raised his eyebrows interrogatively.

'He didn't come forward willingly. He's one of the bums in the square by the station and was brought in because two undercover men had heard rumours that he knew something about the murder in Loenga,' Gunnarstranda went on. 'The man's name is Steinar Astrup. On the night in question he was sleeping in cardboard boxes. What he says is very interesting. He says he was awoken by the sounds of someone breaking into the container nearby. There were three men.'

'Very promising. Any results with the rogues' gallery?'

'They were all wearing balaclavas. Outside the wire fence there was a car, a BMW estate. The three men had started to cram the loot into black plastic sacks. Then they ran to the fence and threw over the sacks. And now get this: the witness maintains a fourth person was sitting behind the wheel of the car. This person had left the driver's seat and lifted the sacks into the boot of the car twice. That means the men ran over to the fence twice. But suddenly the three inside the perimeter hid behind a pile of pallets. Because the security man, Arnfinn Haga, drew up in his little Ford. He slowed down as he passed the BMW even though the two cars were on opposite sides of the fence. The Ford stopped, then reversed. The guard got out of the car with a powerful torch and shone it through the fence at the person sitting in the BMW on the other side. But then something even stranger happened.' Gunnarstranda paused for effect before continuing.

'The person behind the steering wheel in the BMW got out – hands in the air.'

'Hands in the air? These guards aren't armed, are they? The car was on the other side of the fence and the man could have just driven off.'

'I haven't finished. Though you've got a point. According to Astrup, the guard asked the person what they were doing. Then there was a bang.'

'Bang?'

'Yes, one of the men wearing a balaclava had charged out and smacked the guard over the head with a baseball bat.'

'And then?'

'What he says about the baseball bat is important. It means the witness is telling the truth. No one knows about the murder weapon – except for trusted members of the force.'

'And he talks about four people. That suggests we might be barking up the wrong tree.'

Gunnarstranda shook his head. 'Then the three of them climbed over the fence and jumped into the BMW, which shot off,' he concluded.

'Four people?'

Silence settled over the room. Frølich could hear ticking. It was Gunnarstranda's Swatch. He coughed. 'What do you make of that?'

'Not sure,' Gunnarstranda murmured. 'Either it was those four: Faremo, Rognstad and Ballo plus an unknown fourth man who committed the robbery and murder – or the whole line of enquiry involving Faremo, Rognstad and Ballo is simply a wild goose chase.'

'What about if the three were using a driver for this particular job?'

'A container at the harbour? There's no reason for the three of them to recruit a fourth man for this job. The trio are well known for sticking together, for not taking on anyone else.'

'When were they arrested?'

'Ballo and Faremo were picked up at the Faremo flat just before five in the morning. Rognstad was collared outside the Hell's Angels clubhouse in Alnabru. In their statement they said all three of them had been playing poker in Jonny and Elisabeth Faremo's flat, accompanied by Elisabeth from two o'clock onwards until they were arrested. And the clincher for the judge was that Elisabeth Faremo was in the flat when the police arrived.'

'What about Rognstad?'

'His explanation was that he left the flat ten minutes before the arrests. He went on his motorbike to Alnabru and that matches witnesses' testimonies in Alnabru.'

'No one saw them arrive during the night?'

Gunnarstranda shook his head.

'What about the car, the BMW?'

'A stolen BMW, which might have been the car used in the robbery, was found in Sæther the day after. There had been an attempt to set it alight.'

'What's your take on this then?'

'The only thing connecting these three men to the murder of Arnfinn Haga is Merethe Sandmo's tip-off. If Sandmo and Ballo are lovers, the chances are she'll withdraw her statement and then we'll have nothing.'

'But what do you think? Did these three kill the guard?'

Gunnarstranda stood up. 'Right now I don't believe anything.' He went towards the door. 'What bothers me is another mystery,' he mumbled.

'What's that?'

'If four men broke into the container that night, why did Merethe Sandmo only mention three names?'

Frank Frølich shrugged his shoulders.

'You agree it's a little odd?'

'Yes.'

'There are three possibilities. Either she didn't know about the fourth man or she's keeping stumm about him or the tip-off was a fabrication.'

'Maybe Astrup is pulling a fast one? And there were only three men?'

'Doubt it. His statement clarifies the course of events, gives a motive for the murder and the explanation fits in with the burned rubber on the road outside the fence.'

'So there were four men.'

Gunnarstranda nodded. 'If you succeed in finding her – Elisabeth Faremo – try to coax a couple of relevant names out of her.'

'Belonging to whom?'

'The fourth robber.'

17

Inspector Gunnarstranda drove along Drammensveien and turned off at Lysaker. He was going to see Reidun Vestli and wasn't happy about it. *Why was he going?* he wondered. Was it to do Frølich a favour? No. Even though he was aware of the value of Frølich's instincts. The problem was that initiatives to do with Reidun Vestli didn't fall within the jurisdiction of his investigation.

That was why he had decided to justify this initiative by telling himself it was important to establish Elisabeth Faremo's trustworthiness. Reidun Vestli might be able to give them more information so that they could assess the defence's main witness. He parked alongside a red picket fence and strolled up the drive to her house. It was cold. The sun, almost colourless and cold, shimmered between two roofs covered with hoar frost. He stopped in front of the brown teak door with the lion's-head door knocker and reflected for a moment before he rang. Nothing happened. There wasn't a sound to be heard. He grabbed the handle in the lion's jaws, brought it down hard and discovered that the front door was unlocked and ajar. He listened. There was a small bang, like something, an object, falling onto the floor. He looked around him. Everywhere lifeless windows reflected back at him. The light breeze caused the front door to close with a clunk against the bolt. He knocked again. Again there was that thud.

Gunnarstranda made up his mind, pushed the door half open and shouted: 'Hello!'

But then he hesitated. Tomatoes lay strewn across the floor. He stared. There was a bunch of grapes in a transparent plastic bag in front of the tomatoes. A banana had been trodden flat in the doorway to the next room; in front of the door a shattered bottle lying in a large pool of wine – some still in the carrier bag.

Should he go in?

'Hey you. Man.'

Gunnarstranda turned round. A small boy in a ski suit with snot running from his nose peered up at him.

'Are you looking for the old dear?'

'The lady who lives here, yes.'

'She'th gone in an ambulanth.'

Frølich had got into his car and was on his way down the Ryenberg slopes towards the city centre when Gunnarstranda rang.

'I shouldn't contact you like this – it might give the wrong signals,' Gunnarstranda said.

'Didn't know you were a moralist,' Frølich said, his eyes peeled for a place to stop.

'It's my job to moralize. What kind of cop would I be if I weren't sceptical about people's morality? Our profession, Frølich, is based on the same authority as speed cameras at the side of the road: if we don't see people doing something wrong we think they're doing something wrong anyway.'

It occurred to Frølich that the man was being unusually garrulous. He pulled into the first bus lay-by and stopped so that he could speak. He didn't know where this corny line about speed cameras was going, so he replied: 'I don't agree. It's unethical to pre-suppose as yet uncommitted breaches of the law. Speed cameras are an entirely different matter. After all, they prevent traffic accidents.'

'Brilliant, Frølich. You've seen through the state's legal rhetoric. They call installing speed cameras a precautionary measure. As long as it's done under this label, it doesn't make any difference if the photograph is used as evidence in the consequent prosecution. You and I and the rest of the civil servants are paid for doubting the nation's morality. But that isn't my main purpose in ringing.'

'That's what I suspected.'

'I'm wondering about the real reason why you wanted me to contact Reidun Vestli.'

'I told you.'

'But I don't exactly buy it.'

'Better tell me what's happened,' Frølich said wearily.

'The lady may not survive.'

A couple of hours later he found somewhere to park in Skovveien. He crossed Bygdøy allé and continued towards the Norsk Hydro buildings and the Hydro Park. When Frank Frølich had been small, he had visited his uncle here; he had worked in the purchasing department of Norsk Hydro.

The security men in reception seemed to be bored. They were throwing playful punches at each other until he knocked on the plastic window. He asked to see Langås. The older of the two men picked up the telephone and called. The younger man hid behind a tabloid, *Verdens Gang*. The guard on the telephone cupped the receiver with his hand and asked who he should say was there. Frank Frølich introduced himself. The man held his hand over the receiver again. 'Langås says he isn't familiar with the name.'

Frank Frølich said: 'Tell him I want to meet now. I'd much rather discuss things with him personally than with you.'

Shortly afterwards the entrance gate flashed green. Frølich went in and crossed to the lift. The lift door opened and he looked straight into the face of a man in his fifties. He had a central parting in long grey hair tied into a ponytail at the back. His beard was clipped short, and a conspicuous crown in his top row of teeth lent charm to a crooked smile. The man's ex-hippie image combined with an expensive suit. Frølich, who could feel his prejudices rising, immediately took against him.

'You wanted to talk to me?'

Frank Frølich introduced himself.

'So what's this about? I have a tough agenda and not very much time to spare.'

'It's about your ex-wife, Reidun Vestli.'

'And who are you?'

'I'm a policeman, on leave.'

They faced each other for a few seconds without speaking. 'All right,' Langås said finally. 'I'll look for a free room.'

Frølich trailed Langås down the corridor, passing office doors and a room with a flashing photocopier. A man and a woman were talking in a glass cage, both fidgeting with their paper cups.

Langås showed the way to a small room where they sat down on either side of a neglected, withered potted plant in the middle of a table.

Frølich went straight to the point. 'She's in hospital,' he said.

'I know.'

'She was attacked in her own house.'

'I know that too.'

'I have reason to believe the attack is connected with a case I'm working on.'

'While you're on leave?'

Frølich didn't answer. They sat weighing each other up. Langås tilted his head. Not in any ironic way, more an appraisal.

Frank Frølich broke the silence: 'The attack is being investigated by others. I have reason to believe that . . .'

'Actually, I have nothing to say,' Langås interrupted. 'The policeman who rang me about Reidun indicated that there had been a break-in. I can tell you what I told him: Reidun and I've been divorced for years. I know as much about her daily routine as I know about our TUC chairman's next-door neighbour.'

'Although she's named you as her closest relative.'

'The word relative is a technical term on this occasion. And I didn't ask for this role. It is Reidun's choice, which I respect but fail to understand.'

'So you and Reidun do talk now and then?'

'Now and then sounds more frequent than is the case with us. But listen, Reidun and I . . .'

'Has she ever mentioned the name Elisabeth Faremo?' Frølich broke in.

'Not that I can remember. But listen to me. I don't want to be involved in your private matters, especially not via my ex-wife.'

'Have you seen this woman?'

Frølich pushed a photograph of Elisabeth Faremo across the table.

Langås craned his head to look, wordless.

'I take your silence to mean that you've seen this woman before.'

Langås nodded.

'Where and when?'

'At Easter. She went to the weekend chalet with Reidun.'

'Where's the chalet?'

'In Valdres, Vestre Slidre.'

Frølich held back in the hope that he would be more forthcoming. Langås leaned forwards and said: 'Is this your woman? Did she leave you for Reidun? Are you jealous? How am I to know it wasn't you who broke in and beat her up?'

'It wasn't me. But yes, I have occasionally been jealous of your ex-wife. She was having a relationship with Elisabeth at the same time as I was. That isn't why I came here though. The fact is I'm fond of this woman and have reason to believe she's in serious trouble. For that reason she has gone to ground. I think the serious trouble has something to do with your ex-wife being taken to Ullevål hospital.'

Langås rolled his wrist and squinted at his watch – a macho job: classic diver watch meets James Bond.

Frølich pointed to the photograph. 'My motive for talking to you is to find this woman, and help her out of her predicament. I've tried to talk to your ex-wife. Other policemen have also tried. She refuses to answer any questions. That means that your ex may also have got caught up in the mess. I'm only asking you to . . .'

'I have to go,' Langås said. 'Whatever Reidun is caught up in, it has nothing to do with me. I'm happily married, Frølich. And I'll be quite open with you. In fact, one of the reasons we got divorced when we did was Reidun's predilections. We married too young. We grew apart, intellectually and . . . well . . . in other areas. That meant that Reidun and I have almost nothing in common, not even children. And we were miles apart when we divided all our possessions. In fact, one of the things at the time that created bad blood between us was the chalet I was talking about. It's been in my family for two generations and was built by my grandfather. But she was downright dishonest and grabbed it when we got divorced. I was very depressed at that point and incapable of standing up for myself. For sentimental reasons, I've bought another chalet not so far from the one she cheated me out of. This is where I most often meet her. We occasionally bump into each other when we go skiing at Easter.' He tapped a finger on Elisabeth Faremo's picture. 'I saw this woman when I was out skiing. They were resting alongside the piste on a slope and I chatted to them for maybe three minutes perhaps, maybe five – to be polite. Not long enough to ask her name. I assumed she was having problems because she was young, probably half Reidun's age. That's all I know, all I can say. If you would excuse me now?' He stood up, flipped open the clasp of his fancy watch and closed it again, like a secondary schoolteacher rattling his keys.

'Thank you,' Frølich said, realizing why Langås was fidgeting with his watch: he wanted to avoid shaking hands.

18

She was ensconced in a chair by the window. Staring out. Her back appeared narrow and lonely in the white dressing gown. Her brown hair was brushed. In the window Gunnarstranda saw his own reflection – and the profile of her face.

He stood like that without saying anything.

'I know who you are,' she said. The voice was quiet and concentrated.

He met her eyes in the transparent mirror. 'May I buy you a cup of coffee?' he asked and added: 'If you're strong enough to go down to the café.'

Finally, she turned round. 'Do you think this face is fit for a café?'

He didn't answer.

'What do you want?' She was forced to talk out of the corner of her mouth. The skin around her eyes was covered with red and blue contusions.

'I wanted to know how you were. It looked pretty bad . . . in your house,' he hastened to add. 'Can you remember any of what happened?'

'I remember the ambulance. Just a vague recollection.'

'Have you any idea how much time passed between the ambulance coming and . . .?'

'No.'

Gunnarstranda involuntarily put out a hand as she stood up. He wanted to support her, but she rejected his approach and hobbled off towards one of the low coffee tables by the wall. He sat down at the other side.

'It looks worse than it is,' she said.

'Did you see him?'

The question disconcerted her for a second. She lowered her gaze.

He waited.

'Who?' she asked finally.

'I won't force you to answer. Instead, I'll say how I interpret your silence and your attitude. Either you saw your attacker and you're frightened of reprisals if you describe him to me or you saw him but you don't wish to see him punished.'

She was silent.

A nurse in a white uniform appeared at the door. She came into the room and asked if everything was all right.

Gunnarstranda gestured towards Reidun Vestli. 'You'll have to ask her.'

Reidun Vestli regarded the nurse with a distant look. 'Yes, everything's fine. Could I have something to drink, though?'

They sat in silence watching the nurse go to the unit in the corner, take out a bottle of mineral water, thoroughly rinse a glass in cold water and then return with light steps. She handed a glass with a straw to Reidun Vestli. They watched the nurse cross the room and leave.

'How did he get in?'

'Through the door. How else?'

'He rang the doorbell?'

She was silent.

'Or was he waiting for you when you came back from shopping?'

She was still silent.

'Do you want to report him?'

She shook her head slowly.

'Why not?'

No reaction.

Gunnarstranda leaned forwards. 'Who hit you?' he asked doggedly.

Reidun Vestli didn't answer.

'Can you describe the person?'

She put down her glass on the table. She made rings with the bottom of the glass. The silence persisted. A large clock on the wall clicked as the minute hand moved on.

'I think,' Gunnarstranda said finally, 'that the person who did this to you is extremely desperate. If you don't wish to say who he is, or describe him, I'd like you to tell me what he wanted – apart from causing you injury. It's imperative that we have this man under lock and key, imperative for us, for you and particularly for Elisabeth Faremo.'

The name threw a switch in Reidun Vestli's consciousness. She slowly raised her head; her eyes were focused on something far away. 'I want you to go,' she said.

Gunnarstranda produced a photograph of Vidar Ballo. 'Was this the man who gave you the beating?'

Reidun Vestli looked at the picture without saying a word.

Gunnarstranda took out another picture. This time it was Jim Rognstad, a prison photograph, a front and a profile.

Reidun Vestli was quiet.

Gunnarstranda showed her a photograph of Frølich.

No discernible twitch on Reidun Vestli's face.

The policeman pulled out a newspaper cutting about her ex-husband – Langås the investor.

No reaction this time, either.

'Anyone else?' the policeman asked softly.

Reidun Vestli peered up.

Gunnarstranda leaned back in the chair and said: 'Was it someone you didn't see a photo of?'

Reidun shouted in a hoarse voice: 'Nurse, sister, hello! I can't take any more.'

Gunnarstranda stood up. 'Just one minor thing before I go,' he said before putting back the pictures in his inside jacket pocket. 'You and your husband both had an interest in a chalet in Valdres, but who is actually the owner?'

The door opened. A nurse came in. 'I'm going now,' Gunnarstranda said to reassure her.

'Wait!' Reidun Vestli looked at him with a troubled expression on her face.

The nurse left, closing the door behind her.

Reidun Vestli was breathing heavily. 'Why do you want to know?'

Gunnarstranda thought this over. Eventually he said: 'For several reasons actually, but let's start with the insurance premium. I'm wondering who gets the payout if anything should happen – something unforeseen.'

'What are you trying to say?' she whispered.

'You're going to be discharged today, aren't you?' Gunnarstranda asked. 'Shall I drive you home so we can talk about it?'

She nodded slowly.

'We can call the nurse then,' Gunnarstranda said.

19

When Gunnarstranda came into the office, he just managed to nod to Yttergjerde and wrestle off his coat before the telephone began to ring. He picked up the receiver and barked into it as usual: 'Please be brief.'

'Frølich here.'

'Good morning. Up early and no weeping?'

'I talked to Langås yesterday, Reidun Vestli's ex-husband.'

'You're not letting go, then?'

'He said something about a chalet. Elisabeth had stayed with Reidun Vestli in a chalet in Valdres.'

'So?'

'I thought I was supposed to play with an open hand, as you requested. I intend to go there now and find out whether Elisabeth is hiding in the chalet. She might be. I think . . .'

'I know about the chalet,' Gunnarstranda said, immediately regretting his interruption. The line went quiet and he knew he would have to bring the silence to an end. He said: 'It was in Vestre Slidre.'

'It *was*?'

'It burned down a few days ago.'

'Burned?'

'I happened to be in the area by chance.'

'And which chance was that?'

Gunnarstranda stretched back in his chair. He pulled a cigarette out of his pocket and stuck it between his lips. He was silent.

'Hello,' Frølich yelled impatiently. 'Are you there?'

'Frank Frølich, have you got a chair to hand?'

'Out with it! Tell me!'

'Perhaps you'd better sit down. I received a report yesterday, addressed to the Institute of Forensic Medicine, and I wouldn't have taken any notice, had it not been for the land registry document. A property burned to the ground, a chalet belonging to Reidun Vestli. The Nord-Aural police report talks about finding long bones in the ashes of the chalet.'

Silence again.

'Long bones, Frølich. Do you know what that means?'

'It doesn't have to be her.'

'Of course not.'

Silence again.

'But Reidun Vestli's chalet burned down a few days ago. What is special about this is that someone was in the chalet at the time of the fire. If Reidun Vestli hadn't lent the chalet to Elisabeth Faremo, it might have been a thief who broke in, went to sleep with a fag in his mouth and caused the fire. But that's not what we thought, is it? We both thought there was a chance she might have let Elisabeth use the chalet, didn't we?'

Frølich's voice, clearly strained: 'How are you going to approach this case?'

'Standard procedure. Look for DNA to establish the identity of the remains.'

'How?'

'We've been to the Faremo flat.'

'Find anything?'

'A hairbrush. On her bed. I've requested a DNA profile and I'll match it with that of the bones in the chalet.'

This time there was a longer pause before Frølich's question: 'When are you expecting an answer?'

'Any time now.'

After Gunnarstranda had put down the receiver he sat looking glumly at the telephone. Yttergjerde turned to him. 'How did he take it?'

Gunnarstranda lounged back and said: 'How do you think he took it?'

20

That night Frank Frølich didn't sleep. The duvet was drenched with sweat, as if he'd had a fever. When he tried to get out of bed, his legs almost gave way. His head was buzzing. He was thinking: *I have to go there, have to find the chalet.* He had no idea where it was, no idea where he should start searching. Yet he couldn't just lie there doing nothing.

He had to find out where the chalet was. There was only one person he could ask.

So he got dressed and left the house. It was freezing, although he didn't feel the cold. The ice on the car windscreen was as hard as the road surface. He found a scraper, but it had no purchase. He banged on the ice with his fist, hammered away, but that didn't help. In no time at all he was out of breath and tired, to no effect. He got into the car, started it up and put the defroster on full. He waited apathetically behind the wheel until the ice had melted. Then he drove off. He went through the city to Vækerø and took a right turning into Vækerøveien.

He parked alongside one of the many picket fences. Oslo West lay in the dark, apart from the odd lamp posts casting yellow-grey cones of light between the terraced houses. After getting out of his car, he went over to Reidun Vestli's house. It was night, but he couldn't care less. He regarded his hands for a few seconds. They were shaking. Would it be right or wrong to talk to her now? He had no idea and continued on his way, passing a couple of cars with iced-up windows. Shortly afterwards he banged the door knocker. Nothing happened. He listened, but couldn't hear any sounds inside. Went back down the steps and walked slowly around the house. The night frost had scattered crystals of ice over the soil in the flower beds. He retreated and stood back a few metres, studying the house. It was the last in the row. He walked back onto the frozen lawn, leaving clear footprints in the hoar frost. He went to the veranda – it was poorly maintained, a kind of decking made with pressure-impregnated wood. The railing had been put together with stained slats which were going rotten. A couple of withered potted plants had been shoved into the corner. In the centre of the veranda there was a green pot half full of sand and old cigarette ends. *Long bones in the ashes.* He walked to the window and spied through a crack between the curtains. Came face to face with two white feet sticking up in the air. The nail of one big toe was varnished. He knocked on the door. No reaction. The feet didn't move. He tried the veranda door. It was unlocked.

She was lying on her back with her mouth in a rigid grimace, her eyes staring up and behind her as if trying to catch eye contact with someone residing in the wall. She was dead. He didn't need any doctor or forensic scientist to confirm that side of the matter. But he did feel tired all of a sudden. *Who will mourn you?* he thought and felt the nausea rising. *Long bones in the ashes of the fire.* Sleeping pills scattered around the upturned glass on the bedside table. Some had fallen on the floor; some were in the pool of vomit on the pillow. *Cause of death: poisoning* or *suffocation as a result of vomit produced by the body's reaction to poisoning.* The odds? 1 : 2. He guessed suffocation. However, the nausea he felt could not be attributed to her, to the stench of the dead body, the stench of dried vomit or the stench of stale air and old cigarettes. Nausea was his body's reaction to this universe of death, of mutilation; the absence of grief, the absence of normality. *Where was Elisabeth's grief when she lost her brother?* He sank back against the wall. *Who will grieve over you?* he thought again, contemplating the pitiful feet protruding from under the blanket. *Your ex-husband? Who will presumably hate you more now that the chalet you quarrelled over has burned down.*

He wanted to be sick. *Long bones.* He slid down the wall until he was sitting on the floor. Breathed in deeply. Where was the suicide note? No envelope, no shaky writing on a piece of paper, no indication of any leave-taking in the immediate vicinity. He cast a glance at the computer. It was switched off. But Gunnarstranda was bound to seize it. Nausea was rising in him again, but this time it was a reaction to himself. His own pitiful condition. *Long bones*. Here he was, next to a corpse and fearing for the life of another. And what if it *was* Elisabeth who had died in the fire? Could that explain why Reidun Vestli would kill herself? He swallowed his queasiness, stood up, went out onto the veranda and gulped lungfuls of fresh air. Supporting himself on the rotten railing, he sat down on the edge of the veranda and phoned Gunnarstranda.

PART THREE

The Key

21

Frank Frølich sat up in his all too spacious double bed, looking at the pillow and duvet beside him. No one had been there since Elisabeth – the night she vanished and Arnfinn Haga was murdered in Loenga. The bedding had not been changed; the creases in the sheet had been made by her body. She had left behind one single black hair, a line winding over the crumpled pillow like a path across mountainous terrain on a map. Next to the bed, on the bedside table, there was an empty wine bottle with a candle stump in the top. A makeshift light – her work, one night when there was a power cut. Afterwards the flickering light had cast dramatic shadows of their bodies on the wall.

This reminiscence could equally well have emanated from a book he had read, or a film he had seen a long time ago. The drawer in the bedside table on her side was not properly closed. Naked, he got up and walked around the bed. No earrings, no rings left behind on the table top. He was about to close the drawer properly when he spotted something. He pulled out the drawer. It was a book. Poetry. Her book. The one she often had her nose in. For a brief instant he saw himself coming into the bedroom from the bathroom: Elisabeth naked on the bed, her chin supported by her arms; she looked up at him and closed the book.

Her book. The images were no longer faded. It was like holding a fragment of Elisabeth between his hands. He perched on the bed, excited by his discovery.

He opened the book with trembling hands. There was a bookmark. The sight of it caused a shiver to run down his spine. It was an embroidered bookmark – delicate – white silk with black designs embroidered in tiny stitches. The image the signs formed gave him a shock. It was the same motif as Elisabeth's tattoo. He moved the bookmark to one side and read:

> I forget no one
> pain also passes
> along a snapped twig
> I forget no one
> if I kiss you

He sank back down onto the bed. The words evoked their decisive encounter: the evening she had followed him home. The crush on the Metro, the sound of footsteps on the tarmac, the image of her silhouette against the street lamp. He could feel her warm breath on his cheek.

He flicked back. The words were the last verse of a long poem written by the deceased lesbian writer, Gunvor Hofmo.

He read the first verse of the poem:

> I have lost my face
> In these wild rhythms
> Only my white body dances

Was that how she saw herself? A body without a face? He read again: 'I forget no one if I kiss you'. The image of Elisabeth dissolved as he read. Had she left the book on purpose? Or had she simply forgotten it? A replica of Elisabeth's tattoo, so peculiar to her, and unlike anything else, an intimate signature taken from her body, placed over the sentence she had used to initiate their relationship – *I forget no one if I kiss you.*

He could hear Gunnarstranda's voice in his head: *long bones.* The words were immediately drowned by the noise of the crackling flames in his head. An image: a gigantic bonfire, a house aflame, a glowing heat, window panes exploding. Nothing else visible except the contours of a body enveloped in flames. Zooming in. The contours materialize into flesh – flesh blistering, melting, body fat hissing, burning with a yellow flame until it is carbon. His thoughts stood still, paralysed by the vision until he began to feel the book in his hands again.

If they were Elisabeth's remains in the ashes of Reidun Vestli's weekend chalet, if Elisabeth was dead, how was he ever going to recover?

He read the poem again. New images in his consciousness: him in the act of making love, a long time ago, the image duller, no colours. Elisabeth putting down the book and saying it wasn't possible to read the same book twice.

Then he knew: it was about an old love. The sentence referred to one person in particular. He stood up and gazed blindly out of the window: Elisabeth initiating a relationship with him back then had to mean betraying someone else. But whom had she betrayed? Reidun Vestli? Could it be so simple? No, it couldn't. This was about forgetting. This was something from the distant past. But who was it she didn't want to forget?

And who was unable to answer? Her brother was dead. Reidun Vestli – dead. He weighed the embroidered bookmark in his hand. Embroidery. A motif tattooed on Elisabeth's hip. There was a chance that someone had seen this tattoo before.

After a long shower and some breakfast, he switched on the computer and logged onto the net, Yellow Pages, Tattooists, Search. The list of outlets was long: Purple Pain in Heimdal, Odin's Mark in Lillestrøm, Ow! Tattoo and Piercing in Bergen, Hole in One in Bodø. He narrowed the search down to the Oslo region and printed out the list. He looked at it. *Almost like working as a cop again. A house-to-house job.*

Perhaps he should do that? Report back to work and continue the investigation as part of his job? He dismissed the thought, left his flat and went down to his car.

It was a trek, in and out of tattoo parlours, walls covered with kitsch – motorbikes, skulls, sword and flames, roses, scorpions. In most of the places young girls were lying on their stomachs having a decoration tattooed onto the small of their backs. In others they lay on their backs and had roses or calligraphic symbols on their groins and thighs. One man wanted a crown of thorns around his arm; another wanted the name Leif Ericson on his leg. The routine was repeated: first of all, Frank Frølich showed the photograph of Elisabeth, then the bookmark with the unusual motif on. It looked like crow's feet: strange lines with curls on. He didn't find anything remotely similar. Many of the tattooists supplied photographs of their body decorations. Most of the practitioners looked like followers of the motorbike culture. But not a nibble anywhere.

In between visits, he stayed at home continuing the search on the net. He searched the words from the poem, a variety of word combinations, but without success. It was while he was going through the list on the printout for the third time that his eye was caught by a business called the Personal Art Tattoo Studio. What was special about the shop was that it was located in Askim.

It was a shot in the dark, but Jonny Faremo's body was found there – in Askim. He might as well try there as anywhere.

He got ready, picked up his car keys and took the lift down. Out on the street, he breathed in the damp, heavy air. It had turned mild again. It wasn't raining, but the air was full of vapour, a grey moist consistency, tiny drops of water, hovering in the mist and gently, ever so gently, floating to the ground.

After getting in the car, he took a wrong turn and ended up driving towards Olso city centre instead of towards Ski. So he headed for Simensbråten, went up Vårveien, over the hump and turned right, down Ekebergveien. He braked just before Elisabeth's apartment block. A sudden impulse almost made him come to a complete halt. *You aren't dead. I refuse to believe that.* It was pathetic, but the emotion was strong. He was certain she was there, in her flat. He reversed into the car park, got out and ran down the steps to the Faremo apartment. The door hadn't been sealed. He stood gasping for breath. And rang. Not a sound. He rang again, listened and knocked. The apartment was dead.

But there were sounds coming from the neighbouring flat. He turned towards the adjacent door. The sounds from behind it died away. He went over and rang the bell. The sound of feet. A shadow flitted across the peephole in the door. More seconds ticked past until the chain rattled and the door was opened.

'Nice to see you again,' Frølich said.

The old man stared at him. His lips were quivering; his face was distorted into a grimace with a fixed squint into a sun long since disappeared.

'We met a few days ago. I was making enquiries about Elisabeth Faremo. You said she had packed a rucksack and had gone away. You've spoken to the police about the same conversation. Do you remember me?'

The man nodded.

'I was wondering about something,' Frank Frølich said. 'You've lived here longer than the Faremos, haven't you?'

The man nodded again.

'Do you know how long they lived together here? Did they move in at the same time?'

'Why –?' The man spluttered and found his voice. 'Why are you here asking questions?'

Frølich chewed that one over. In the end he said: 'For personal reasons.'

The man gave him a long, hard look. Eventually the answer seemed to pass muster. At least Frølich was unable to detect any scepticism in the other's eyes when he said: 'She moved in first. The brother came a few years afterwards.'

'Can you remember what year it was when she moved in?'

The man shook his head.

'Try.'

'It must be a good ten years ago. Must be.'

'And she lived on her own at first?'

The man shook his head. 'There were a number of chaps, of course, particularly one, before the brother came to live here.'

'Chaps?'

'Yes, well, she's a good-looking girl and there have been men, you know, but there was one who lasted quite a long time. I don't think he lived here; he just stayed here for stints. I remember because I was a bit doubtful. He was one of our new countrymen, you know. He went off, thank God. At first we thought Jonny had given him the heave-ho, but Jonny was her brother, wasn't he?'

'One of our new countrymen?'

'Yes, not a Negro, more like a Turk or a Slav. Slightly rounded head and long nose. Can't remember what his name was, though. Something with an I . . . or was it an A . . . Ika? Aka? Nope.' He shook his head. 'Time passes; we get older.'

The information wasn't a lot of use. Frank Frølich was being a policeman now. He had a job to do. *Elisabeth Faremo, ex-lover, long bones.* No resonance in his head, no fever, no disturbing images, no crackling flames. He pinched his arm and felt pain.

It was still early morning as he crossed Mosseveien driving towards Fiskvollbukta and Mastemyr. The journey to Askim took three-quarters of an hour. He was driving against the rush-hour traffic and the late-winter sunrise. He passed Fossum Bridge and the motorway construction site. When he turned off the roundabout on Europaveien, down towards the station and into Askim town centre he found the tattoo studio right in front of him. It was next to the offices of Lilleng Frisør in a solitary yellow building beside the railway crossing gates which divided the small town into two. On the other side of the railway line, opposite the beginning of the pedestrian area, there was a cafeteria which looked like a red military barracks.

The tattoo shop hadn't opened yet. Frank Frølich decided to go for a walk around the town. He wandered through the pedestrian zone and turned right along a winding road which finally ended in a crossroads with traffic lights. Large square buildings dominated the landscape. This town could have been anywhere – flat land broken up by barrack architecture and special offers on groceries. But behind it he could glimpse greater ambitions: adventure pools, a manufacturing plant – the old Viking factories which had, as usual, been converted into a shopping centre.

As Frank Frølich was strolling over the railway lines on his way back, ten minutes later, he heard the familiar roar of a Harley in the bend by the station.

The man was a rotund, jovial type with long curly hair. Frølich showed him the photograph of Elisabeth Faremo, but he didn't recognize her. Then he gave him the bookmark with the design of Elisabeth's tattoo on. Which he did recognize.

22

Frølich had taken up a horizontal position on the sofa and was studying the ceiling yet again – a black mark beside the lamp. Might have been a fly. But it wasn't moving. It was something else. He had stared at the ceiling from this position at least a million times, seen the mark and thought: perhaps it's a fly. But not even this time could he be bothered to get up and find out what it actually was.

He lay on his back mulling things over. You know she had a tattoo done in Askim four to five years ago. What else? You don't know what it represents or why she did it. The tattooist who had injected the ink into her skin had been supplied with a design and didn't know what it symbolized. So he was no further forward: the man remembered the design, but not her face.

Frølich realized he was fumbling around at the edges of a puzzle, unable to make the pieces fit any longer. He would have to try another corner. But which one?

What set the whole business rolling? That one night, the murder in Loenga, the arrests based on the tip-off.

Question: Who tipped them off?

Answer: Merethe Sandmo.

Question: Why?

Answer: Not a glimmer. A mystery. It might have happened because Merethe Sandmo had first been with Elisabeth's brother, then had gone off with Vidar Ballo. So there may have been some unknown factor in the group, an internal force driving these two events: Merethe Sandmo moving from one man to another and contacting the police when the three of them become responsible for a murder. However, when she blows the whistle, why does she give them only three names instead of all four?

Only one person could give him the answer to that: Merethe Sandmo.

And Merethe Sandmo worked as a waitress.

Frank Frølich, lying on the sofa and contemplating the black mark beside the lamp, knew he would be heading for the city centre.

He looked for a shirt and tie. When he had blown the dust off his suit, he realized he should have had it cleaned a couple of years ago. He left it in the wardrobe and instead chose a pair of dark linen trousers and matching jacket. Posing in front of the mirror, he mused: a little hair gel and he might make the grade.

He took the only taxi parked at the Ryen rank. The driver was reading *Verdens Gang* and was visibly startled when Frølich opened the door.

To the city centre, he said, and left the cab in front of Bliss, whose existence was announced by a flashing pink neon light on the wall. For a weekday, it was too early to go out. The doorman wasn't in position yet, and apart from him there was only a single customer in the room. The customer was trying to strike up a conversation with the woman serving him. She was an exaggerated solarium-brown colour and had her hair in Rasta dreadlocks. Apart from a green mini-skirt and red fishnet stockings, she wore nothing. She must have been in her late twenties – a nicely compact stomach beneath her breasts.

Frølich sat down at a table in the corner. A poster said the show was due to start at nine. The text was illustrated with the regulation picture of a stripper climaxing, wrapped around a fireman's pole.

The woman in the fishnet tights came over to his table and asked him what he wanted. Her nipples were the colour of chocolate mousse. Frank Frølich didn't know where to look.

The befuddled man at the bar scowled; he obviously didn't like any competition for the lady's attentions.

Frølich decided to focus on her eyes, which shone like tram lights out of her solarium-tanned skin. He ordered a large beer and asked if he could speak to Merethe.

'Merethe who?'

'Sandmo.'

'She's left.'

Frølich determined to make the most of the opportunity: 'Left?'

'Yes. Stupid really. She was making good money here.'

'Where's she working now?'

'In Greece. A club in Athens or somewhere like that. She got a good job. I was just a little jealous of her, working in Greece, wasn't I? It's warmer down there now than it is here in the summer.'

'Damn!' Frølich could feel himself getting into the role. 'I'd have known where I was with her, if she'd said she was going to Greece, just to work . . . Left a long time ago, did she?'

'About a week ago. Wait a moment – I'll just get your beer.'

She crossed the floor like a ballerina, her breasts doing a jig as she swung round for a glass to draw his beer. The man at the bar was having difficulty balancing on the stool.

He reminds me of myself, Frølich thought glumly.

'Do you know Merethe well?' he asked, when the woman came back with his beer.

'No, I'm a friend of Vidar's, Vidar Ballo.'

'Poor Merethe. I feel *so sorry* for the girl.'

'And I know Jonny's sister,' Frølich said. 'Elisabeth Faremo.'

The man at the bar yelled something or other.

The woman craned her head and screeched. She whispered to Frølich: 'He's *so* wearing.'

'Right. I was with Elisabeth for a while. That was just after she went with that – hell, what was his name again? . . . some Iranian or Moroccan or wherever he came from . . .'

'Ilijaz?'

'Yes, Ilijaz, that was it.'

'I'm fairly sure he's a Croat.'

'That's right.'

The man at the bar roared again.

'Coming!' The woman went back to the bar and poured him a large beer which he took with a shaky hand.

Soon she was back. 'Good to see a few new customers once in a while,' she said. 'Are you here for the show?'

'Well, no, actually I came to talk to Merethe.'

'I'm on at eleven. There are a few more people around then. Stag parties and that sort of thing. Just *so* naff. But you can come and see what you think.'

Frølich caught himself studying the hard lines around her chin, the first signs of a harrowed face, the glint of steel a long way behind her tram-light eyes.

'Do you know what happened to Ilijaz?' he asked and instantly knew he had blundered. She sent him a different, a strange look. All the scars and overgrown paths he had been examining in her face stood out in the same way that the autumn countryside takes shape when the early-morning haze lifts. He was the one she was avoiding now. The silence between them grew heavy and uneasy. She went back to the bar and stayed there.

Which landmine was it I stood on? he wondered and finished his beer.

She didn't return to his table.

When he went to the cash desk, he put a hundred-kroner note on the bar and said she could keep the change. She looked away.

Sitting in the Metro, he rang Yttergjerde and asked him if he knew any criminals by the name of Ilijaz. He suggested a few alternative spellings. Yttergjerde said he would follow it up.

Yttergjerde didn't ring back.

He found out for himself.

It was three o'clock at night. He woke up with a start – he had been dreaming about Ilijaz.

23

Next morning he couldn't get to the police station quickly enough. Lena Stigersand met him in the corridor. She shook her head patronizingly, but also squeezed his arm. 'I know that man . . . good to see you again.'

'Easy, easy,' Frølich stammered, feeling the sweat break out over his whole body. 'I just want to pick up a couple of things before I go back on leave.'

He unlocked his office and closed the door. That was lucky. Gunnarstranda wasn't in yet. No one was there. He couldn't face meeting anyone. It had been enough of a physical strain exchanging the few words with Stigersand. He shook his head like a punch-drunk boxer and went over to the desk with the computer on. Logged on and searched for his report about the break-in at Inge Narvesen's in Ulvøya on 4 November 1998. Afterwards he looked for a report by the Bærum police about a shooting incident in Snarøyveien a few days later.

The moment the reports had been printed out and he had them stapled together, Gunnarstranda walked in through the door. The older policeman didn't bat an eyelid, just took off his overcoat and hung it up.

'Leave over?' he asked, briefly.

Frølich shook his head.

'Wouldn't it have been more practical to find the body of Reidun Vestli in your capacity as a policeman rather than a tourist?' Absent-mindedly, Gunnarstranda continued: 'It's been playing on my mind. I talked to her about that burned-down chalet of hers and the minute I left she took a stack of pills and passed away. Crazy.'

'It probably wasn't losing the chalet that drove her to it.'

'You're thinking about the bones?'

Frank Frølich nodded. He could feel the sweat trickling from his brow. Talking about Elisabeth as *bones* was unpleasant.

'The girl must have been special,' Gunnarstranda said.

Another nod.

'What have you got there?' Gunnarstranda asked, gesturing at the papers Frølich had stuffed under his arm.

'A case from six years back. The Snarøya murder.'

Gunnarstranda took a few moments to reflect. 'Folkenborg,' he mumbled. 'Wasn't he working at a petrol station?'

'He owned and managed it.'

'Taken hostage, wasn't he?'

'No. Should have been a straightforward arrest. Folkenborg was shot and killed by the man under arrest. I went with the guy from Sandvika to arrest him. He was working at the garage in Blommenholm. I had the papers for his arrest – a burglary in Ulvøya. When we got there, our man was behind the counter, but he drew a gun from his pocket.' Frølich flicked through the report. 'A Colt Python, short barrel. He waved it around, ran through the car wash and into the shed with the grease pit where Folkenborg was changing oil. Neither of us had considered this a dangerous job and neither of us had requisitioned a weapon. We had to stand by and watch the man run in with the shooter in his hand. Then we hung back. Unfortunately for all of us Folkenborg went into action. He probably thought he knew the man and had the situation under control. There was a bang. Folkenborg was hit in the chest. Then the man panicked, threw the revolver away and ran for it – straight into our arms.'

Gunnarstranda was deep in thought.

'The man who fired the gun was Ilijaz Zupac,' Frølich said.

'Immigrant?'

'Second generation. Mother and father from the Balkans. Both dead. Zupac is a Norwegian citizen.'

'Why are you digging up this stuff now?'

Frølich put the papers in a bag and said: 'Zupac was arrested because he had taken part in a burglary in Ulvøya. A fat cat called

Inge Narvesen had his safe stolen. It was in a cupboard in his bedroom and there was half a million kroner in it. Ilijaz Zupac was seen by a neighbour. There were a number of people involved, but Zupac's appearance gave him away.'

'All right,' Gunnarstranda said impatiently. 'But why rake it up now?'

'He was found guilty of aggravated burglary and wilful murder. Even though he wasn't the only one involved in the burglary, no one else was charged. Zupac kept his mouth shut. I'm interested in witnesses and the investigation itself.'

'Why?' snarled Gunnarstranda.

Frølich hesitated.

Gunnarstranda's irritation grew and the furrow above his eyes deepened.

'Ilijaz Zupac was living with Elisabeth Faremo when he was charged and sentenced,' Frølich said quickly.

They stood staring at each other. Gunnarstranda's hands fumbled for a cigarette.

Frølich grinned. 'I've made you curious, haven't I,' he mumbled.

'I'm thinking something I've thought for a long time,' Gunnarstranda said slowly.

'What's that?'

'The relationship between you and the girl was a set-up.'

There was silence. Which Frølich broke: 'If you're right, I don't understand the logic behind it.'

'But even though you don't understand the logic, you're following up this link with Ilijaz Zupac?'

'Of course.'

'Why?'

'The murder of the security guard. In my opinion, this clears up a little problem.'

'Which problem?'

'The fourth robber. Ilijaz wasn't on his own when he robbed Narvesen's safe. Ilijaz was Elisabeth's lover, she was Jonny Faremo's sister. I would bet a hundred kroner that one of the others was Jonny Faremo. If that's right, Faremo has worked with other people apart from Ballo and Rognstad one or more times. So it's no mystery that there were four of them the night the guard was killed on the quay. We have a fourth man involved in the Haga killing, but we don't have the slightest idea who.'

'If you come back to work, you may have a case now,' Gunnarstranda said pensively.

'Not so sure about that. I would still be disqualified as long as the trail leads through Elisabeth Faremo.'

'Don't tinker with this case while you're on leave.'

'I haven't done anything else since I've been away.'

Silence again. They could read each other's thoughts well and neither of them was going to waste words on the obvious. Frank Frølich was breaking all the rules, but he would continue to do so whatever measures Gunnarstranda took to stop him.

'The car has turned up,' Gunnarstranda said.

'Which car?'

'Jonny Faremo's Saab, the one we thought had been seen near the Glomma the day he was released.'

'What about it?'

'The car was abandoned on a deserted logging track near Sollihøgda – a hundred kilometres from Askim. A farmer passing by in his tractor every day finally became irritated enough to ring in.'

'Has it been examined?'

'Kripos are working on it. Now don't do anything stupid,' Gunnarstranda said. 'And keep me posted.'

Gunnarstranda waited until the door closed behind Frølich before swivelling round to pick up the phone.

He rang the detective he knew best in Eco-Crime – the Economic and Environmental Crime division: 'Chicken Brains' Sørlie. But before Sørlie managed to answer the telephone Gunnarstranda had one of his sporadic coughing fits.

'Is that you?' Sørlie asked amid the coughing. 'Are you OK, Gunnarstranda?'

Gunnarstranda nodded and gasped for air. 'Just these rotten lungs of mine.'

'Perhaps you should give up smoking?'

'Perhaps sheep should stop bleating?' Gunnarstranda suggested breathlessly and sat erect again. 'There was something I wanted to ask you.'

'Fire away.'

'Inge Narvesen. Does that name mean anything to you?'

'Businessman.'

'Nothing else?'

'I know he's an art lover.'

'What sort of art?'

'Paintings. He's spent a lot of money on art. His collection must be a bit like Stenersen museum at its peak, only Narvesen doesn't go in for modern art much.'

'But what does he live off?'

'He's a trader on the stock exchange. Buying and selling.'

'Buying and selling?'

'And he's got POTS of money,' Sørlie said. 'Invests a lot in property. The last I heard he'd bought up large areas of the forest Norske Skog had put up for sale. He's planning to build mini-power stations on a number of the rivers, I believe. That's pretty popular now as energy is expensive and the authorities don't give a damn about environmental issues.'

'Nothing illegal, though?'

'Doubt it. He's an upright sort. Never heard of him being involved in anything disreputable. Has a good reputation at the stock exchange as well.'

'No weaknesses: never touched up young boys, exposed himself to girl guides –?'

'Inge Narvesen is clean. Believe me.'

'Well, he's a very unusual person then.'

'If there are any irregularities, they'll be financial.'

'Yes, yes,' Gunnarstranda said, irked. 'Talk to you later.'

On entering the hall of the apartment block, Frank Frølich made straight for the post box. The box was so full you could hardly turn the lock. When he opened the door, a pile of bills fell out.

One letter slid across the stone floor. His name and address were written in beautiful looped handwriting. No sender's address.

He managed to curb his curiosity in the lift, but impatiently weighed the letter in his hands. Could it be from Elisabeth? He closed his eyes and struggled to think clearly. *Long bones. Flames.*

He was perspiring as he opened the lift door. To have a hand free to unlock his front door, he put the letter in his mouth. Once inside, he ripped open the envelope and read:

> The most difficult thing about writing a letter is the salutation, as Elisabeth used to say. She always thought long and hard before she decided what she would write: Hi or Dear, or perhaps nothing at all. The first words of a letter actually said as much as the letter itself, she thought, because they signalled the emotional relationship the writer was communicating to the receiver. For me it was always reassuring to read her letters. She always started them with Dear Reidun. In this way she calmed my nerves enough for me to be able to absorb the message – even though what she had to say on occasion had a bitter taste. She told me about you first in a letter. But I don't want to get sentimental now, and I assure you that all Elisabeth's letters to me have been burned. As you see, I have left the salutation out completely this time. It feels right. I haven't started taking the pills yet. First of all, I want to get this letter out of the way. I don't know who will find me, nor do I really care. But I am writing to you because I have realized that you are driven by the same passion that I have struggled with. Therefore, I have a tiny hope that you will understand me well enough to fulfil a last wish. I don't know whether Elisabeth will be able to stand up to these terrible people. I hope she can, but I have no illusions. Nor did I have any illusions when they came here. Elisabeth warned me about them and, arrogant as I so often am, I took no notice, believing I would be able to stand firm. However, I have always had a fear of pain and I couldn't hold out. Although I knew that revealing her hiding place would lead to what I am doing now,

I still couldn't stand firm. So I told them where she was hiding. Hence I am responsible for whatever might happen to her. My fate is sealed. I hope she will survive, but I have neither the illusions nor the courage to wait for an answer. Should this nightmare end well for Elisabeth, tell her from me: My darling, forgive me. I tried, I really did.

Reidun

Frank Frølich slumped into a chair. It was difficult to unravel his feelings. Before he began to read he had supposed the letter would be from Elisabeth. So, to hear Reidun Vestli's voice in his head was a shock. *Forgive me*, he thought. *These terrible people*, he thought. *A last wish*, he thought, and sat up. He read the letter through again.

He jumped when the telephone rang and seized the receiver.

'I've just had a chat with Sørlie from Eco-Crime about the fat cat who was robbed by Ilijaz Zupac, this Narvesen person,' Gunnarstranda said.

He's beginning to ring a lot now. 'Oh yes? Did Sørlie come up with anything?'

'Nothing, as usual, except that Narvesen is loaded. He's a stock market trader, owns a lot of art and has swathes of forestry property in Hedmark.'

'I knew that.'

Gunnarstranda coughed. 'But Sørlie has just rung me back. He must have had Narvesen's name on the brain when he put the phone down. Eco-Crime receives a list issued by banks when there has been a large withdrawal of money. And Inge Narvesen's name is on it. From Nordea Bank, to be precise.'

'Large withdrawal?'

'Five million.'

'Why does that kind of information go to Eco-Crime?'

'Routine matter. Banks are obliged to report large transactions, cash withdrawals and that sort of thing to intercept potential money laundering.'

'Has Narvesen said what the five million was for?'

'No one has got round to doing anything yet. What is mind-boggling is that this withdrawal took place on a very particular day.'

'Which day?'

'The same day Jonny Faremo was released and his sister made off for the woods.'

Frølich was staring out of the window as a couple of cars on the roundabout several metres below avoided a collision by a hair's breadth. 'What do you think?' he asked. 'You wouldn't be talking to me if you didn't have a theory.'

'There doesn't have to be any connection at all, but you know how I feel about so-called coincidences.'

'Gunnarstranda's Coincidence Theorem,' Frølich said with a tiny smile. 'There's no such thing as a coincidence. The word co-incidence is a construct to replace and thus conceal the logical explanation of how things happen.'

'You're recovering, Frølich. When I die you can write my obituary. But if my theory is correct, Narvesen has taken out the money for a reason, and I'm guessing blackmail.'

'Why?'

'Narvesen has been blackmailed before.'

'What?'

'On a cruise. I looked up Narvesen in the archives. There was some story in 1991. Narvesen was one of the main shareholders in one of the shipping companies who sail American tourists round the Caribbean. It happened right after the fire on the *Scandinavian Star*. Everyone was talking about security and describing passenger ships as death traps, weren't they. Someone was trying to blackmail Narvesen for ten million. If he didn't pay up, information about inadequate security on the cruise liners would be leaked. The blackmailer was a Norwegian ex-captain from one of the cruise liners. The man had been fired for drinking and apparently wanted to get his own back.'

'What happened?'

'He was caught. Got three years.'

The two cars on the roundabout had caused a bottleneck. Someone honked their horn. Then the traffic started flowing again. A clenched fist shook from one of the car windows and the two cars were soon lost in the traffic.

Frølich said: 'If the man was arrested, Narvesen must have gone to the police for help on that occasion. He hasn't done so this time.'

'That's clear. But why else would anyone take five million out of the bank?'

'No idea. But if Narvesen is such a whizz-kid in the stock market as you said, he would have been much more sophisticated with regard to money laundering. He could have used a trusted solicitor's private account or something like that. Simply withdrawing cash suggests honourable intentions or extreme haste.'

'Haste is a word I like,' Gunnarstranda said. 'Especially with respect to the day the money was withdrawn.'

'What does Sørlie say?'

'Sørlie considers Narvesen as pure and spotless as a freshly scrubbed baby. And he believes it too. But I've never met anyone like that. I think anything is possible. Maybe Narvesen has been posing for photos in a G-string with an apple in his gob.'

'No one is shocked by anything any more.'

'Perhaps he likes little boys and was caught red-handed by his wife's private detective?'

'He was single at the time,' Frølich said. 'And I doubt he's interested in anything other than women. Regardless of whether he's married or not, there's no shortage of single wannabees in *Dagens Næringsliv* who spend their time screwing each other and drinking champagne in the breaks. No, sex is too old-fashioned. I would put my money on some financial hanky-panky.'

'The problem is,' Gunnarstranda said, 'that Narvesen passes for an honest man – a model businessman for many people, I've heard said. At the stock exchange on top of that.'

'There's no honesty in the Oslo Stock Exchange, and Sørlie should be the first person to know that.'

'Yes, but we're talking about the part of the honesty spectrum covered by the law. Inge Narvesen is always on the right side of the line – with a good solid margin in between. Though there are not many options open when you have to justify a withdrawal of that kind of money.'

'What about kidnapping?' Frølich said.

'He hasn't got any children or any valuable racehorses or prize-winning hunting dogs. But I suppose Sørlie will put in a formal enquiry. Then we'll see what Narvesen comes up with.'

After putting down the phone, Frank Frølich stood looking into space. He was wondering about Narvesen, about procedures. Sørlie and the formal approach. *Tick-tock*, he thought with irritation. *Tempus fugit. Time drags, everything goes slowly. Nothing happens.* He looked at the clock on the wall. Soon it would be one o'clock. Lunchtime for the workers. One thing he did remember from the kerfuffle surrounding the break-in at Narvesen's in 1998 was an almost surrealistic conversation during the man's lunch break at his permanent table at the Theatre Café.

Lunch. Theatre Café. The time.

It was a long shot. But was there anything else he could do?

Frølich took the underground to the National Theatre station. From there he quickly crossed Stortingsgata and walked with lowered gaze past the windows where Theatre Café customers sat having their lunch – absorbed in themselves and each other. Turning the corner of Klingenberggata he peered in and spotted Narvesen sitting at his usual table – alone as had always been his wont. He was taking coffee – so he would soon be finished.

Frølich checked his watch again. It was approaching a quarter to two. He walked around the block and joined the queue of people waiting for the tram outside the National Theatre, opposite the windows of the Theatre Café. There was snow in the air. Tiny, dry snowflakes lifting on the wind and settling like fragments of dust on people's shoulders and sleeves. He could make out Narvesen's brown hair through the windows on the opposite side of the street. At two o'clock precisely the man rose and joked with the waitress clearing the table. *Good friends, good tips*. Frank Frølich waited until Narvesen had moved into the corridor towards the cloakroom. Then he sprinted away from the wall and crossed Stortingsgata. When Narvesen had eased on his winter coat and was on his way through the entrance, Frølich had one foot on the pavement.

He said: 'Well, I never! Hello and nice to see you again! Long time no see!'

He grabbed the hand that Narvesen automatically stretched out.

'Do I know you?' The man's whole being radiated bewilderment. In his winter coat, with his upper body bent forward and his gloves rolled up in his left hand, he resembled an old photograph of John F. Kennedy. Small granules of snow landed on his hair.

'I'm a policeman. We met after a break-in at your house some years ago. Somebody had stolen a safe.'

The confused expression on Narvesen's face changed to one of irritation. 'The money which never reappeared?'

'Half a million is nothing,' Frølich said with a smile. 'Compared with five million in cash.'

Narvesen's eyes narrowed. He didn't say anything.

'Nordea registered a withdrawal of five million kroner in small notes in your name less than a week ago.'

'And what has that got to do with you?

'Maybe nothing with me, but with Eco-Crime.'

Narvesen stood facing him, thinking. The gloves he had held rolled up in one fist changed hands. Then he began to thwack them against individual snowflakes on one arm.

'You're a policeman,' he said. 'What was the name?'

'Frølich.'

'Right, now I remember you. You looked a little different then.'

'I had a beard.'

'Exactly, now it's coming back to me. Well, then, you know I am a wealthy man?'

Frølich nodded. He was puzzled. *The man sees the cop who investigated a theft of half a million of his money and he says: 'Right, now it's coming back to me.'*

Inge Narvesen started edging away. They walked side by side along the pavement. Narvesen said: 'If I gave you a number – say, one million eight hundred thousand – what would that mean to you?'

'A really nice apartment in one of the satellite districts – where I live now, for example.'

'If I said eight million kroner, what would *that* mean to you?'

'That would be harder to have any kind of genuine relationship with.'

Narvesen glanced at Frølich and gave a wry smile. They turned down Roald Amundsens gate towards Klingenberggata and Haakon VIIs gate. 'I feel the same,' Narvesen said. 'Exactly fourteen months ago the value of a small part of my portfolio increased by 150 million kroner. Tomorrow, at this time, the same portfolio will be worth 300 million kroner more. This has nothing to do with me, but with a series of factors: current low interest rates, my own long-term investments, the breadth of my portfolio and, not least, how the general economy is performing in the market place. And it's not the first time this has happened. On the roller coaster that is the stock market, I have experienced lots of what seemed to be endless boom times. But I've always come through the ensuing crises with both feet on the ground and a good base for further business. And I'll tell you a little secret as far as that is concerned.' Narvesen stopped. They had come to the corner of Klingenberggata and Haakon VIIs gate.

'Well, tell me,' Frølich said impatiently.

'A good antidote to eternal optimism with stocks and shares is an occasional trip to the bank. Then I take out a pile of money. I stuff all the notes into a supermarket carrier bag and put it in a cupboard in the office. The last time I did this is less than a week ago. Yes, I withdrew five million in cash. It's in my office. In a plastic bag. Whenever I make a transaction of such unreal proportions, I go to this cupboard and look into the bag and say to myself: "Inge Narvesen," I say. "This is what it's all about, this is real money. With the contents of this bag you can buy a reasonable home, an above-average car and a fair-sized holiday chalet. You can put the rest of the money in the bank and live on the interest."'

'You've got five million in a cupboard?'

Narvesen nodded. 'And now I have to go back to my office and earn more money. Nice to meet you, Frølich. Have a great day.'

Frølich watched him go. Two minutes' chat about money and 'What's that got to do with you?' turned into 'Have a great day'. *Five million in a cupboard in the office? Don't make me laugh.*

He did some mental arithmetic: *five* million kroner, that's fifty thousand hundred-kroner notes. Is there enough space for them in a carrier bag – or if he had used thousand-kroner notes – five thousand notes? How many bags did he need? OK, Inge Narvesen wanted a genuine relationship with money, so why not confine the sum to a hundred thousand? Or two hundred thousand? That would be much more in accord with the logic behind the act. First of all, make a staggering profit and afterwards check how many notes make up just one hundred thousand. But – five million?

He thought back to the time six years ago. The atmosphere in Narvesen's house. Deadly serious. The worry in his mother's eyes – she had been there to represent him. Yes, that was what had happened: Narvesen had been on holiday, somewhere hot – Bahamas or Pitcairn Island or something like that – and his mother had turned up after the break-in. The crime had been committed in the son's house. Must have been night time or early morning. Narvesen's mother had sat like a lonely little bird in the corner of the sofa imagining all sorts of bogeymen while Narvesen sent his telephone instructions from the southern seas.

Frank Frølich thought about Ilijaz Zupac. So far he had served more than five years of the sentence for a second, more serious crime. Perhaps it was time to have a chat with Ilijaz Zupac.

24

It was a freezing cold morning. A narrow margin of cloud resembling red lava presaged daybreak over the mountain peaks. Frank Frølich was heading north on the E6 towards the rush-hour traffic and the sun rising in the east. He pulled out his sunglasses from the glove compartment. As his car sped over the ridge, Karihaugen and Nedre Romerike revealed themselves as a large patchwork quilt of farmland in hibernation. Three lanes, 120 kilometres an hour and only oncoming traffic. The scene seemed almost American. He pushed a Dylan CD into the player – 'Slow Train Coming' – and clicked forward to the title song. It was a long track and the driving guitar complemented the scenery. On top of that, there was something fateful and invigorating about the repeated refrain of a train coming. He felt he could be that train. It was moving slowly but it was making progress. When Dylan finished singing, he played the track again, until he arrived outside the high walls of Ullersmo prison.

After passing the gate in the internal prison wall, he was met by a young man with big, blond, curly hair, who said: 'Are you the person who wants to meet Ilijaz?'

Frølich nodded.

'I'm Freddy Ramnes, the prison doctor.'

The man's handshake was firm and he looked Frølich steadfastly in the eye. He said: 'Do you know Ilijaz Zupac from before?'

Frølich raised both eyebrows and considered the question briefly before deciding to answer honestly: 'I arrested Zupac in autumn 1998. I questioned him at various times the same day and then gave evidence at the trial. Those are the only times I've seen the man.'

Ramnes hesitated. 'Are you here on police business?'

'I'm on leave at present.'

'May I ask why you're here?'

'For personal reasons.'

They weighed each other up.

Frølich waited for the unpleasant question: *Which particular personal reasons?* But it never came.

Eventually Frank Frølich said: 'Is there a problem? Doesn't he want to talk to me?'

The doctor took his time to answer. 'This has nothing to do with me,' he said in the end, sticking his hands in his pockets as if the words he was searching for were down there. 'It's more the situation. Ilijaz is sick. He needs, *really* needs psychiatric treatment, a facility we are unable to offer.' He went silent, apparently still searching for words.

'Yes?' Frølich said, expecting more.

'We're dealing with a *very* needy person here. I thought I should prepare you for that.' Pause. Ramnes finally added: 'Hmm. Shall we go?'

The echo of their footsteps resounded against the concrete walls. *This is unusual. The doctor is accompanying me on the visit. But then he's young, probably an idealist.*

They came to one of the more comfortable visiting rooms where inmates can meet their partners and there are condoms in the cupboard. The room was not very inviting, however. It contained one cheap sofa, one table and one armchair. Bare walls. In front of the radiator, between the wall and the armchair, a man was squatting on the floor. Frank Frølich didn't recognize him. The previously golden skin was now grey. His hair was a greasy, tangled mess reminiscent of a crow's nest; his back wretchedly rounded in a T-shirt full of holes. The man was squatting like a Hindu in meditation along the banks of the Ganges, hiding his head in his hands.

Frølich and Freddy Ramnes exchanged glances.

'Ilijaz,' Freddy Ramnes said.

No reaction.

'Ilijaz!'

The figure stirred: a hand, filthy, with narrow fingers and long nails, began to wind strands of hair.

'Ilijaz, do you want a Coke?'

The situation was ridiculous. Frølich looked across at the doctor whose expression was serious and empathetic.

'Ilijaz, you have a visitor.'

A look, hunted, like a frightened cat's, before his head hid itself again.

'Ilijaz, would you like to come and say hello to Frank?'

The head didn't budge.

Frølich cleared his throat. 'Ilijaz, do you remember me?'

No reaction.

'I arrested you that time six years ago, at the petrol station. I'm the policeman who talked to you afterwards.'

No reaction.

'You had a Norwegian girlfriend called Elisabeth. I wanted to talk to you about . . .' He paused when the figure on the floor moved. The crouching body turned away completely, into the corner.

Frølich and the doctor exchanged glances again. Frølich said: 'Elisabeth Faremo. Jonny Faremo, Vidar Ballo, Jim Rognstad . . .' He stopped. No discernible reaction. He cleared his throat and proceeded: 'I have a photograph of Elisabeth Faremo. Would you like to see it?'

No reaction.

Frølich and the doctor looked at each other. The doctor had his hands in his pockets, waiting.

'Perhaps this isn't such a good idea,' Frølich said.

Freddy Ramnes shook his head. He took a plastic half-litre bottle of Coke out of the pocket in his roomy jacket and put it on the table. 'Bye, Ilijaz,' he said, moving towards the door.

They walked back down the same corridor without speaking. 'If I were to die while working here,' Freddy Ramnes said in a voice quivering with anger, 'I would like my gravestone to say I was killed by the Norwegian penal policy. Those with political responsibility have given *me* the happy dilemma of either securing him with straps or doping him up every evening so that he doesn't do away with himself.'

'Was he doped up now?'

'Naturally.'

'Does that mean he would have problems remembering names?'

'No. It means he's calm, but absolutely indifferent to what you or I might say. A lobotomy is much the same, according to those who are au fait with such things.'

'What's he suffering from?'

Freddy Ramnes walked on a few metres. Now that he had vented his fury, he was collecting himself and trying to regain the dignity his emotions had blown to pieces a few moments ago. 'If I were a specialist in psychiatry, I might be able to tell you. The only thing I can do is apply for a place for him in an institution and receive rejections. After all, he *is* in an institution, isn't he?' Ramnes pulled a bitter face.

Frølich didn't know what to say.

'Well, I don't know,' Ramnes continued in a gentler vein. 'They're just labels anyway. Psychotic personality disorder, bipolar personality disorder, schizophrenia, you name it, he might have it. Cynics might call it prison psychosis.'

'As I said, I had some contact with Ilijaz six years ago and he was a very different person.'

Ramnes breathed in. 'The only thing I know is that the illness and the symptoms have developed while he has been serving his sentence. It had already started when I first came here. Intense fear, withdrawal, paranoia. And it's simply getting worse.'

'Does anyone visit him?'

Ramnes stopped and gave him a sceptical look.

'You seem like a decent person, Frølich. However, we're now moving into an area where I'm bound by professional secrecy and you'll have to direct your enquiries to others.'

25

This was the first time in eighteen years that Inspector Gunnarstranda had taken time off work. The evening before he had discovered that Kalfatrus wasn't swimming straight. Afterwards he sat down with a glass of whisky in front of the goldfish bowl and watched the fringetail swim in and out of the magnifying glass that the curve of the glass created. The fish was lopsided. He fell asleep in the chair and when he awoke he simply neglected to go to bed. Just sat there watching the goldfish, illuminated by the street lamps outside the window. He could feel that something was wrong. For one tiny insane moment he saw himself walking with the fish in a plastic bag; he saw himself sitting with the red fringetail in the vet's surgery:

And what's the matter with this chap?

Well, you know, it doesn't swim straight.

The situation was not the most satisfying. But at the same time he couldn't rid himself of a sense of unease. He had been sure that the tiny fringetail would outlive him. It was worrying that the contrary appeared to be the case. He attempted to work out what this worry was based on. Was it concern for the fish or concern for himself? Was his worry an expression of his fear of loneliness – a life without Kalfatrus – or was this unease in some specific way more altruistic, in that he was actually concerned about the fish's general condition? He wondered if a fish could feel pain.

The previous evening he had tried everything: changing the water, washing the bowl, washing the sand at the bottom, adding prescribed conditioners and food. Despite this, it swam even more askew and the characteristic gaping mouth was less in evidence.

If it dies now, he thought, it might be from old age. Was that likely? He tried to think back. When had he bought the fish? He couldn't remember. And he had no idea how many years a fish like this could live. The only thing he could remember was that it cost seventeen kroner. The next moment he imagined himself standing by the telephone, dialling and asking the following question: *Um, I was wondering if you could tell me how long a fringetail costing about seventeen kroner could live?*

He lit up a cigarette and reflected as he blew smoke rings in the direction of the goldfish bowl. For the first time in many years he felt a diminishing commitment to work. And what displaced all that was the sight of a red and yellow fish swimming askew. *Damn you, damn you, if you die now, before me!*

26

Frank Frølich regarded himself in the mirror in front of his bed. He reconstructed the sequence of events in his head:

I had discovered someone was in my flat. Elisabeth had let herself in before I arrived. She had taken a shower. She sat cross-legged in the living room. She was sitting in front of the hi-fi listening to music, dressed only in underwear.

He stood up and went into the living room. Stared at the stereo. In the TV screen a reflection of himself and the furniture he had bought for the room.

He went to the doorway and stared at his hi-fi equipment again. *She was sitting with her back to me as I came in and said she had let herself in with the key from the key dish.* He saw her back in front of him as she stalked over to her clothes on the chair. He remembered the brush of her lips against his. He saw the sway of her hips as she walked across the floor. The clink of the key as it dropped into the bowl in the kitchen. He went to the kitchen door. Stood staring at the bowl of keys, small coins, various steel screws, drawing pins, the odd krone coin and other bits and bobs. *No house key.*

So she hadn't put the key back.

Why not? But he *had* heard the clink of the key in the bowl. If she hadn't put the house key back, what had she put in it instead? He took hold of the bowl with trembling hands. It was a piece of hollowed-out birch, a so-called wooden nipple with delicate carvings on, a dish he had bought at an art-and-crafts fair when he went fishing on Lake Osen in Trysil. He tipped the contents of the bowl onto the kitchen worktop: coins, some screws, a safety pin, a dud 5-amp fuse, an anti-nuclear-weapons badge, another badge against joining the EU. One of the coins rolled off onto the floor – a euro. A green marble rolled after it. He caught it. *Yes, there was a key.* He took the key. *It's not mine!* It wasn't a house key. And he had never seen it before. It was a long, narrow key with a strange cut, a key to a special kind of lock. *What is going on here?* Why had she put back a completely different kind of key? And why had she *not* put back his house key? Why had she lied to his face? What would this key fit?

A key. But what was it hiding? Where is the lock?

Frank Frølich walked stiffly back into the living room and dropped into a chair. *She hadn't put back the key.* In a flash he saw bones glowing in the ashes. *The key has been burned. No, stick to the facts! The house key is irrelevant. What is relevant is the key she left in the bowl.*

Once again he saw the contours of her body moving away from him – across the floor. The clink in the bowl. Everything had been a bluff, a red herring. Either the bluff was because she wanted to hang onto the house key – or perhaps it was because she wanted to put the other, strange key in his bowl. Third option: she wanted both, to deposit this key and keep his key so that she could collect it later.

That was the answer. He was sure. She had intentionally hidden this key in his flat so that she could pick it up later.

But she hadn't managed to accomplish her plan. She had been killed, burned to death in the chalet where she was hiding.

The phrasing in Reidun Vestli's suicide letter bit into his consciousness: *Fear of pain. I couldn't hold out.*

Was this the key these *terrible people* were after? If so, *who was looking for the key? And why?*

He gave a start as the telephone rang. It was Gunnarstranda. Without any preamble, he said: 'Positive DNA.'

'Where?'

'The fire – Reidun Vestli's chalet. It *was* Elisabeth Faremo who was burned. My condolences, Frølich. You'll be getting another visit from Kripos soon.'

'Hang on,' Frølich said.

'Relax,' Gunnarstranda said. 'Take more time off or apply for a week's holiday so you can ride the storm.'

'I have to talk to you.'

'What about?'

'A key I've found.'

'Is it very important?'

'Yes.'

'Come over this evening – after eleven.'

Perhaps he just wanted to kill time. Or something else in him had triggered the initiative. But he went back to Merethe Sandmo's ex-workplace. It was almost eleven o'clock. The place was filling up. The gathering was a motley group of individuals, several of them belonging to a stag party. One man – presumably the bridegroom-to-be – was dressed in a bunny outfit. He was in such a drunken state he needed three chairs to sit on. Two young whippersnappers wearing dinner suits were giggling and trying to dip his hand in a bowl filled with water. An older guest with a waxed moustache and a chimpanzee jaw cast furtive glances while rolling a schnapps glass between his hands.

On the stage a buxom woman with chocolate-brown skin was rotating her breasts to the sound of Tom Jones's 'She's a Lady' booming out of the loudspeakers. Frølich went to the bar and ordered a large beer from a pimply youth in a dinner suit. Frølich took his beer, reflecting that he had always considered dinner suits ridiculous. *Item in his favour: I have never worn a dinner suit. Item no longer in his favour: I have never seen a striptease.* The woman with the rotating breasts had finished. Eyes followed her as she ran off the stage and the lights were lowered. Frølich manoeuvred his way to a table right in front of the stage.

He scanned the audience. Stag party or not, these men were serious. Welcome to men's country, he thought, and looked up at the ceiling where he discovered a flashing disco ball the like of which he had not seen outside seventies John Travolta films. He looked at the faces in the room. Yes, he was in the arena of shadows, the hour of the rats, the wedding procession of the cockroaches: in this light, all the faces were lent the same blue and yellow hue. This was a place where it didn't matter whether you were sick, healthy, Aryan, Indian, Chinese or just uncomfortable. This was the place where there was no room for reflection or appraisal, where lonely souls would reap pangs of guilt, bitterness or self-contempt the following day – or another time, later anyway – for everyone here can deceive themselves for a few seconds that welfare is a fruit that grows out of your own wallet. The password of the void here was: 'Another drink, please.'

And here I am sitting in the front row! he thought, raising his tankard and drinking while the next number was being announced. The glass at his mouth, he met the gaze of the woman making her entrance on the stage. She had covered her face with a mask moulded into the shape of a face. Nevertheless, he recognized the hourglass figure and the dreadlocks. She danced to Percy Sledge's 'When a Man Loves a Woman'. The lady knew her audience. Even the hecklers in the stag party quietened down. She was wearing long tight gloves over her arms, but the most striking effect was the contrast between the cold, lifeless porcelain of the mask and the living skin, of which she was gradually revealing more and more. After a while she let go of the firemen's pole and glided off the stage. With her eyes behind the mask fixed on his, she released her top. A couple of the guys in the room couldn't stand the pressure and roared rutting cries. A young man sporting a grey suit and a formidable fringe threw a hundred-kroner note folded into a paper aeroplane. The note hit her in the stomach. She took no notice; but in one gliding movement she was back on the stage. The eyes behind the mask were still fixed on him. She held eye contact even while she was taking off her gloves. Not until she had spun round and run off stage did she relinquish his eyes. The music was drowned by whistles and applause. Only the bridegroom in the bunny outfit had missed the finale. He was on all fours under a table throwing up.

Frølich was fascinated by the fact that she hadn't taken off the mask.

He went to the bar.

He had almost finished his next beer when she was beside him, dressed, without a mask, and transformed into a completely different woman from the one who had left the stage without a stitch. He asked what she wanted to drink.

'Just water,' she shouted through the din.

'Well, I must say,' he said, aware that he had no idea how to compliment in situations like these, 'you're good.'

She said: 'I've been keeping an eye open for you for a few evenings now.'

'I didn't think the invitation was still valid.'

'And *I* didn't know who you were.'

'But you do now?'

She nodded.

'Do you know Elisabeth?'

She nodded. 'I have to go,' she said. 'Give me your hand.'

He shook her hand. 'That's my phone number,' she said and let go. 'I mustn't be seen with you.'

He put the slip of paper in his pocket and asked: 'Who are you frightened of?' She was drinking water and could not answer. When she had put down the glass, she slid off the barstool.

'When they ask you what I said,' Frølich yelled, 'tell them I have a message. I have the key.'

She wanted to go.

He held her back.

She sent him a wounded look. 'I have to go, I mean it.'

'I have the key,' Frølich repeated.

She squeezed his wrist lightly and was gone, the heavily made-up, fake-tanned babe from the working classes who stripped to earn money in this grotty place. *What am I doing?* He was dismayed to meet an echo of his earlier thoughts, and put down the glass with trembling hands. He walked away from the bar, up the stairs and out. Outside, he stood breathing in the air, which was cold and refreshing. He jumped into the first taxi. It was just gone eleven.

It was an odd feeling to be trudging up these particular stairs, noticing the smell, passing door after door with peepholes, in a stairwell that he felt such an affiliation with, but had never entered. He stopped and studied the battered door, the brass nameplate, the aluminium newspaper flap. He lifted his finger to the white doorbell and pressed it. The bell rang like a sixties telephone. The echo hung in the quiet stairwell until he could hear his boss coughing on the inside shortly before the door was opened.

Gunnarstranda stared coolly up at him without any expression.

'Now it's my turn,' Frølich said, embarrassed.

Gunnarstranda held open the door. 'Would you like a whisky?'

'Yes, please.'

'Which brand do you prefer?'

'What have you got?'

'All of them.'

Frank Frølich raised his eyebrows.

'At any rate, the ones you know.'

'An Islay,' Frank Frølich said, watching Gunnarstranda going off to a worn old trunk on which it was still possible to read the faded label of MS *Stavangerfjord*. He opened the lid; the brown bottles were tightly packed in.

'Bowmore?'

'OK.'

Frølich had a look around. Almost every square centimetre of wall space in the living room was covered with books. Specialist literature, encyclopaedias, ballistics, botany. He read the titles: *Alpine Flowers in the North*, *Flowers of the Alps*, *Flowers in Iceland*, *Flowers of the Faroese Islands*. The only break in the rows of books was a glass bowl in which a red fringetail was belching water. He stood up and looked at the fish through the glass.

'Here you are,' Gunnarstranda said, passing him the glass.

Frølich took it.

'They cost thirty-five kroner,' Gunnarstranda said.

'Hm?'

'Fish like that one. Cheap, isn't it?'

'Looks a bit listless.'

Gunnarstranda didn't answer.

'You don't have a lot of fiction,' Frølich noticed.

'Fiction?'

'Yes, novels, poems . . .'

'Arts?' Gunnarstranda shook his head and smiled. 'I don't like the arts.' He raised his glass. '*Skål.*'

They sipped their whisky.

Frølich swallowed his with relish.

'That doesn't tally with your ability to quote literature.'

Gunnarstranda shrugged, put down his glass and said: 'Have you got the key?'

Frølich buried his hand in his pocket and then passed it to him.

They were sitting in two deep chairs which must have dated from at least the first EU referendum in 1972.

Gunnarstranda studied the key. 'A bank safety-deposit box,' he said.

'Why do you think that?'

'Because it's exactly the same as the key for my own safety-deposit box.' Gunnarstranda passed him back the key. Frølich sat pondering it in his hand. 'No name of bank, no number of box.'

'That's how it usually is.'

'So we've got a few thousand banks to choose from and a few hundred thousand safety-deposit boxes,' Frølich burst out dejectedly.

Gunnarstranda nodded. 'It's not meant to be simple.'

'But why don't the banks mark their keys?'

Gunnarstranda shrugged. 'I assume because having a safety-deposit box is a fairly solemn business. When I acquired one all those years ago I was provided with two keys and informed that the bank didn't have any copies. If I wanted to authorize someone to open the box, it would have to be registered in the bank's own authorization register.'

'But what the hell am I supposed to do with the key if it's not possible to find out which bank or safety-deposit box it belongs to?'

Gunnarstranda smirked and said: 'Where has the key come from?'

'She left it at my place.'

'Who did?'

'Elisabeth.'

'Sure?'

'A hundred per cent.'

'The odds are that the key was issued to either Elisabeth Faremo or someone in her circle – Jonny Faremo, for example. Perhaps to both of them. The only snag you might encounter is that there is no central register of holders of safety-deposit boxes – something you would definitely be glad of in other situations.'

Frølich sipped his whisky while the other detective brooded.

'You said you found a tattoo parlour in Askim where someone had decorated Elisabeth Faremo's hips?'

Frølich nodded.

'Did you find that out on your own?'

'Of course.'

'What made you search there – in Askim?'

'Because Jonny Faremo was found dead in Askim.'

'Would you be interested to know that Ilijaz Zupac once lived there?'

'Where?

'In Askim.' When Gunnarstranda saw the bewilderment in the other's eyes, he added: 'I took the trouble to do a little digging around Ilijaz Zupac. He went to the FE College in Askim and took the basic mechanics course. In the seventies his father was working at the rubber-goods factory in Askim. There must have been a whole colony of Yugoslav immigrants there.'

'Yugoslav?'

'This was before Tito's death and the Balkan wars. These Yugoslavs are now Croats, Bosnians, Serbs and Montenegrins. Where Zupac's parents came from, only he knows. They're both dead. However, he has Norwegian nationality and he did the basic and the advanced course at this college from 1989 to 1991. He's a qualified panel-beater and was working in that capacity at the garage where you arrested him.'

Gunnarstranda motioned towards the key. 'I have a safety-deposit box in Den norske Bank NOR in Grefsen. As I said, the keys are very similar.'

'You mean we should go to Grefsen and try all the safety-deposit boxes there?'

Gunnarstranda shook his head. He said: 'Faremo was killed in Askim, his sister got a tattoo in Askim, her ex-lover has lived in Askim. And I happen to know there is a branch of DnB there.'

They both lapsed into silence. Frølich was still holding the key in his outstretched hand. 'It's worth a stab,' he said.

'But it has to be done officially.'

'Why's that?'

'I'll have to use the case I'm investigating. I'll call in Jim Rognstad and Vidar Ballo for more questioning about the Arnfinn Haga murder – and about the death of Elisabeth Faremo. I have a strong suspicion that neither of the two will turn up. If they don't, there's nothing to stop me –' Gunnarstranda was tapping his chest with his forefinger '– from confronting the employees of the Askim branch of DnB –' he leaned forward and snatched the key out of Frølich's hand '– with this key.' He put it in his pocket. 'From now on you and I are playing in the same team on this case,' he concluded. 'I assume you'll be making it into work tomorrow.'

Frølich deliberated. He didn't like the direction Gunnarstranda's outline of events was taking. He said: 'What if the key doesn't fit?'

'Then you've got something to work on in the days to come.'

Frølich stood up. He put out his hand.

Gunnarstranda glanced up. 'What is it now?'

'The key. If this is supposed to be official, it will have to be official. I'll hand it in tomorrow.'

After leaving Gunnarstranda, he decided to go from Bjølsen to the city centre on foot. He strolled along the pavement by the timber houses in Maridalsveien and took a left turn down by the old mill on the Akerselva. The bridge over the waterfall was illuminated now in the dark. He wandered over the bridge past the Hønse-Lovisa house and on to Grünerløkka. He had to think. Gunnarstranda's snatching the key out of his hand had irritated him. But what did this emotion signify? Was it a kind of ingrown allergy to being given orders? To handing over the key and being obliged to go to work tomorrow, clean-shaven and properly breakfasted, ready to conform religiously to all the rules and regulations? Perhaps that was the cause of his irritation: the fact that he was disqualified by his personal involvement and this would make further work on the case difficult. So perhaps he wasn't ready to go to work yet. The key weighed heavily in his trouser pocket. It had been left in his flat by *her*. This key was *his*. And this pressure from Gunnarstranda to go to work, to perform his function in the orchestra and allow himself to be conducted, he wasn't ready for that. Not now. Not *yet*.

Autumn chose this night to demonstrate its damp side. The streetlamps in Birkelunden had an orange aura in the mist. A man wearing a parka and pyjama trousers was taking his dog for a walk. A dark car drove slowly past. Frank Frølich quickened his step, heading for Grønland Metro station.

He caught the last train. It was about one o'clock at night. He still wasn't sure whether to go to work or not. For one thing, he would have to be up in a few hours. And for another he would have to tolerate the looks, the silence and the unspoken – not just for a whole day but every single day from now on. Would he *ever* be able to get back into the swing of police work?

He got off at Ryen station and walked slowly down Havreveien. The weather had become even milder. It was drizzling. He stopped – held the palm of his hand out to feel the drops falling. But he didn't feel anything.

He heard the motorbike, but didn't see it. He only felt himself flying through the air. Then the cold, wet, hard tarmac as his hands broke his fall. He didn't feel the crack on his head either. But he heard it and it stunned him. As the air was knocked out of his lungs, he saw the rear lights of the motorbike. The powerful figure in the leathers and helmet rested the bike on its side-stand. He had been run over. The air had rushed against his face as he flew. *The man had run into him deliberately*. He tried to get up, but was too slow. A kick and he was down again. The man with the motorbike helmet was holding something in his hand. A voice in his head screamed: *Get to your feet! Run!* But his legs crumbled. He held his hands over his head as the man struck. Everything went black and he could feel hands groping his body. He lay there with his eyes closed and everything was still. He blinked but couldn't see. He dabbed his face with his hand. Wet. *Blood. You have to get help!* He dragged himself up on all fours, but passed out and collapsed in a heap. He ran his hand over his face again, caught a brief glimpse of the street and the parked cars. The motorbike started up. The red rear light and the exhaust. The outline of a rider who didn't look back. He managed to crawl. Slowly he clambered up onto the pavement as the sound of the motorbike faded into the distance. His clothes were soaked. He leaned back against a parked car. He felt his scalp with his fingers, found the wound and took his fingers away. He patted his pockets. The wallet was there. *What had he stolen?* He knew the answer and didn't bother to check his pocket. Instead he searched for his mobile phone. No one would have seen anything here between the blocks of flats. He would have to call emergency services himself.

It wasn't yet five o'clock in the morning. Gunnarstranda hadn't eaten, hadn't had a cup of coffee. He was irritated and irascible. Not even the sight of his sorry-looking colleague sitting beside him in the car could lift him. Frølich had been bandaged up with all the expertise at the disposal of Oslo Accident and Emergency Department, but was still in shock from the attack and stank of beer and vomit.

'Didn't you even catch a glimpse of his registration number?' he asked.

'No.'

'No idea who it was?'

'No.'

'You said it was just one man. Are you sure there weren't more?'

'I'm not sure, but I think there was only one man.'

'And he took the key. That was bloody clever of you to take it with you.'

Frølich didn't reply.

'The thing that disturbs me most is the fact that they knew when to strike.'

'What do you mean?'

Gunnarstranda opened the car door and said: 'Come on.' He half-guided and half-supported the heavy Frølich out through the door of the Skoda and into the entrance of the apartment building. It was morning. A newspaper boy on his bike rattled past. A man who came shooting out of a door stared wide-eyed at Frølich's distressed condition.

They stumbled into the lift. The door closed with a bang and the lift jolted into action.

Frølich repeated: 'What do you mean?'

Gunnarstranda narrowed his eyes with annoyance. 'Do you think I'm daft, Frølich? These men struck tonight, pinched the key but didn't touch your money, your phone or your watch. How could they know you had the key on you? They haven't made a move before tonight. I didn't talk to anyone about the key. If you want any sympathy from me in this case, I want to know how they knew that tonight of all nights was the time to attack.'

'There was just one man. I suggest you ask him.'

'Bloody hell, you're pathetic.'

Frølich went quiet. The lift stopped. Gunnarstranda pushed open the door. They went out. Frølich searched his pockets for his bunch of keys, found it and opened the door.

'You were allowed to keep *those* keys then?'

Frølich glared at him. 'I haven't got anything to offer you, I'm afraid.' He sank down into the sofa.

Gunnarstranda stood in the doorway. His eyes were aflame. 'You came to me with the key for help. You serve me up some idiotic justification for wanting to take the key with you. Then you almost get yourself killed, only to ring me and wake me up instead of calling emergency services. Well, you got some help. But if deep down you're the man I take you for, and you still want my help, I have to bloody know what you've been up to!'

'I can't tell you.'

'And why can't you tell me?'

Frølich went quiet again. He put a cushion behind his neck.

'Answer me! Why can't you?'

Frolich closed both eyes and let out a heavy sigh. 'Before going to yours last night I went to the club where Merethe Sandmo used to work. I talked to someone working there, a woman.'

'A woman.' Gunnarstranda pulled a face, as if he had been eating lemons. 'A woman,' he repeated with revulsion. 'What is it with you and women?'

'Wait a moment – she put me onto Ilijaz Zupac. I went there a few days ago on a pure hunch and had his name presented on a silver platter. And yes, I went back there last night. But she'd been told to keep away from me. I took a risk. Thought I could smoke them out by asking her to tell these people – no idea who they are – that I had the key. She must have done that, at least it wasn't very long before the motorbike smacked into me.'

'What's the lady's name?'

'No idea.'

'Frølich!'

'It's true, I don't know. She's got red hair, or black hair dyed red, a pretty fiddly hairstyle – you know, Afro locks and so on. She's about twenty-eight, give or take the odd year. But what's more important is that the banks open soon.'

'I knew it,' Gunnarstranda said, exasperated. 'You think I'm stupid.'

Frølich breathed out.

Gunnarstranda turned in the doorway and said: 'I've thought a lot about the work we've done together, Frølich, and it's gone well. I sort of thought we complemented each other. But now – it's no good you keeping things to yourself and going round behaving like an idiot. There are too many dead people in this case: Arnfinn Haga, Jonny Faremo and Elisabeth Faremo. Add the academic at Blindern who killed herself and we're up to four. You're a policeman. I would never have believed I would see you lying there with one foot in the grave or that you'd be telling me tales during an investigation.'

'I would never have believed it either,' Frølich said. 'But I know who it was,' he mumbled.

Gunnarstranda shook his head. 'Even if we've arrested a man on a motorbike before, it's not certain he was the one who knocked you down.'

'How much do you bet?' Frølich mumbled. 'I bet you a hundred it's Jim Rognstad.'

'Maybe he lent his bike to someone,' Gunnarstranda said. 'If he did you've lost a hundred kroner.' Gunnarstranda shut the door and left.

27

Inspector Gunnarstranda had opted to go by train. One glance at the timetable told him that the journey would take a good hour. He would arrive there at roughly the same time as the bank opened. Yttergjerde and Stigersand had already taken up positions nearby.

The train journey was a long, tedious business. He remembered he had done the trip before – it must have been in the sixties, to see a cup match between Vålerenga and a team from Sarpsborg. With the exuberance of youth and faith in technology he and a friend had caught the train, only to arrive in Sarpsborg well after the match had started. Forty years on, he had forgotten that the railway track had been laid between the majority of the milk-churn collecting points in central Østfold. But now – before the October sun rose – there was neither the chance nor the time to enjoy the view of stubble, farmyards or the black-ploughed fields. Gunnarstranda was co-ordinating the troops by phone and running through his logbook.

When he had been travelling for a little more than half an hour, the phone rang again. It was Lena Stigersand who said simply: 'Bingo.'

'More,' Gunnarstranda said.

'I'm sitting here with the bank manager. They have a safety deposit box which was issued to Jonny Faremo and Vidar Ballo in 1998.'

'Who has authorization?'

'Jim Rognstad and someone called Ilijaz Zupac.'

'And the vault containing the boxes?'

'In the cellar.'

'Is there a camera down there?'

'No.'

'OK. Let's cross our fingers they turn up. If not, I'll get a court order for the box to be opened. Whatever happens, I'll keep a low profile. Ballo and Rognstad both know me.'

Lena Stigersand tentatively cleared her throat.

'Yes?'

'If they do come, should they be arrested?'

'Of course.'

'And the charge?'

'Reasonable cause for suspicion of violence towards a public servant.'

The railway station was opposite the bank building. It was a fairly modern brick building which also housed a chemist's shop and a medical centre. Gunnarstranda joined the queue in front of the ATM and noticed Yttergjerde sitting in a car outside the large station kiosk. It was his turn at the cashpoint and he took out five hundred kroner. Then he went to find somewhere to have breakfast. He walked beneath some tall trees by the railway line. The dead leaves lay in frozen rosettes on the sticky tarmac. On the other side of the lines he found a coffee bar in a combined picture-framing business and gallery. He ate a ciabatta sandwich and drank a cup of black coffee while keeping an eye on the pedestrian area where warmly dressed people hurried to and fro. A bearded man came cycling along with both red-gloved hands ostentatiously stuffed in his pockets and his eyes fixed rigidly ahead of him.

He had finished his coffee and was fuming about the politicians' ban on smoking in restaurants and cafés when the glass door flew open and Yttergjerde rushed in and ordered a new-fangled coffee from the menu hanging on the wall behind the young girl at the cash desk.

'I've just seen someone with worse up-and-over hair than you, Gunnarstranda,' Yttergjerde said.

'Congratulations,' Gunnarstranda answered, straightening individual strands over his bald head while studying his appearance in the window.

'Peder Christian Asbjørnsen,' Yttergjerde said.

'He's been dead for over a hundred years.'

Yttergjerde waved a fifty-kroner note. 'He's alive on this.'

Gunnarstranda glanced at the portrait of the man on the note and snapped: 'Aren't you supposed to be watching the bank?'

At that moment there was a crackle on Gunnarstranda's shortwave radio. It was Stigersand from the command car.

She said: 'I've got good news and bad news. Which do you want first?'

'The bad news.'

'Only one person came.'

'Where is he now?'

'He's making himself comfortable on the back seat here with me – so you've got your good news at the same time.'

Yttergjerde grinned.

The girl behind the counter poured Yttergjerde's coffee into a paper cup. They went out. Gunnarstranda lit a cigarette in the cold and inhaled greedily. Yttergjerde turned and then stopped. 'What do you think about when you stand like that?' he asked.

'I think about a novel I once read,' Gunnarstranda answered. 'Nordahl Grieg's *May the World Stay Young*, written in 1928.'

'Why that one in particular?'

'Somewhere he wrote how dangerous it was to smoke in the cold of winter.'

'And?'

'The writer maintained that what was dangerous was inhaling the cold into your lungs, not the smoke.'

'So the world's no longer young,' Yttergjerde said, grinning at his own witticism.

'You could say that.'

They walked slowly towards the railway line. The blue lights from the police cars flashed across the wall of a brick building on the opposite side. 'Does nothing surprise you, Gunnarstranda?

Having one of these guys pop up is actually like winning the lottery.'

'There are far too many things which surprise me.'

A train was coming. The bells at the crossing rang and the gates were lowered with a creaking noise. Gunnarstranda waited. Yttergjerde, who was already on his way across, stopped and went back to wait for the train to pass too.

'What, for example?'

'Well, for example, how much people know about television programmes. They talk about this or that series. Not just people at work; people interviewed in the papers talk about TV. People on TV talk about TV.'

'Nothing surprising about that, is there?'

'My opinion has always been that you should never expose yourself to that sort of thing.'

Yttergjerde smiled thinly. 'If you were ever forced to cut down on anything, I suppose it would have to be your consumption of whisky and tobacco, wouldn't it?'

'I don't know. I would have problems existing without tobacco, but a life with an excess of low-quality TV would be worse. Bad TV cripples people's sense of aesthetics in the short term and in the long term creates decadence.'

The train rolled up the slope from the west remarkably quietly. It click-clacked past, came to a halt in front of the yellow station building and once again the gates of the level crossing were raised to the accompaniment of creaking noises.

Two police cars were outside the bank. They had been sent by the Follo police division. The third car was civilian and it was the one with the flashing blue light – a discreet lamp on the roof and one inside the grille. There were two bulky shadows in the back seat. The door on the driver's side opened and out stepped Lena Stigersand.

'Who is it?' Gunnarstranda asked.

'Jim Rognstad.'

Gunnarstranda bent down to have a look inside. Rognstad sat, massive and unmoved, on the back seat.

'Was he riding a motorbike?'

'Yes.'

'Tow it in. Material evidence.'

'You're the boss.'

'When did you catch him?'

'We let him go down to the vault unchecked, he collected what he was after, and then we arrested him on the way up.'

'What have you confiscated?'

'A briefcase full of money.' Lena Stigersand lifted up a document case. 'Lots and lots of money.'

Gunnarstranda glimpsed through the car window again. 'And the safety-deposit box?'

'It's empty now.'

'Did he say anything?'

'He hasn't been asked.'

They stood for a few seconds without saying anything. Lena Stigersand spoke up. 'Well, what shall we do?'

'We'll bang him up. The public prosecutor will decide what to do with the money.'

Yttergjerde opened a car door. 'Are you coming back with us?'

Gunnarstranda shook his head. 'No,' he said. 'I'll take the train. I've got some thinking to do.'

He watched the procession of cars drive away. Finally, he turned and wandered past the railway station, continued past a bus stop and over to a large car park. He stopped, raised a hand and waved.

An engine started, and a silver-grey saloon reversed out of a row of cars and drove towards him. The car pulled up.

Gunnarstranda opened the door and sat inside without a word.

'How did you know I was here?' Frølich asked.

'I don't think you even know how ridiculous this is,' Gunnarstranda answered. 'But since you're here anyway, you can drive me to Oslo.'

'What was in the safety-deposit box?'

'Money.'

'So Inge Narvesen will be happy?'

'Presume so. The box was issued immediately after his safe was stolen. And Zupac is an authorized keyholder.'

'So Narvesen will probably be able to claim the money. Could be complicated, though, digging up an old case, from 1998, and charging another man.'

'Two.'

'Two?'

'Ballo may have stayed away, but he's not innocent.'

Frølich drove off. They took the E18.

Gunnarstranda added: 'But Rognstad will get off this time.'

They didn't speak, until Frølich could no longer stand it. He said: 'Why should he go free?'

'What are you going to charge him with? You didn't see your attacker, did you?'

'But he had the key to the safety-deposit box. He obviously stole it from me.'

'If you report him for assault.'

'I will.'

'As far as I'm concerned, go ahead. But do that and you're off the case. Any evidence that has passed through your hands will be totally worthless in a case against Jim Rognstad.'

Frølich drove in silence.

'Besides, Rognstad can always say he borrowed the key from Vidar Ballo and he has no idea where Ballo got it from. And we can't check that story out because Ballo is nowhere to be found.'

'You're a real optimist, you are.'

'Wrong, Frølich, I'm a realist. Rognstad's going to the safety-deposit box to collect the money changes nothing. Jonny Faremo and Vidar Ballo have had free access to the box for six years. The only thing Rognstad needs to say is that he got the surprise of his life when he saw the money in the box and he doesn't know where it came from. It could have been put there by Jonny Faremo, who is dead, of course, and so cannot answer any questions. See? All that has happened today is that probably Narvesen's money has turned up again. We haven't got enough on Rognstad to make any charge stick.'

After another silence Frølich said:

'Couldn't you use the torched chalet, Elisabeth's murder?'

Gunnarstranda shrugged. 'We'll have to wait and see. The local Fagernes police have got photos of Ballo, Faremo, Rognstad and even Merethe Sandmo. So we'll see what they can uncover.' Gunnarstranda looked over at his colleague and said: 'There's one thing we haven't discussed, Frølich.'

'What's on your mind?'

'Could your lady friend have set fire to the chalet?'

'No.'

'Why not?'

'Elisabeth, set fire to herself? The idea is absurd.'

'Let me put it a different way. Could she have killed herself?'

'Why would she kill herself?'

'That sort of thing happens.'

'But no one chooses to burn themselves willingly.'

'Suicidal types might, Frølich. They're not as lucky as Ophelia. They don't all have a romantic millpond in the moonlight to hand when misfortune beckons.'

'Listen to me. Elisabeth did not take her own life. You cannot make me believe that she set fire to herself.'

'But she might have taken sleeping tablets and fallen asleep with the candle lit.'

'What makes you say that?'

'The fire in the chalet was probably started by a candle, a candle in a bottle.'

Frølich said nothing.

'The local police and the fire investigators are agreed on that,' Gunnarstranda added. 'And it's not so unlikely that she was depressed after the death of her brother, is it? She didn't have any other family. Just imagine, she's on the run from some roughnecks, then her brother dies, her protector, the anchor in her life. Many would become emotional for much less.'

Frølich deliberated before speaking. 'I tend to the view that the candle was helped on its way, by someone who first of all dealt with Elisabeth – by Rognstad, for example. There was a fire because someone wanted to conceal a murder.'

'Naturally that is a possibility, but it is no more than a hypothesis.'

'Hypothesis?'

'Kripos find human remains subsequent to a chalet fire. The cause of the fire seems to be a candle which has toppled over. So the sequence of events is: someone reading in bed falls asleep, the candle is lit and she dies of carbon monoxide poisoning before the fire really takes hold.'

'Do you believe that?'

'I don't believe anything. I'm just telling you the theory Kripos have come up with.'

Frølich took a deep breath. They had arrived in Spydeberg. He indicated right and stopped at the petrol station. 'I'll show you something,' he said finally and pulled out Reidun Vestli's suicide letter from his inside pocket.

Gunnarstranda finished reading the letter, then took off his glasses and chewed the ends. 'Why didn't you show me this before?' he asked gently.

'It came a couple of days ago. The crux is . . .'

'It came? To your post box?'

'I hadn't opened it for days. The crux is what you can read between the lines. *These terrible people* etc etc. Reidun Vestli didn't find any romantic millpond. She took recourse to a bottle of pills because . . .'

'I can read too,' Gunnarstranda interrupted. 'But all this just sounds like a radio play.' He put his glasses back on his nose and read aloud: '*I don't know whether Elisabeth will be able to stand up to these terrible people. I hope she can, but I have no illusions. Nor did I have any illusions when they came here. Elisabeth warned me about them – these terrible people* . . .' He lowered his glasses. 'I've never read such dross.'

Frølich didn't know what to answer.

Gunnarstranda said: 'If this lady was beaten up so badly she told her attackers where Elisabeth was, and then, on top of that, sent a letter through the post to a policeman, why on earth would she not say who was responsible so that they would be punished?'

'Don't know,' Frølich said lamely. 'But I would assume out of loyalty to Elisabeth.'

'Loyalty? Elisabeth Faremo was dead when Vestli wrote this.'

'I have no cause to doubt the authenticity of the letter. The opening sentences, about the salutation. That's like listening to her speak. Reidun Vestli killed herself, and no one, not even you, can make me believe anything different. It's true there isn't much information of any value in the letter, but, in my opinion, it is genuine. Now you've got Rognstad. I'm sure he's partly responsible for Reidun Vestli's death.'

'Reidun Vestli is no longer able to testify against Rognstad. But – if you're right about the letter and it is genuine – why send it to you?'

'I thought it may have been something as basic as a need to communicate to someone the cause . . .'

'What cause?'

'What caused her to take her life.'

'So your version of events is that *someone* – possibly Vidar Ballo and/or Jim Rognstad searching for Elisabeth Faremo – beat the information out of Reidun Vestli and this *someone* made their way to the chalet, killed Elisabeth Faremo and set fire to the chalet? This had such a dreadful effect on Reidun Vestli that she took a load of pills and died?'

'Yes. I think Vidar Ballo and Jim Rognstad beat up Reidun Vestli to find out where Elisabeth was. I think they succeeded. I think the fire was intended to cover up Elisabeth's murder.'

'But why did they kill Elisabeth Faremo?'

'They wanted the key to the safety-deposit box, but she'd left it in my flat.'

'So they bumped off Jonny Faremo, gave Reidun Vestli a pasting and saw off Elisabeth Faremo to get their paws on the briefcase with the money?'

'Yes.'

'The two of them? Rognstad and Ballo?'

'Yes.'

'There are two things that bother me, Frølich,' drawled Gunnarstranda. He opened the car door and put one foot on the ground. Then he got out, buttoned up his coat and lit a cigarette before leaning into the car to say: 'First of all, if these two are such bosom buddies, as you claim, why did only one of them steal the key from you and why did only one of them turn up to take the bloody money?'

Frølich shook his head. 'We've talked before about an unidentified fourth man, haven't we?'

'Unidentified or not, Frølich, you've got to wake up. If you're well enough to sleuth in Askim, you're well enough to sit at your work desk.' He stood smoking and gazing thoughtfully at the sky.

Frølich was the first to break the silence. He said: 'What shall we do with the letter?'

'We?' Gunnarstranda shook his head in desperation. 'I'm going to do what you should have done a long time ago. I'm going to give Kripos a copy of this suicide letter so we can see whether it is enough to revise assumptions about how the fire started. If they do that, someone may ask Jim Rognstad where he was when the chalet burned down. But I won't be enormously surprised if he coughs up an alibi.'

'What was the second thing?' Frølich wondered.

'Second?'

'You said there were two things bothering you.'

'Yes. It was your version of events. If Rognstad and Ballo beat up Reidun Vestli to find out where Elisabeth was hiding, why did they do it *after* the chalet burned down?'

Neither of them said anything for a long while.

Frølich broke the silence. 'You're sure?' he asked.

'At least she was found after the chalet burned down.'

'So you aren't sure?'

'I'm just myself, Frølich. Theoretically speaking, maybe it was possible for Rognstad to beat up Vestli, drive to Valdres, kill Elisabeth Faremo and set the chalet on fire before Vestli was found, but to have managed all that he must have been out of *bloody* breath. And then there is the phrasing: *terrible people*. The anonymity of it reminds me of Hamlet: he could smell when there was something rotten in the state of Denmark.'

28

Inspector Gunnarstranda sat inert on his swivel chair, staring at the office wall lost in thought. He was still tormented by the death of his fish. It had lain at the bottom of the fish bowl, on the stones and the sand, dead. This sight had destroyed his perception of how fish died. He had always imagined that fish lay on the surface of the water when they died, that they didn't sink to the bottom. But Kalfatrus had been dead, that much was obvious. No movements of the mouth and no reaction when he took it out with the fish slice. It was also somewhat macabre: his goldfish lying on a fish slice, almost like a piece of fish cooked to perfection and ready to serve. But what tormented him now was the way it had been despatched. He had thrown the fish in the bin, something which – given his period of reflection, doubts and remorse – he considered an unworthy mode of valediction for a companion of many years' standing. This thought tormented him. However, on the other hand, burying the fish would have been ludicrous. The alternative would have been to throw it down the toilet. Caught between these two courses of action he had felt the solution was obvious and he had thrown the fish in the dustbin on the way to work. The dubious ethical dimensions of his action played on his mind nevertheless; he couldn't concentrate at work, he went off into reveries, and so when the telephone rang it was like being woken up by a furious alarm clock. He jumped and snatched at the receiver: 'Please be brief'.

Nothing at the other end.

'Hello,' Gunnarstranda yelled impatiently.

'This is Inge Narvesen speaking.'

'Yes?'

'I would like to express my gratitude to you for . . .'

Gunnarstranda interrupted him. 'Ring *Verdens Gang* and tell them. I'm just doing my job.'

'On the other hand . . .'

'There is no other hand. Goodbye.'

'Just wait a moment, will you!'

'Narvesen, I'm very busy.'

'I'm a busy man, too, for Christ's sake. Do you suppose I'm ringing to pass the time?'

'Well, come on, get to the point.'

'I'm grateful to have the money back – even though I lost six years' worth of interest, five hundred thousand kroner.' This was said with a chuckle.

'I thought we'd finished talking about the money,' Gunnarstranda snapped.

'I just wanted to make sure that the matter was closed.'

Open sesame. For the first time Gunnarstranda started to get interested in the conversation. His fingers scrabbled around for cigarettes. He knew he wouldn't smoke the cigarette he found, but this was special. His nervous fingers fidgeted with the cigarette while he pondered and waited for the man's next words: the bastard had got half a million back and was wasting valuable time stamping down the earth over a hole which had already been filled. What Inge Narvesen had just done was to switch on a blue lamp in Gunnarstranda's head, a lamp that flashed a clear message: *Find a spade and start digging!*

Narvesen must have sensed this instantly, though. His voice said: 'Well, I'm wasting your time. I have my money back and the culprits have been arrested.'

'So why are you ringing?'

'As I said, to . . .'

'I heard you. To make sure the matter was closed. Why?'

Narvesen's silence lasted exactly two seconds too long. He said: 'You misunderstand. As I pointed out at the beginning, I wanted to express my sincere gratitude . . .'

'I heard that too. So it doesn't matter to you that the case has *not* been closed?'

Two seconds too long once again. 'Isn't it?'

'The case has never been reopened. The money turned up as a result of an investigation into a completely new matter. A murder enquiry. And the investigation is in full swing.'

'Right.'

Gunnarstranda was quiet.

Inge Narvesen was quiet.

Gunnarstranda was beginning to enjoy himself. 'Nice to talk to you,' he said softly and put down the receiver.

He sat, deep in thought.

The door opened and Lena Stigersand came in.

'I'd like you to do me a favour,' Gunnarstranda said. 'Check all the airline passenger lists for Merethe Sandmo. According to a colleague she was supposed to have caught a plane to Athens a few days ago. Go back two weeks. Don't limit the search to Athens.'

Lena Stigersand gave a deep sigh. 'And what about you?' she asked.

'I'm going to have a chat with Chicken Brains Sørlie and tell him that Inge Narvesen is feverishly trying to protect his house of cards against winds and wearisome ground tremors,' Gunnarstranda said with a grin.

There was a soft tap at the door. Yttergjerde poked his head round. 'Am I disturbing you?'

'No more than you usually do,' Gunnarstranda said cheerfully.

'Do you know a solicitor by the name of Birgitte Bergum?'

'Had I known her, I would have felt obliged to call her Bibbi, and I would never call anyone Bibbi, least of all a fifty-year-old blonde who does interviews for weeklies and talks about her liposuction experiences.'

Lena Stigersand's head shot up: 'I didn't know you read weekly magazines, Gunnarstranda.'

'Just as it is impossible to find perfection on earth, it is impossible to comprehend what Norwegian culture correspondents find fit to communicate to the silent majority.'

'Do I detect prejudice against journalists or liposucted blondes?'

'Just general stupidity. What do you think of a person who imperiously proclaims that life is too short not to surround yourself with beautiful objects?'

Yttergjerde and Lena Stigersand exchanged glances: 'What passion!'

'Let's get down to business!'

'Birgitte Bergum is defending Rognstad,' Yttergjerde said.

'You talk to her. I don't feel up to it.'

'I have done. She says Rognstad wants to plea bargain. Rognstad wants to get something off his chest. This Bibbi babe is simply acting as a mediator.'

Gunnastranda started putting on his coat.

Lena Stigersand plucked up courage and asked him straight out: 'What's wrong with surrounding yourself with beautiful objects?'

'Does it really interest you what other people care about?'

'Yes.'

'What Birgitte Bergum cares about?'

'No.'

'Who interests you, for example?'

'You, for example,' Lena Stigersand said.

'Me?'

'Yes.'

Gunnarstranda gave her a long searching look. 'Personally,' he said stiffly, 'I spend all my time keeping myself healthy and well by avoiding keep-fit classes, moderation, courses on how to give up smoking, new diets and a good night's sleep.

Yttergjerde said: 'I've thought of something.'

The other two turned to him.

'If Rognstad knows something . . . no, forget it.'

'What were you thinking?' Gunnarstranda insisted.

'Forget it. It might not be anything. I mean Rognstad is in custody and now he wants to get off the hook. He could just say anything.'

'But you *were* thinking of something.'

'I was thinking the only thing that has happened since he knocked Frank down is that he's been arrested – that he's on his own. I mean, Ballo didn't turn up at the bank. Perhaps Ballo . . .'

'Yes?'

Yttergjerde shrugged. 'Not sure. We don't know what Rognstad's pitch is going to be anyway, do we?'

Gunnarstranda mused. 'There's something in that,' he said. 'Ballo has gone. Merethe Sandmo has gone.' He looked at Lena Stigersand. 'Check for Ballo's name on the airline flight lists too.' Then Gunnarstranda walked back to his desk with slow, deliberate steps. He sat down, reached for the phone and tapped in a number.

The other two stared at each other. Lena Stigersand hunched her shoulders forward as Gunnarstranda asked to speak to the bank manager.

They exchanged further glances when they heard the question he asked: 'Could you find out from your employees whether there has been a documented visit to this safety-deposit box over the last three months? Yes, please, ring me back.'

29

Frank Frølich was in his car reading the report on the 1998 Narvesen burglary. *The great mystery,* he thought, putting down the papers and starting the engine to keep warm. A break-in. Five hundred thousand kroner in a small safe. The thieves hadn't managed to open the safe in the house, so they took it with them. They stole the safe from a house in Ulvøya. What had struck him at the time was how *clean* the whole job had been: nothing else stolen, no silver, no jewellery, not a scratch on the Bang & Olufsen hi-fi, no fancy ornaments touched, no vandalism, no tagging, no crapping in jam jars or thieves' other original calling cards. Only the safe was spirited away, containing half a million NOK. Serious enough or unusual enough for the investigating team – himself included – to form alternative hypotheses, such as Narvesen making up the whole thing for a potential insurance payout. But since there were no specific items in the safe, the contents were not insured. There was only cash in it, and Ilijaz Zupac had been identified coming out of the house that night – as one of a group of many. And where had Narvesen been that night? Far away. He had been on holiday – according to the report – on the Mauritius islands.

He called to mind his thoughts in 1998. First of all, the break-in had to be genuine. As luck would have it, a vigilant neighbour had been alerted by the unusual activity in Narvesen's garden and his house, which she knew to be empty. She had called the police, who arrived too late. Later, from the files of photos, she pointed out Zupac as one of the men she saw getting in the car which drove away. Frank Frølich had thought at the time that the burglary must have been an inside job. *Someone* must have known about the money, *someone* must have known where the safe was *and* the same person must have known Narvesen was away, thus the coast was clear. However, the arrested man, Zupac, hadn't uttered a word, neither about the robbery nor about his accomplices.

Frank Frølich took a decision: he put the car into gear and drove off. It was a dark December afternoon. Cloud cover over the Ekeberg Ridge resembled a heap of discarded oily rags. He took Mosseveien to Ulvøya, not knowing whether Narvesen would be at home or what he could say to the man.

Driving across Ulvøya bridge, he passed an elderly man in a beret and a woollen coat fishing from the bridge. That, Frølich reckoned, could be one approach – cast a line into the water and just stand in the cold with your mind in observer mode.

Frølich swung into Måkeveien, braked and parked behind a Porsche Carrera. He surveyed the sleek car, thinking: *If this car belongs to Narvesen, he's a bigger buffoon than I took him for.* The house behind the fence was large and detached, post-war, with a huge injection of cash at a later point. He opened the wrought-iron gate, walked up to Narvesen's front door and rang the bell. Loud barking from inside. A woman's voice shouted something. Next there was the sound of claws on the parquet flooring. The door opened. A woman in her thirties with long, raven-black hair, an oriental appearance and a smile worthy of a film extra in Hollywood. She had a distinctive three-centimetre-long scar running from her chin to her cheek. It did not mar her face in any way; it was the kind of mark which invited you to look twice, which lent her appearance a touch of mystery, even of mysticism. The dog she was restraining was a delicate-looking, lean English setter. It wagged its tail and wanted all the attention.

'Yes?' the woman said, and to the dog: 'Come on, now. You've said hello, you can relax now. Come on, in you go!' She grabbed the dog's collar and lifted it more than pushed it behind the wide door, which she closed afterwards. 'Yes?' she repeated in a friendly voice. 'How can I help?'

Frank Frølich thought she matched the Porsche. He said, and it was the truth: 'I'm a policeman. I once investigated a burglary here, about six years ago.'

'Inge isn't at home right now.'

'That's a shame.'

The dog was growling behind the door. Its paws were scratching.

She smiled again. The little scar at the corner of her mouth retreated inside a dimple. 'He's only being playful. What did you do to yourself?'

Frølich fingered the contusions on his face and said: 'Accident at work. When will he be back?'

'At about eight.'

They stood looking at each other. She made a gesture to conclude the conversation and go into the house.

'Are you his partner or . . .?'

'Partner,' she nodded. She stretched out a slim hand: 'Emilie.'

'Frank Frølich.'

He didn't mention the reason for his visit. She was only wearing light clothes, her legs bare, sandals. She must have been freezing standing there like that.

As if she had read his thoughts, she gave a little shiver. 'Shame he wasn't in since you've made the effort.' She lowered her gaze. 'Is there a message, a telephone number –?'

'No, no,' Frank Frølich and went straight to the point. 'The money that was taken at that time has reappeared, but he knows all about that. I just had a few questions. Do you know anything about the matter?'

She shook her head. 'Inge and I go back only two years. You should really talk to him.'

'He was in Mauritius when it happened,' Frølich said. 'On holiday. You don't know if he was travelling alone or if he was with someone, do you?'

Her facial expression was more strained than friendly now: 'I know nothing about such things. Sorry.'

'Well, I can come back later,' Frølich said and left. By the garden gate, he looked back. She hadn't moved from the spot; she had been staring at him the whole time. The dog behind the door was forgotten. She must have forgotten she was freezing cold too, he thought.

30

Gunnarstranda arrived late for their dinner date, as always. They had agreed to meet at Restaurant Sushi in Torggata. Tove loved sushi; didn't want anything else except sushi – sometimes. The restaurant was tucked away on the first floor of the most ethnic street in Oslo. That was why she preferred to eat here. The food was exactly as it was in Japan. However, unlike in the sushi restaurants in Aker Brygge or Frogner, the guests here were real people – in fact, it was very difficult to spot brokers with a Dow Jones complex or hip-looking youths dreaming of a role as an extra in a commercial.

He looked at his watch. This was a little competition between them. Ten minutes late. He went up the wooden stairs, through the door on the first floor and looked around. She wasn't there. He gestured to the head waiter, a Japanese-looking man in black. 'A window table reserved for seven o'clock,' he said, hanging up his coat. This was her game. He had no idea whether she had reserved the table, or under whose name. He knew only one thing: when they ate ethnic food, she would never reserve a table under his name.

The head waiter consulted the book. 'Rarsen? Table for four?'

Gunnarstranda shook his head.

'Table for two? Kar Rinaeus?'

Gunnarstranda nodded. 'Carl Linnaeus. Has the lady arrived?'

'Not yet.' The man picked up two menus and led the way into the room.

He had hardly sat down and ordered when Tove came through the door. A second later she was by his table, bringing with her a waft of cold winter air.

'Sorry, but I couldn't find anywhere to park.'

'So you won this time, too.'

She grinned and took a seat.

'I've ordered,' he said.

They gazed at each other. She observed him with laughter in her eyes – when she was like this she could always force a self-deprecating slant on life out of him.

'The reference to a botanist . . . does that mean you're going to be Helen Keller next time?' he asked.

'Do I look like Helen Keller?'

'Do I look like Carl Linnaeus?'

'You sound like him sometimes. Apart from that, I thought you would be flattered.'

The waiter came with the trays of sushi.

'There would be a closer resemblance if you did something about your hair. You could buy a periwig instead of combing your hair like that,' she said. 'Periwigs with a pigtail are sexy.'

'I might look more like Linnaeus,' he said. 'But I wouldn't be any sexier.'

She grinned again.

'Well, you can say who you're going to be next time.'

'No, you choose.' She smiled playfully, because she knew he didn't like games like this.

'Meryl Streep,' he said.

'Thank you, but I don't think the head waiter will believe you,' she said. 'Anyway, why aren't you eating? Aren't you hungry?'

He looked at the red salmon covering the cylinder of rice he was holding in his hand. The similarity was intimidating. 'Kalfatrus died yesterday,' he said, peering up. *Big mistake*, he reflected.

Tove was out of control. She was laughing so much she was gasping for air.

31

Frank Frølich found Inge Narvesen's private telephone number on the Internet. When it was eight o'clock, he waited for another half an hour and then rang.

'Emilie speaking.'

'It's me again. Frølich, the policeman.'

A hand was placed over the receiver. Mumbling voices in the background. Emilie came back. 'Inge is a little busy. Can he phone you back?'

'It'll take two seconds.'

Hand over the receiver again. More mumbling. Then an irate man's voice:

'What do you want?'

'There were just a couple of things I wanted to ask about the burglary six years ago.'

'Why is that?'

'Just a couple of things to clear up.'

'You're on leave. Whatever you may find unclear is of absolutely no interest to me.'

'It's simply a matter of clarifying things which may cast light on . . .'

'It is not. It is a matter of you sneaking around my neighbourhood and harassing a person I care for.'

'Harassing?'

'Asking Emilie questions about things she cannot possibly know. On top of that, you make insinuations.'

'What I'm trying to do is view the burglary in the light of the reappearance of the money.'

'Wrong,' Narvesen said curtly. 'And now I think it's time to bring this conversation to a close.'

'If you would let me finish. The stolen money turned up in the possession of someone who was not investigated at the time of the burglary. It means the burglary can be cleared up now . . .'

'You're working in a private capacity without the power to prosecute and this case *has been closed*.'

'Where do you get that from?'

'Your boss. And, Frølich, let's not mince words. The sole purpose of this conversation is that you take note of the following: STAY AWAY FROM MY HOUSE.'

'The break-in was too clean a job,' Frølich persisted. 'Nothing was stolen, nothing in your house was touched.'

The line went quiet.

'Someone knew about the money, knew where it was and knew the house was empty. That means someone gave Ilijaz and his gang the information and they struck while you were away.'

'Where do you live, Officer Frølich?'

'Where do *I* live?'

He said nothing. Narvesen had put the phone down.

Frank Frølich stood gaping at the wall. These were not the best terms to part on. But there was no point ringing again.

As he was going to bed that night he sat down and looked at the pillow beside his own. Elisabeth's long, black hair contrasted with the whiteness of the pillow. *A book of poetry*, he thought, *a bookmark, a hair*. He opened the book at the same place: *I forget no one*. He took the hair, lifted it up and laid it carefully on the page like a fine bookmark. He thought: *long bones in a burned-out chalet*. He tried to picture her face. But the image had faded. *I'm a sentimental idiot*, he thought, and went to the bathroom.

While he was cleaning his teeth, the doorbell rang.

He met his own eyes in the mirror, turned off the tap and put down the toothbrush. Checked his watch: it was past midnight.

The bell rang again.

He walked into the hall and squinted through the peephole. No one there. He opened the door. No one there. He went to the door leading to the stairwell. He opened this door too. No one there, either.

He listened but heard nothing.

He went back to his flat. *Probably some young brats ringing the bell and then running off. Except for one thing. It's past midnight.* He stared at the button which opened the front door downstairs, but hesitated. Instead he took the intercom phone and said: 'Hello?'

Nothing. Just crackling noises.

He hung up the internal phone, went into the living room and looked out. If anyone was down at the bottom, it would be impossible to see them from up here. Outside, everything seemed normal: parked cars, sporadic traffic on Ring 3 further away. But in the line of parked cars he could see a pair of red lights glowing. An engine was idling.

It didn't necessarily mean anything, but he went into the bedroom anyway and took the binoculars from the cupboard. The car was a Jeep Cherokee, but the registration plate wasn't visible. And the windows were matt, impenetrable surfaces.

He put it out of his mind, finished cleaning his teeth and went to lie down. He lay looking at the ceiling until he could feel tiredness gradually catching up with him. He turned off the light and lay on his side.

Then the telephone rang.

He opened his eyes, contemplated the dark and listened to the phone ringing endlessly. In the end, he reached out his arm and lifted the receiver. 'Hello.'

Silence.

'Hello,' he said once more.

There was a crackle until whoever it was at the other end cut the connection.

32

He slept badly and was tired when the alarm clock went off. Woke up with one idea on his mind: to get the burning chalet out of his system. To go and see it with his own eyes. He set out early, before seven in the morning, and was in Steinshøgda before eight. On the stretch to Hønefoss, he kept to the speed limit. He didn't begin to put his foot down until he was driving alongside the river Leira in the Begna valley. Chris Rea was singing 'The Road to Hell'. The irony of it, he thought, and turned up the volume. Norway's valleys lay in winter shadow. The sun shone on the mountain peaks. In the Begna valley fir trees towered up like flagpoles on either side of the road. He tried to imagine Elisabeth's face, body, but could only think about *long bones*. Someone had set fire to the chalet and to her. Someone had been out there in the night and seen the timber being consumed by the fire, someone had raised an arm in defence against the wall of heat, had heard the window panes exploding in a crescendo of howling flames and the crackle of countless bursting fibres in the timber as the fire enveloped it. Someone had stood there breathing through an open mouth in order not to smell the stench of scorched flesh in the yellow-black smoke from burning roofing felt, books, woollen fabrics and paraffin lamps exploding with showers of sparks into further flames which devoured down duvets, the kitchen interior, a timber store in a shed; flames melting the seat of a biological toilet before it caught fire with all the other chalet furnishings and one single overturned candle. Skin which is scorched black; flesh which melts and catches fire; hair which goes up with one tiny inaudible puff.

He was sweating. His knuckles on the wheel went white and he had to stop, had to get out. He pulled into a bus lay-by, got out and gasped for air, breathless, as if he had been on a long march with a heavy load on his back. *What is happening, what the hell is happening to me?*

He had to go there, to the charred ruins. He wanted to see the remains with his own eyes. He lay across the roof of his car, looking like a prisoner in an American movie. He wanted to retch, but his stomach was empty. A car on the road passed by, two eyes ogled the man by the car in amazement, which made him straighten up and take a deep breath.

When, eventually, he was able to breathe normally, he got back into his car and drove off. This time he drowned his melancholy in Latin rock: *Mana – unplugged.* A suitable number of guitar riffs, enough emotions and, since he didn't speak Spanish, it was absolutely impossible to understand what they were singing about. He drove into Fagernes market square before the clock struck twelve. Hungry, but restless, he bought a piece of fruit from a large kiosk and hurried on. The December darkness was drawing in. It would be light until half past three at the latest. He drove north – accompanied this time by Johnny Cash's 'The Man Comes Around' and his crunching guitar riffs. It was like eating vitamins: every line of verse made him feel stronger. He turned off towards Vestre Slidre and took Panoramaveien up to Vaset. The snow on the highest peaks began to take on its wintry blue colour. The birch trees were bare and stubbly on both sides of the road. He arrived in Vaset. There was still quite a way up to the tree line on the mountains. He kept driving until he found the collection of chalets, then let the car roll slowly in between the small houses towards the ruin.

A chimney, about five metres in height, towered like an obelisk staked into the middle of the black heap of cinders.

So this is where you hid. Where you were discovered. Where you shouted for help.

The ruins were cordoned off with red and white police tape. There was a smell of soot and dead smoke. He looked around.

No view. The chalet lay in a kind of hollow. It was only twenty or thirty metres from the other chalets. An impenetrable birch thicket prevented others looking in, like a singed pin cushion bristling skywards. He kicked the ashes. His foot hit a soot-soiled pot of paint. It rolled around and came to rest. Around the pot were blackened coil springs. *Here, right here, there must have been a bed.*

He could feel nausea rising and falling.

Standing, looking at the black pile of soot, he was suddenly aware how tired he was of all this. Of Violence. Fire. Death.

He turned, went back to his car and started the engine. He had his own chalet. That was where he would go.

It was a calmer person who drove the few miles back to Fagernes. Who stopped to fill up with petrol. While he was standing with the petrol nozzle in his hand, he heard someone shout his name. Frølich turned round, but initially didn't recognize the man. Then it dawned on him who it was: fiery red face, red hair and air of authority, it was 'Cranberry' or Per-Ole Ramstad, as he had been christened.

'Per-Ole!' Frølich shouted in response. The man was on his way through the petrol station door and waved for him to follow. Frølich gestured that he had to finish filling the tank first.

They had been at Police College together, he and Per-Ole, alias Cranberry on account of his red hair and cheeks. Per-Ole was working at the Nord-Aurdal police station. A solid soul in a solid body. He was the police force's answer to Postman Pat – a man who knew everyone in his line of work and was kind to all. Frølich drained the last drops of the nozzle, screwed on the petrol cap, steeled himself for tricky questions and went to pay.

'Hear you've been under the cosh,' Per-Ole said after the opening chit-chat.

'Which means?' Frank Frølich said, putting the change in his pocket.

'Heard you were an item with the lady who died in the chalet fire in Vaset.'

'And what else?'

Per-Ole grinned. 'Heard about your time off, the murder of a security guard, an inappropriate acquittal and all the bollocks. But, apart from that, are you OK?'

Per-Ole's expression was tinged with concern and genuine sympathy. Frank Frølich blew out his cheeks. 'Do I look it?'

'You look like you need a holiday from the holiday, Frankie.'

'Right first time. And I've been trying to relax for almost two weeks now.'

'And now? Have you just been up there?' Per-Ole motioned with his head. 'At the ruin?'

Frølich nodded.

They exchanged glances.

'Do you want to know a secret?' Per-Ole asked. 'Just received a statement which certainly ought to interest your boss. Heard of someone by the name of Merethe Sandmo?'

Frølich nodded again.

'Thought so. You see, we had an enquiry from Oslo. This Sandmo woman was seen at Fagernes the same day the chalet burned down.'

'Sure?'

'Sure,' Per-Ole said slowly. 'She was in a restaurant. I can't say any more than that, actually.'

'Was she on her own?'

Per-Ole shook his head. 'The woman had dinner at the hotel with a man.'

'Was she staying at the hotel?'

'No.'

'The identity of the man?'

'Not known. Your boss, though – don't remember what his name is, but the fiery-tempered one with the wrap-over hair – he's faxed over a pile of photos.'

They looked at each other again.

'You could stay here for a couple of days, couldn't you?' Per-Ole suggested. 'We could go into the mountains, go fishing in Vællers? Catch a few fat arctic char, smoke them and eat them with a dram or two. No better battery-charger in this world.'

'That's tempting, Per-Ole, but . . .'

'But?'

'I've got my own chalet to keep an eye on. On my way there now. To Hemsedal.'

Frølich could read in Per-Ole's eyes that he had seen through him. But Per-Ole was a fine fellow. He didn't say anything. 'Another time,' Frølich said. He wasn't in the mood to be sociable now. 'It was tough – I mean, seeing the ruins.'

It was dark as he drove up the mountain road towards the family chalet. The headlights caught the screens of spruce on either side, making the universe seem as if it was a narrow path enveloped by spruce walls. This was terrain with isolated houses and farms, game and bird-life. He knew that because he had been here innumerable times. *Perhaps that's my problem. I see this case the way a driver sees reality, as objects the headlamps pick out and illuminate. Perhaps I ought to shift my perspective, find a different angle?*

It was, as usual, colder inside the chalet than outside. He opened all the windows and doors to create a through-draught and change the cold air while he strolled down to the well for water. A well was probably an overstatement. It was a trickle which had been developed into a spring. He and his father had dug up turf and soil to make a hole big enough for surface water to collect after being filtered through a mound of cleansing sand. Then they had sunk a cement ring which they had bought from a farmer in the village. So they had a well one and a half metres deep, a well which never went dry. And, in addition, stayed frost-free longer than the ground surrounding it. He had cut a slate slab lid to fit on top of the cement ring, mounted hinges and a little handle. All you had to do was pull the slab to the side and drop the pail into the dark water. Crystal-clear water, full of minerals and taste.

As always, he quenched his thirst before walking back slowly with the pail.

Then he closed the doors and windows and lit the old wood burner. It would take time to heat the large space under the high ceiling. So he went out onto the veranda and unlocked the sauna. The wood stove in there would be boiling hot in less than an hour. He fetched some finely chopped birch, tore off the bark and used it to light the fire. As the flames caught hold, he put on the birch and watched it catch before closing the stove door with the draught on full. Now he just had to wait. From the veranda he looked at the water, which hadn't frozen over yet. He went to the shed and took his fishing rod, a couple of spinners and a sheath knife. Then he ambled down to the pond to pass the time. The moon was shining like a white Chinese lantern in the sky. All the birch trees had lost their leaves. The moon reflected on the black surface of the water and the rising frost smoke. The water was probably too cold to catch any fish. Even the leaves of the pond lilies had begun to prepare for winter. He cast the line a few times, the reel squealed and the spinner broke the surface of the water like the leap of a trout. But not a bite. It didn't matter. He continued to cast a line. The water was cold and the fish were deep. He let the spinner sink until the line was slack and looped, then wound it in slowly. This was his favourite spinner, the one with the red tassel and red spots. He reeled in, lifted the rod, threw, let the spinner sink, reeled in – and got a nibble. The powerful jerk on the rod was unmistakable. Trout. It swam off with the bait and he let it run. The line zigzagged across the water until he locked the reel and wound it in. It held. Perhaps half a kilo. Perfect size. Perfect for frying in the pan.

The fish took a decision and swam to the shore. Frølich let it swim, reeled in until there was another jerk. Thirty seconds later he hauled it onto land; it wriggled around like crazy, squirmed and leapt into a juniper bush. He placed both hands over it. Held it tight. The fish had eaten all the bait. He quickly broke its neck and weighed the fine specimen in his hand. Looking up at the moon, he realized that he had been far away – for as long as it lasted – not thinking about anything else apart from the pleasure of being here in the dark by the lake.

He headed for the chalet reckoning that the sauna was probably hot enough. But the thermometer on the sauna room wall showed only 60 ° C. He put on more dry birch and some spruce. Dry spruce burned like matchsticks, quickly and fiercely, with flames which would soon boost the heat. Afterwards he went to the well to collect water to pour on the stones in the sauna stove. When he next looked at the sky, it had clouded over. He stood on the veranda, sipping at half a bottle of Upper Ten whisky. The temperature in the sauna had reached 80 ° and the first raindrops fell.

He undressed and lay naked on the bench. The sweat poured off him. He thought about Elisabeth. Her hands which had flitted across his body like nervous squirrels. He threw water on the stones. They hissed and the steam adhered to his skin, boiling hot, smarting. But he forced himself to lie still. He watched the flames through the glass pane in the stove and thought of the flames burning the long, glowing bones. Soon he wouldn't be able to stand any more heat. He sat up. The temperature was approaching 90 ° when he burst through the door and sat naked on the stump of a spruce tree in the rain. This was half the pleasure of the sauna, being rinsed down by the rain, which was a degree or two off falling as snow, but still feeling as hot as before. Rain and sweat mingle as one. The rain kept him drenched, but when he licked his arm it tasted of sweat. The raindrops ran down his body, found their way down his stomach, thighs, let go and found a resting place on the cranberry leaves. But then the wind picked up and caressed his body, a new form of well-being, reducing the temperature a tiny bit, enough for him to stand up and pick his way down to the water: the ice-cold pond, where he glided in and swam between the water-lily leaves, an undulating white monster. Cooled and shivering, he ran back on sensitive feet to the sauna and the sweltering heat. He lay down on the bench and planned the meal for afterwards: trout grilled with salt and pepper, some mushrooms he had brought with him and a little cream, then a lager or white wine from the store in the room under the floor. Lying on the bench, he thought about Elisabeth again. He should have brought her here, shown her this, because this was him, this was the existence he occasionally yearned for; where he came to find his fulfilment.

Once again he was drenched with sweat. His body had almost reached the limit of its tolerance when he heard a sound on the veranda. He raised his head and listened. Something must have fallen, but there was nothing to fall. Yes, there was. The fishing rod. A small bottle of Upper Ten. He got up and went to push open the door. It wouldn't budge. He applied pressure. The door seemed to be locked. Then he heard another noise. The sound of footsteps. He sat down on the bench. Naked, close to exploding with the heat, sodden with sweat. Inside: 98°. Outside: fresh air, cold, car keys, clothes, money. Someone had locked the door. *What is going on?* He stood up and shoulder-charged the door. It didn't stir. The door was wedged shut. *Someone has locked me in. But how?* He shoved again. But the door held firm. He looked up at the little window in the wall, fifteen by thirty centimetres. Impossible. *I can't take any more!* He put the whole of his body behind the door. It didn't move. Then he smelt it: *Smoke.*

He looked through the little window. There was no doubt. Flames were licking up at the walls. *They're trying to burn me to death in here.* He blinked the sweat out of his eyes. The yellow door quivered in his vision. He kicked it. Nothing happened. Yellow-grey smoke was filtering through the cracks in the floor. The floorboards were warmer now than they had been two minutes before. They were singeing the soles of his feet. *Long bones.* He could see the headlines in his mind's eye: *Man found dead in chalet fire.* He took a run-up and launched himself against the door. His shoulders hurt everywhere, but the door frame gave with a crack. *This is me*, he thought. *This is my bloody chalet. No one's going to fucking burn it down!* He threw himself against the door again. The smoke was in his nose and eyes. He couldn't see anything, he over-balanced and fell against the burning hot oven. The scream of pain as the flesh on his shoulder hissed. But the burn woke him up too. Another run-up. And this time the door panel caved in. It cracked with a deeper, hollower sound. He filled his lungs with the air that seeped in, tensed his muscles to the maximum, put all his ninety-five kilos behind the punch and smashed his fist through the door panel. His knuckles and forearm were bleeding. But he had one hand through and groped towards the door handle on the outside.

It was the snow-clearer. The shaft had been wedged under the door handle and the blade had been forced down into an opening between two tables on the veranda. The door was effectively locked.

But whoever did this didn't know how flimsy the door was, didn't know what a skinflint his sister was, didn't know that she had bought the door in a sale, a door with a plywood panel and not boards. Once his hand was through, the rest was easy. He felt around for the shaft, took hold, pulled it away and kicked the door open. He spilled out onto the veranda gasping for air. Ran off, rubbing smoke out of his eyes. He expected to be attacked. But no attack came. He looked around. The fire under the sauna had been made with old roofing felt and semi-rotten pieces of wood from the pile by the shed, all raked together. Frølich hurried over to his clothes and used them to smother the fire. He had to douse a fire single-handed, naked, on a December day in the mountains. But he put out the fire and was helped by the rain. *How could that rotten wood burn so fiercely?* he wondered and then smelt paraffin. It took time for the cold to eat into the soles of his feet as he concentrated his energy on extinguishing the fire. The jacket, his large jacket suffocated the flames. He could feel time passing. His feet were numb. But when – bleeding, black from soot and naked – he finally gulped in air and was confident that the damned fire had done no more than scorch the outside wall of the sauna, blacken the window pane and destroy the floorboards, he was happy. He was trembling with cold and put on his wet clothes, aware that he had been the easiest target in the world for any ill-wishers for God knows how long.

He focused vigilant eyes on the area around him. However, all he could see was the outline of black trees in the dark. The job had been executed in such a terrible, amateurish way: deciding to burn someone alive, blocking the door to the sauna, making a fire from wood and paraffin, lighting it and running off before the job was complete. Instinctively he knew: the perpetrator had not run off. *Someone was standing somewhere staring at me, right now.*

Frozen and shivering in the dark he rotated on his own axis and yelled: 'Come out! Show yourself, you fucking bastard!'

Silence. Black spruce trees, the patter of rain.

'You spineless piece of shit, come out!'

Nothing.

Frank Frølich shook with cold. He forced his wet, swollen feet into the mountain boots which seemed much too tight. His fingers trembled and he listened. Then he heard the sound: a car engine. Then headlights shone through the screen of spruce trees.

He sprinted towards his own car, tripped over a root, fell headlong and scrambled up again. He tore open the door of the car. Bugger. The keys! *Had he left them in the ignition?* He had no idea, but ran off down the gravelled road. It was a bad road; the other person would be forced to drive slowly. But the hum of the engine faded in the distance, and the car lights behind the trees disappeared. He stumbled on the gravel, panting, a taste of blood in his mouth. Then he sensed the contours of the mobile phone in his trouser pocket. Who should he ring? He thrust his hand in his pocket for the phone. He held it in two trembling hands. The display showed: no coverage. His hands fell helplessly to the ground.

He lay like that for a long time, shaking, aching for warmth and dry clothes – for perhaps an hour, perhaps an hour and a half. He didn't know. In the end he pulled himself together, sat up and searched his jacket pockets for the bottle of whisky. It was with his car keys.

33

The morning sun balanced on the edge of the ridge. It cast sharp meridians of light down the slopes to the bottom of the valley where he was driving home.

It was unreal: a mixture of a hangover, the beginnings of a cold, insufficient sleep and a searing pain. At long last he was sitting in the queue of cars heading for Sandvika, observing men's faces, freshly shaven, upper bodies sewn into finely tailored office clothes, eyes self-assured and secure, cheerfully confronting the morning, mysterious beauties behind tinted windows, sombre clusters of people waiting for buses along the main traffic artery, students and schoolchildren dawdling towards more tedium, long lessons with intolerable obligations and existential meaninglessness. And in the middle of all this was Frank Frølich, not awake, not tired, not ill, not well, none the wiser after his injuries, simply worn out, confused, sick of the whole business and frightened.

When the queue had finally started moving and he was driving up Ryenbergveien, his mobile rang. He drove into a bus lay-by. It was Gunnarstranda. 'Are you coming to work today?'

'That's not on my list of things to do, no.'

'You should come.'

'Got a few formalities to complete first.'

'Then we'll see you tomorrow.'

Frølich glanced down at the piteous state of himself and said: 'I'll give it some thought.'

'You want me to keep my mouth shut about the latest development?'

'I'm tempted to start work again, but Lystad from Kripos has probably got something to say about this, hasn't he?'

'I gave him an ultimatum. If he considers you in any way blameworthy he should have asked Internal Investigations to set up a separate inquiry last night and that didn't happen.'

Frank Frølich sucked in his breath. 'OK, I'll try tomorrow.'

'I want you to think about it,' Gunnarstranda said. 'I got in touch with DnB NOR in Askim. On a hunch. It turns out they have a procedure in place for every time someone with power of attorney wants to go down to the vault. The authorization is checked against the bank's register.'

'And?'

'There are not many visits of this kind. But there are a lot of employees and they have different timetables. The manager talked to one of the shift workers. She says someone with power of attorney opened the safety-deposit box about a week ago.'

'Who?'

'Ilijaz Zupac.'

'That's impossible.'

'Nothing's impossible.'

'Zupac's serving time at Ullersmo and needs medical care. Prison leave is totally out of the question. It cannot have been him.'

'Nevertheless he was there,' Gunnarstranda said, deadpan. 'So you can see you're needed here with those of us who have to solve impossible problems. What I'm curious to know is whether the man left something in the box or took something out. Mull that one over and I'll see you tomorrow.'

He didn't drive home directly. After zipping through the Oslo Tunnel he made for the city centre and then out to Mosseveien. He took the Ulvøya turn-off and drove on to Måkeveien. Outside Narvesen's house he came to a halt. No Porsche parked by the fence today – but in the drive, in front of the garage door, there was a Jeep Cherokee.

Frank Frølich sat and watched. It was a December morning. A woman in a winter coat with a large, brown scarf wrapped around her neck came round the corner pushing a pram. The child was wearing blue winterwear and sucking a dummy. They passed the car. He watched them getting smaller and smaller in the mirror as he thought about the evening two days ago when, through his binoculars, he spotted a car parked outside the entrance to his block of flats.

Narvesen's Jeep was the same colour. Furthermore, it was dirty and streaked after many kilometres on salted roads – just like his own car.

He took his mobile phone and found Narvesen's private number. He called. It rang several times. Finally, a man's voice answered thickly.

'Hello.'

Frank Frølich rang off. He thought: *Our whizz investor isn't at work. Has it been a hard night perhaps?*

He turned the ignition key. Then he caught sight of a shadow in one of the windows on the first floor. He put the car in gear and drove off.

34

They were making love. The flickering candle cast heavy, blurred shadows onto the wall. She was on all fours with her left cheek resting on the pillow. A deluge of black hair. He turned her over onto her back; went on; on and on. Elisabeth's body quivered as she came to orgasm, but he pretended not to notice. He wanted to pound her to pieces, grind her into the ground with his pelvic thrusts, hard, remorseless, lunge upon lunge. When she came for the second time, he could feel the germ of a scream writhing out of a husk somewhere in his abdomen. She immediately sensed it, opened her eyes as if waking to an extreme reality and covered his mouth with hers, searching for the sound, as she held the base of his sex and clung to him. The sound would not stop, the germ of a scream became a vibrating convulsion which started in his toes, consumed its way through his body, took control of the muscles in his legs, thighs, back, stomach – but was controlled by the grip of her hand as she triggered the roar which surged through his windpipe into his mouth where she was waiting with her mouth and lips and hungrily absorbed it. Even though she was underneath, she was the one who was riding. She rode all the wildness out of him, all his fury, until he lay calmly between her legs. Then she came for the third time: a blasé thrust of her groin, performed in lazy triumph, the way a rider finally turns a tamed wild horse to the sun to confirm that the task has been accomplished.

Frank Frølich opened his eyes.

The candle wasn't alight. There were no shadows on the wall. It had been a dream. Nevertheless, he could sense her aroma: her perfume, perspiration, sex. He switched on the light. He was alone. In a few hours he would have to go to work. And the sole indication of Elisabeth's presence was a black hair in a book on the bedside table. He switched off the light and rested his head on the pillow. Staring into the dark with wide-open eyes and wondering: *Why was I so furious?*

There were restrained cheers in the corridor when he opened his office door at eight in the morning. Emil Yttergjerde took a deep bow and Lena Stigersand said, 'You look dreadful – sorry, I didn't mean that.'

Frølich rubbed his face. 'It's been a tough few days.'

'Well,' Lena Stigersand said. 'Today of all days it would be right to break feminism's first commandment. Frankie, welcome back. Can I get you a coffee?'

At that moment Gunnarstranda stuck his head round the door. He coughed and said: 'Frølich, I must have a word with you.'

When they were alone, Gunnarstranda said: 'I've had a meeting with the Chief of Police and various police solicitors. We've agreed to go for the link between Jim Rognstad and the Loenga murder. Thus the murdered man is our only case. Elisabeth Faremo's death is a Kripos matter and so is Jonny Faremo's. And they don't want anything to do with us – for the time being. The Chief will push for a co-ordinated investigation – then we'll see. For the moment we'll concentrate on the murder of Arnfinn Haga. OK?'

Frølich nodded.

'For us, and for you in particular, Reidun Vestli, her chalet and the bones found in the remains are peripheral issues – only of interest if we stumble over some evidence which proves that Rognstad or Ballo beat up Reidun Vestli and/or set fire to the chalet. The Elisabeth Faremo case – if it is a case at all – is still with Kripos.'

'Merethe Sandmo was seen in Fagernes the day the chalet burned down,' Frølich said.

'Kripos are dealing with the Elisabeth and Jonny Faremo cases,' Gunnarstranda repeated slowly and sternly.

Frølich didn't answer.

They stood looking at each other.

Gunnarstranda broke the silence: 'The break-in at Inge Narvesen's has been cleared up. It's not our case and never has been.'

'She had dinner with a man at the hotel.'

'I know,' Gunnarstranda barked with irritation. 'But it's not our case. Do you want me to send you off on leave two minutes after restarting?'

They eyed each other warily.

'You were disqualified from the investigation of the Loenga murder because you were in a relationship with Elisabeth Faremo – for as long as she was alive. Some consider that you should still be disqualified. Several people, me included, feel you're too emotionally involved in the whole business. The conclusion is that you're *not* entitled to take any freelance initiatives on this investigation. From now on you're my errand boy – no more, no less.'

Frølich didn't answer.

'But if we're going to dig any deeper to find links between Rognstad and the Arnfinn Haga murder, we can't walk around with blinkers on,' Gunnarstranda said. 'We have to knuckle down, question witnesses and focus on the suspects we have.'

'Rognstad might have had dinner with Merethe Sandmo.'

Gunnarstranda let out a deep sigh. 'Something tells me it was a mistake asking you to come in this morning.'

Frølich said: 'I was there yesterday, at what's left of the chalet. I wanted to see the place. I met Cranberry Ramstad in Fagernes.'

'I know. He's sent me e-mails and faxes and I don't know what. Now pin back your ears,' Gunnarstranda said and yelled: 'YES, I KNOW MERETHE SANDMO HAD DINNER WITH AN UNIDENTIFIED MAN IN FAGERNES, BUT IT'S NOT OUR BLOODY CASE!'

'I drove from Fagernes to my chalet in Hemsedal. Someone tried to set it on fire while I was inside.'

Gunnarstranda sat down.

Frølich took out his mobile phone and showed him the pictures he had taken. He stood up. 'Here,' he said. 'Are these scorched boards proof enough for you?'

Gunnarstranda breathed in and coughed. 'Tell me more,' he said with a heavy heart.

Ten minutes later Lena Stigersand arrived with the coffee she had promised. She sensed the atmosphere at once and crept in on tiptoe: 'Am I disturbing you?'

Neither said a word.

'Obviously not,' Lena Stigersand said and sneaked out.

Gunnarstranda waited until she had shut the door before saying: 'Continue.'

'After Fagernes I drove to Hemsedal where someone tried to burn me alive.'

'Someone followed you.'

'Of course.'

'All the way from Oslo?'

'Either from Oslo or Fagernes.'

'Could someone have tailed you all that way without your noticing?'

'Anything is possible. I had lots of other things on my mind. I was thinking about the fire, her, I didn't bother about the mirror at all.'

'But why try to murder you?'

'No idea. I can't see the motive.'

'I've been investigating murders for more than thirty years. Motives for murders rarely belong to the *rational* category.'

'Nevertheless there must have been a motive. Either it was revenge or someone was trying to stop me.'

'Stop you doing what?'

'Yes, well, that's the point. Revenge is totally absurd.'

'Could it have been Ballo or Merethe Sandmo?'

'What do they gain by snuffing me out? You're still investigating the Arnfinn Haga murder anyway.'

'You saw your attacker on the motorbike. Maybe someone is trying to silence you for good.'

'But that was Rognstad on the motorbike and he's behind bars as a result of another case. One that's cut and dried. On top of that, if the motorbike had been meant to expedite me into the beyond, they could have done the job there and then. I can't get over the bloody unprofessional nature of it: rotten boards, bits of insulation and damp roofing felt soaked in paraffin . . .'

'Yes, but who else is there?'

'I know someone who is pretty upset by my activities.'

'Who?'

'Inge Narvesen.'

The two of them sat opposite each other without saying a word. Gunnarstranda's face wore a sceptical expression.

'The unprofessional technique would fit in then,' Frølich said.

'It has been on my mind to have a word with Narvesen anyway,' Gunnarstranda said pensively. 'And you might as well come along.'

35

Frølich sat behind the wheel. He waited until Gunnarstranda had settled in before starting the car. 'Something familiar about this situation, it strikes me,' he said, shoving the car into gear.

'Look straight ahead, you,' Gunnarstranda said drily. 'The only positive thing you can say about the past is that it has gone. Hope you can learn that this is also true of women.'

They drove past the bus depot on Ibsenringen and turned towards the Palace Gardens and Frederiksgate as they came out of the tunnel.

'On my way to work today,' Frølich said, 'the Metro had to stop in the tunnel. A man was standing on the rails.'

Gunnarstranda glanced over at him. 'It *is* a long time,' he said. 'You've forgotten that we don't necessarily have to talk.'

Frølich smiled faintly. 'The man on the rails was an Indian, an elderly man, just wearing cotton clothes and early this morning it was *bloody* cold. It must have been several degrees below.'

'So he was freezing?'

'He didn't move a muscle. The man was really old, white beard and white hair. He was just babbling. Couldn't speak a word of Norwegian. There was someone in my carriage who could speak the language and interpreted. Turned out the man was on his way back home – to Calcutta. He was unhappy in Norway, always cold and had no friends.'

'Yes, well, he's not the only one.'

'But this old man had decided to walk home, walk to Calcutta. He wasn't sure which direction to go, but he knew it was possible to get to India by train. And he had thought that if he just followed the rails, in the end he would come to Calcutta. But it turned out the rails he was walking on didn't belong to the railway, they belonged to the Metro. So he could have followed the rails for the rest of his days and never have got any further than Stovner.' Frølich grinned.

'Vestli,' said Gunnarstranda.

'Hm?'

'The terminus on the Grorud line is Vestli, not Stovner.'

Frølich turned into Munkedamsveien. 'It's really good to be back,' he mumbled, swinging in to park behind Vestbane station.

They got out and made their way to Vika Atrium.

Gunnarstranda showed his ID in reception. Shortly afterwards they were received by a dark-haired woman in her early twenties. She was wearing glasses with a thick, black designer frame. The impression you were left with was that the glasses had put her on and not vice versa. She marched in front of them into what must have been Narvesen's section. The contrast was palpable. The smooth glass partitions with the pure steel decor suddenly found their counterbalance in dark paintings and extravagantly decorated gold picture frames. Frank Frølich paused for a few seconds and looked around. It was like being in a museum.

The young woman opened a door. She showed them into a small meeting room and bowed before disappearing.

'I think Narvesen is going to play hard ball,' Frølich said.

'You mean we'll have to wait?'

'Isn't that the classic control mechanism? Think I've used it myself a few times. I think I even learned it from you.'

'We'll have to see how long we're willing to wait,' Gunnarstranda said. 'Those of us who have worked with such techniques know a few effective counterploys.'

On the table there was an empty paper cup with a dried-up tea bag inside. Gunnarstranda grabbed the cup. 'First offensive,' he mumbled. 'The inspector goes looking for coffee.'

With that, Gunnarstranda left the meeting room and walked cheerfully into an office – without knocking. Frølich saw the woman recoil in surprise. He shook his head, went out into the hall and studied the paintings hanging there. It was old art, full of madonnas and cherubs – the motifs reminded him of his childhood scrapbook.

Suddenly Gunnarstranda was by his side, holding a steaming paper cup.

'Can you see what I can see?' Gunnarstranda asked.

'Eh?'

'Inge Narvesen is sitting over there pretending you and I don't exist.'

Frølich followed his line of vision. Correct. Narvesen was behind a glass door apparently unaware of their presence. 'You got yourself some coffee, then?'

'Last night I dreamed about a devil,' Gunnarstranda said as he raised his cup. 'It was a sweet little devil with short curly hair, bashful, sucking its thumb. I remember thinking it couldn't be a good devil. He didn't inspire confidence.'

'I'm not telling you what I dreamed,' said Frølich.

At that moment Narvesen caught sight of them. Initially, he was startled; he then paused for a few seconds before getting up and going over to the glass door.

'Someone back in out of the cold?' Inge Narvesen said frostily. He was staring at Frank Frølich.

'I have some questions to ask you,' Gunnarstranda said and put down the coffee cup.

'I'm busy.'

'It won't take long.'

'I'm still busy.'

'The alternative would be to obtain a court order and summon you to Police HQ for questioning. It would mean we leave here after a fruitless visit and you appear in my office when it suits me and stay for as long as it suits me. The choice is yours.'

Narvesen cast an annoyed, impatient look at the clock. 'What would you like to know?'

'The money you had transferred after we arrested Jim Rognstad, does that correspond to the sum you were missing subsequent to the burglary in 1998?

'Yes. The amount is correct.'

'There were no other items in the safe removed from your bedroom in 1998?'

'Nothing at all.'

'Would you be willing to sign a statement?'

'I already have done so and would happily do so again. The case has been cleared up and I am extremely pleased.'

'Name Jim Rognstad mean anything to you?'

'Never heard of him.'

'The reason Rognstad was targeted is that a few days ago we were given a tip-off linking him with a container break-in at Oslo Docks and the murder of a guard.'

'Really?'

'As a consequence it would be interesting to see whether other suspects can be connected with Rognstad.'

Narvesen nodded impatiently.

'Does the name Vidar Ballo mean anything to you?'

'No.'

'Merethe Sandmo?'

'No.'

'Jonny Faremo?'

'No.'

'Sure?'

'Positive. Was there anything else?'

'One question?'

'Fire away.'

'Physically removing the safe from your house while touching nothing else – that seems remarkably focused. Have you ever wondered about that?'

'No.'

'You were out of the country, on holiday, when the burglary took place. That suggests those responsible probably knew your house was unoccupied. Did it occur to you that a third party may have informed them?'

'No. I leave it to the police to devise such hypotheses.'

'But, if that had been the case, it would necessarily imply that you had a disloyal servant. Doesn't that concern a man like you?'

'It would have done if I had any reason to believe such a hypothesis. But I don't. Since 1998 neither my house nor my office has been broken into. Ergo – as detectives are wont to say – I have no disloyal servants. Would you please excuse me?'

Without waiting, he walked past them and down the corridor.

Frølich grasped his arm.

Narvesen stopped. He stared disapprovingly at Frølich's hand.

'Been to Hemsedal recently?' Frank Frølich asked.

'Will you let go?'

Frølich removed his hand. 'Yes or no?'

Narvesen didn't reply. He walked towards a door further up the corridor.

'Perhaps I should ask Emilie?' Frølich called.

He didn't receive an answer. The door was slammed shut. Narvesen was gone.

They exchanged looks. 'Do you remember the blackmail business I told you about?' Gunnarstranda asked.

'The drunken captain who threatened to go to the press etc if Narvesen didn't stump up?'

Gunnarstranda nodded. 'I tried to find the captain. He got three years and did two of them at Bastøy.'

'What about him?'

'He's dead,' Gunnarstranda said. 'He got involved in a fight the very day he came out. Killed. Knifed by unknown assailant.'

'Narvesen is not clean,' Frølich said.

'No one can allege that Narvesen was responsible for the killing. For the same reason you can't claim he set fire to your chalet.'

'Yes, I can. It was him.'

'How do you know?'

'I just know.'

Gunnarstranda regarded him with scepticism. 'If you're so sure it was Narvesen, then it's up to you to find out *why* – before you go accusing him of things.'

When they were outside in the cold again, Frølich came to a sudden halt.

'What's the matter?'

'That man went too far when he locked me in and lit the match.'

They stood for a while watching the cars hurtling past.

'Calm down,' Gunnarstranda said and started moving. 'We'll get Narvesen, you can take my word for it.'

'But it doesn't look like we will, does it?'

'I trust my instinct. And, in addition, here comes our Eco-Crime man, Chicken Brains Sørlie.'

36

Frank Frølich had met Birgitte Bergum once before. It had been a couple of years ago in courtroom number four and she had been defending a drunken carpenter who was an officer in the reserves. The man had drunk himself stupid in his chalet where he kept his service weapon, an AG3. In the middle of the night he had started shooting it off. Unfortunately, two tourists had pitched their tent in the vicinity. They were scared out of their wits and after climbing up a tree they rang the police from a mobile phone. But the local police station wasn't manned in out-of-office hours. So they had to ring the central police switchboard, who sent out a patrol car from another district. But they got lost and the patrolmen called the tourists back to ask the way. The man with the gun, who was now well out of his skull, heard the tourists' phone ringing and thought the enemy was abroad and about to despatch him. He therefore crawled along the ground wearing camouflage gear and closed in on them – with the invaluable assistance of the policemen who were ringing the tourists at regular intervals. When the police finally did arrive on the scene, the man went absolutely bananas and was only arrested after an exchange of fire, which led to one policeman being injured. Frølich had been summoned as a witness – to speak about the general context of arrests. Birgitte Bergum had been on him like a leech from the word go. He was thinking of this as he sat watching her through a two-way mirror in the interview room: a woman of about fifty with big hair, a big nose and a bust like an opera singer's. With a self-assured, impatient expression on her face, she sat next to Jim Rognstad. He balanced on his seat like a fat Buddha with hair, limp and uncommunicative, wearing a black T-shirt, his hands folded and recently brushed hair flowing down both shoulders.

There were two of them secretly observing Rognstad and the solicitor. Frølich sat next to Fristad, who, as a legal man, was clearly uneasy with the set-up. He kept mumbling: 'Oooh dear, I don't like this. No, I must say, I don't like this situation, Frølich.'

He went quiet when Gunnarstranda came into the room they were observing. Rognstad tried to stand up like a school pupil when the headmaster enters the classroom. Bergum ordered him to stay seated. Then she looked severely at the two-way mirror.

'She's seen us,' Fristad said, nervously adjusting his glasses. 'Bibbi's sharp.'

'Who's sitting in there?' was the first thing she asked, with a nod towards the mirror.

Gunnarstranda didn't answer. But Frølich and Fristad swapped winces. 'Put down the sound,' Fristad muttered. Frølich turned down the volume so low that Bergum's next remark could hardly be heard:

'This is no good, Gunnarstranda. All interrogations should be performed in an atmosphere of total openness.'

Frølich turned up the volume a tiny bit.

'This isn't an interrogation,' Gunnarstranda said tersely. 'You requested this meeting.'

'I want to know who's sitting behind the mirror.'

'Let's call it a day then. Rognstad can go back to his cell and daydream. Either he has something to sell me or he hasn't.'

Birgitte Bergum scrutinized Gunnarstranda sternly.

She turned to Rognstad and said: 'What do you think?'

'Just a moment,' Bergum went on, leaning over to her client. The two of them whispered.

Frølich and Fristad exchanged glances again.

'Bet they pull out,' Fristad breathed. 'Bibbi's as tough as old boots.'

In the interview room Gunnarstranda yawned and looked at the clock. 'What's the decision?'

'There was a painting in the box,' Rognstad said, straight to the point.

'Which box?' Gunnarstranda asked, bored.

'The safety-deposit box.'

'No, there wasn't. There was just money in the box.'

'Right. But there should have been a painting.'

Frølich and Fristad looked at each other. Fristad straightened his glasses; he was getting excited.

'What sort of painting?' Gunnarstranda asked.

'Old. Worth a packet.'

'OK,' Gunnarstranda said wearily. 'Let's start at the beginning. This box we're talking about is pretty small. What kind of painting would fit into the box and how did it get there?'

Rognstad leaned over to his counsel and whispered again. Birgitte Bergum spoke for him.

'Its origin is of no interest. But it is a fact that a missing work of art had been deposited in the box as well as the money.'

'You're forgetting that I determine what is of interest or not. This information is meant to serve as a mitigating circumstance, is it not?'

'My client is not interested in talking about the past history of the painting.'

Frølich grinned at Fristad and whispered: 'The picture's certain to have come from Narvesen's safe. Jim Rognstad took part in the burglary, but he's scared of incriminating himself still further.'

Gunnarstranda stood up and walked over to the two-way mirror. He stood combing his hair while mouthing: 'Shut up in there!'

'What kind of painting are we talking about?' he asked with his back to the lawyer and Rognstad.

Bergum replied, 'A stolen work of art. *Madonna with Child*, painted by Giovanni Bellini. It's a small painting but worth millions. My client says it was in the safety-deposit box and someone must have removed it.'

Gunnarstranda turned. 'Let's take that from the beginning, shall we? You say that someone – thus a person other than your client – made their way into the vault, unlocked the safety-deposit box and took out the painting, but left the money, half a million, behind?'

'Yes.'

'Who?'

'We don't know who.'

'But this person must have used a key. Your client had the key.'

'There are two keys.'

'How did your client obtain his key?'

Fristad and Frølich gave each other a knowing look.

Birgitte Bergum and Rognstad whispered to each other.

Bergum said: 'That has nothing to do with the case.'

'I have reason to believe you acquired the key by illegal means.'

Birgitte Bergum said: 'We have no comment to make with reference to your assertion. However, we consider it appropriate to remind you that my client has full legal access to the box.'

Gunnarstranda addressed Rognstad directly now: 'There are two sets of keys to the safety-deposit box. And there are four people with right of access: you, Jonny Faremo, Ilijaz Zupac and Vidar Ballo. Jonny Faremo is dead. Zupac is in Ullersmo prison. You're sitting there and telling me someone else nicked this painting from the box. So you're saying Vidar Ballo has been there and taken the picture. If he did, why did he leave half a million?'

'That's irrelevant,' Bergum interposed.

'Irrelevant?' Gunnarstranda started to grin. 'Is it irrelevant that a notorious criminal walks legitimately into a bank vault and removes a painting, but leaves half a million untouched?'

'Naturally.'

'Why naturally?'

'The individual in question could well go back and collect the money later, couldn't he? The fact is, Gunnarstranda, that there was a work of art in the box and now it has disappeared.'

'And the man on the moon eats cheese every day,' Gunnarstranda snapped. He turned and walked back to the table.

Bergum sent him a deprecating smile. She had begun to develop a new interest in the mirror and when she spoke she addressed the glass pane: 'We're talking about one of the world's most wanted works of art, Gunnarstranda. Go back to your office and look up the records of "Unsolved Cases" and check for stolen works of art. I'm sure you will find Giovanni Bellini's painting mentioned, the great master of Italian Renaissance painting. The painting was stolen from the church of Santa Maria dell'Orto in Venice in 1993. Imagine what solving a case like that would mean for you and Police HQ. After that, you and I plus the police prosecutor can discuss the definition of mitigating circumstances,' she said, getting up and turning towards the glass. She stood still, adjusting her bra. Then she added in a chill tone: 'Isn't that right, Fristad?'

Two hours later Gunnarstranda and Fristad were alone. The latter scratching his neck in irritation. 'Bellini, who the hell is Bellini? As far as I'm concerned, she might just as well have been talking about mountain walking in north Norway.'

'The Bellinis were a dynasty apparently,' Gunnarstranda said.

'How do you know that?'

Gunnarstranda turned to show him the encyclopaedia he had found on his bookshelf and said: 'It says here there was one father and two sons. Renaissance painters at the end of the fifteenth century. There was also one equally famous brother-in-law, Andrea Mantegna.' He flicked over the page and read on: 'The Bellini brothers: Gentile and Giovanni.'

He cleared his throat: 'Giovanni Bellini had enormous influence on Giorgione and Titian, who were both pupils of his, and towards the end of his life Bellini was himself able to learn from them . . . erm . . . erm . . . there are two motifs which dominate his altar paintings. In one there is a beautiful young Madonna with a child in front of a fixed tableau, often giving onto evocative background scenery. Giovanni Bellini's pictures hang in all the great galleries of the world. There are pictures hanging in several churches in Venice . . .' Gunnarstranda peered over the rim of his glasses. 'Look here. I've seen that one.' He showed Fristad a picture, a portrait of a pale man wearing a hat. With his glasses perched on the end of his nose, Gunnarstranda adjusted his reading distance. 'That's what I thought – the National Gallery in London. There's nothing in this book about a robbery at any rate, but on the other hand this encyclopaedia was published well before 1993.' He examined the year of publication before putting it back on the shelf. 'Nineteen seventy-eight to be precise. Perhaps you could put in a good word for us so we get these reference books updated.'

'No one updates reference books nowadays. They use the Internet, but perhaps you don't know what that is . . .'

At that moment Lena Stigersand poked her head in. She said: 'Just checked a couple of details about Rognstad's story. In fact, a painting by Giovanni Bellini showing a Madonna with baby Jesus *was* stolen from the church of Santa Maria dell'Orto in Venice in 1993. Pretty stupid business. The church was being restored. Someone strolled in under the tarpaulin, put the picture in their bag and walked off.'

'So the picture *is* small,' Gunnarstranda said.

Stigersand nodded. 'It has never reappeared and must be very valuable. Of course, pictures like these are almost never sold on. A similar picture of Madonna with the child Jesus, signed by Bellini, was sold in 1996 for £826,500 at an auction in London.'

'How much is that in Norwegian kroner?' Fristad asked.

'About ten million.'

'Thanks,' Gunnarstranda said.

Stigersand left, closing the door behind her.

'We really modern types use the young ones to check modern stuff on the Internet,' Gunnarstranda said and added: 'If a picture like that went for ten million in ninety-six, it must be worth a lot more today. Prices for art shoot through the roof. Worse than flats in Oslo.'

'But do you believe that?' Fristad broke in. 'Is it likely that the picture was lying in a deposit box in Askim for years? It's rather far-fetched.'

'If Rognstad's pulling the wool over our eyes, then it's a pretty good story,' Gunnarstranda retorted. 'So there has to be proof to underpin it. Rognstad would never have gone in for a plea bargain if he didn't have proof. After all, he wants his sentence commuted. He's got an ace up his sleeve. Now it wouldn't be much of an ace if he didn't know *where* the picture came from, would it. I would bet the picture was with the money in Narvesen's safe. The question of where the painting came from in order to end up in the deposit box is the only ace Jim Rognstad has. But he's waiting before he plays it.'

'If that's the case, how did Narvesen get hold of this picture?'

'Haven't the foggiest. Not particularly bothered either. What is important is the sequence of events. The men we're trying to nail break into Narvesen's place in the autumn of 1998 and steal a safe. The painting and the money are in the safe. The neighbour's wife only sees Ilijaz Zupac and points him out in the police photo files. Had she not done that, I presume the safe would never have been reported stolen – since there was such a famous item in it. The fact that the safe contained an item of such value would explain why it was the only thing that was stolen. Zupac is arrested. During the arrest Zupac fires a shot, one man dies and Ilijaz is charged with murder and sentenced. The safe is never found. In all probability his accomplices open the safe and the contents are deposited in the bank. One look at the names of the signatories and it is obvious that Ilijaz's conspirators were the Faremo gang: Jim Rognstad, Vidar Ballo and Jonny Faremo himself. These three recently broke into the container at Loenga in Oslo . . .'

'There were four of them, weren't there?' Fristad interrupted.

'We have a witness who says so, but let's stick to what we know. The three of them are arrested after a tip-off from Merethe Sandmo, right. All three get off, thanks to Elisabeth Faremo's testimony. Her statement is disputed by Frank Frølich who is willing to swear she was in his double bed after one o'clock in the morning. However, since he was asleep when she went home, theoretically she might have been telling the truth. She might have waited until he was asleep before going home and organizing the game of poker with her brother and his two pals.'

'However, Frølich's testimony should not be used under any circumstances,' Fristad said with force.

'The question is whether we can avoid it,' Gunnarstranda objected. 'Brigitte Bergum will fight hard for Rognstad. She has all the gunpowder she needs to stage a regular fireworks display: a cop on leave who queers his pitch by humping the sister of a criminal and a story about some mysterious world-famous work of art, which she will have no problem selling to the press – to name but two.'

Fristad cleaned his glasses in silence. He opened his mouth, breathed on his glasses and rubbed them energetically. 'Continue, Gunnarstranda.'

'Directly after the court hearing Elisabeth Faremo goes home and packs her things. She contacts her female lover, Reidun Vestli.'

'Poor old Frølich,' Fristad sighed. 'What a wretched story.'

'If I may continue?' Gunnarstranda asked politely.

'Of course.' Fristad put his glasses back on his nose.

'Elisabeth Faremo hides in a chalet owned by Reidun Vestli. Then something in the clan gives. Jonny Faremo is found drowned in the Glomma. One theory, then: Faremo knew they had been arrested because someone grassed on them. After his sister provided them with an alibi, Faremo went looking for the grass. Perhaps he points the finger of blame at Merethe. She immediately allies herself with Ballo, who kills Faremo, which binds Merethe to Ballo. Elisabeth may have anticipated this row and therefore flees. To protect herself against the men, and as a security, she takes the safety-deposit box keys with her. The two remaining men, Rognstad and Ballo, feverishly start searching for them.'

'That begs a question,' Fristad said. 'Why didn't these two men bother to ask Frølich for Elisabeth Faremo's whereabouts?'

'Frølich was also searching for her. He had asked her neighbour and Jonny Faremo. Besides, he's a policeman. No, they go for the easiest target: beat the answer out of Reidun Vestli. At least one of them travels with Merethe Sandmo to the chalet. They stop off for a meal in Fagernes – she is seen there with a man. They go on to the chalet . . .'

'There's something out of sync here,' Fristad interrupted. 'I read in one of your reports that the chalet fire was reported before Reidun Vestli was taken to hospital.'

'Her injuries had been sustained within an unspecified period of time. Unfortunately she clammed up tight afterwards. She wouldn't tell us a thing about the assault. Consequently we don't know when she was attacked. On the other hand, I can't see how Ballo or Rognstad would have found the chalet without going through Reidun Vestli.'

'And their intention was always to find the key to the safety-deposit box containing the painting and the money?' Fristad interrupted again.

'Yes. They knew Elisabeth Faremo had access to the key. But she outflanked them – and put the key in a safe place. She put it in Frølich's flat.'

'Where's the other key?'

'We don't know. That's why Elisabeth Faremo doesn't have a key when Sandmo and co. arrive at the chalet. There's a row, which culminates in an arson attack and Elisabeth being burned.'

'Where can the other key have been?'

'All we know is that it was used by someone pretending to be Ilijaz Zupac – it happened the same day the three were acquitted at the murder hearing. The person pretending to be Ilijaz Zupac opened the bank box, took the painting, we presume, and disappeared.'

'It could have been Ballo, as Rognstad suspects?'

'Of course. The problem is that Ballo had access to the box anyway. Why would he pretend to be Zupac?'

They reflected for a while. 'Why did this person only take the painting?'

Gunnarstranda opened his palms. 'Either there is a banal explanation – he wanted to collect the money later – or he left the money so that we would ask ourselves precisely that question, *should* the story of the painting leak out. It seems unlikely that a thief with access to half a million would leave it there. If the painting never turns up, though, whoever claims there was a painting in the safety-deposit box can *neither* prove it was there *nor* make a credible case for it having been there. Leaving the money is in fact an unusually clever move – assuming that Jim Rognstad is telling the truth.'

'And we should add that he does seem to be telling the truth. So who took the painting?'

'I have no idea. But I assume the same person was on the container raid, the man who was seen with the other three when Arnfinn Haga was murdered.'

'It couldn't have been Ilijaz Zupac? The man himself?'

'He hasn't been out of prison since he was sentenced approximately five years ago.'

'Well,' Fristad sighed heavily. 'An unidentified person at the scene of the crime. Could it have been this man who killed Jonny Faremo?'

'It might have been. Why do you think so?'

'I don't think so,' Fristad said. 'But this business with the keys is interesting, isn't it? Let's say Elisabeth and Jonny Faremo had a key each. Elisabeth hides her key in Frølich's flat. The mystery fourth man has a fight with Jonny Faremo, grabs Jonny's key and Jonny drowns. This fourth man drives to the bank in Askim, pretends to be Ilijaz Zupac and picks up the painting. The others don't know this, however. They only know Jonny is dead and they can't find his key. So they reason, shit, now they'll have to get hold of the last key. They know Elisabeth has it and they know she has some relationship with this woman at the university. Whom they turn over to find out where Elisabeth Faremo is hiding, etc, etc.'

'Anything is possible,' Gunnarstranda said. 'We know there were two keys. One of them was in Frølich's flat all the time. The other was used by someone also known as Ilijaz Zupac. We know Ballo teamed up with Merethe Sandmo immediately after Jonny Faremo's death. I talked to them myself. This Ballo is still missing – and we have no reliable information as to his whereabouts. My feeling is that Faremo was killed as a result of the row he started when Merethe Sandmo grassed on them.'

'It really does very much look like an alliance between Ballo and Merethe Sandmo. They could have joined forces, pinched the painting and ridden off into the sunset, couldn't they?'

'But why would Ballo pretend to be Zupac when he could have strolled into the bank vault as himself?'

'To hide his identity. The police are on the lookout for the painting all over the world. Criminal logic: snatch the painting under an alias. And, on top of that, leave the money so that any potential talk of a stolen painting by the others is undermined. Unless the prosecuting authorities manage to get their hands on it, that is.'

'You may be right. But we still have this witness who maintains there were four people at the crime scene where Arnfinn Haga was murdered.'

'So there is a man whose identity we don't know. Who do you reckon it is, this fourth perpetrator?'

'No idea,' Gunnarstranda said, in brief summary.

'Could it have been – please forgive me now, but giving rein to your fantasy can be quite useful in this job – could it have been Frank Frølich?'

The room went quiet. The sun shone through the blinds and Gunnarstranda found time to light a cigarette. He lit it without a word of protest from Fristad.

37

Gunnarstranda and Fristad were in the former's office. Frølich had been summoned without a word of explanation. Gunnarstranda and the prosecuting lawyer each sat in their chair.

He noticed two things: Gunnarstranda was smoking and Fristad was not complaining. Frølich looked from one to the other.

'We would like to discuss the facts of the case with you,' Fristad said concisely.

'Oh yes?'

'Does that strike you as strange?'

'Not strange, simply different.'

'Well . . .' Fristad lowered his gaze, but decided against commenting on his response. Instead he said: 'What do you consider the most important thing to do now – at this stage of the investigation?'

'In my view, the smartest move would be to talk to Narvesen again,' Frølich said.

'You'll have to stop this business with Narvesen,' Fristad exclaimed angrily.

'You asked me what *I* would do,' Frølich retorted. 'And my opinion is that Narvesen should be asked whether he knows the painting Rognstad was talking about.'

'You believe Rognstad was telling the truth then? Ilijaz and company took the painting when they robbed the safe in 1998?'

'Rognstad didn't say that. He said the painting was in the safety-deposit box. He didn't say one word about the break-in, but I'm sure he was holding back about the Narvesen burglary so that he wouldn't be charged. On the other hand, if Rognstad was telling the truth about the painting, the odds are that it came from the safe. I believe both the painting and the money were in the safe when it was stolen in 1998. I believe Jonny Faremo was involved in the theft. So for this gang it wasn't just half a million in the safe, but many more millions. And they deposited the contents in the bank.'

'But why did they do that?' Fristad asked.

'They wanted to wait until Ilijaz got out before dividing their spoils. The usual musketeer motto amongst gangsters: One for all and all for one, and all that crap.'

'A little while ago this painting was taken from the vault by an . . . an unknown person. But why? The picture is unsaleable.'

'Not at all. There is a market for this kind of art. And clearly we have a buyer here. A man who withdrew five million in cash from his account less than two weeks ago.'

'Narvesen? Was he going to buy the picture back? From whom?'

'Vidar Ballo and Merethe Sandmo.'

No one said a word for a considerable time.

Frølich broke the silence. 'Let's take it from the beginning. The three of them are acquitted after the Loenga murder hearing. Then Jonny Faremo is killed. Suddenly his lover Merethe has the hots for Ballo. Furthermore, she is seen in Fagernes the same day Jonny Faremo's sister dies in an arson attack on a chalet.'

'You're probably still a bit fixated on this Elisabeth Faremo, but I like the idea that Narvesen buys back the picture,' Fristad said. 'Then again, five million is a fairly low figure. A picture of this kind would have sold for ten million ten years ago.'

'Yes, but the figure is dependent on negotiations,' Frølich said. 'This gang of robbers had something on Narvesen after the theft of the safe in 1998. They opened the safe and discovered that Narvesen owned a stolen painting – one subject to investigations all over the world – art which was considered part of Italy's cultural heritage. Narvesen also had something on them: they had stolen items of great value, and grand larceny is a punishable offence. So both parties had a vested interest in keeping stumm. The painting may be worth fifteen or twenty million today, no one knows for sure. But it can *only* be sold to individual collectors. The only collector Faremo, Ballo and Rognstad knew was Narvesen.'

'Wait, wait, wait,' Fristad raised his hand in objection. 'What are you saying? Are you saying that Narvesen could be sitting on the picture now?'

'I believe so,' Frølich said. 'I believe the reason he followed me to Hemsedal and tried to set fire to . . .'

'Wait a minute. No unfounded accusations.'

'OK. I can try to reformulate the reasoning. If Narvesen has the picture, it would explain why he's so angry with me. He wants to shift attention away from the 1998 break-in and himself. If he has the picture – for all we know, he may be keeping it at home – it is particularly inconvenient for him that I look him up, go to his house and start digging and asking questions.'

Fristad looked across at Gunnarstranda, who was smoking slowly and deliberately.

'Narvesen rang me to check we weren't continuing the investigation connected with the robbery of his safe. It makes sense – if he's sitting on the painting. But even if he is,' Gunnarstranda said, 'we can't prove it.'

'But who sold the picture back to Narvesen?' Fristad asked.

'Ballo,' Frølich said. 'Everything points to him and Merethe playing the others off against each other. We know the two of them were an item the day after Jonny died. Even Jim Rognstad, who knows Ballo best, suspects him. You and I heard that.'

Fristad looked at Frølich. 'Thank you, Frølich,' he said.

When Frølich had gone, the two men studied each other's faces for an impression.

'What do you think?' asked Fristad.

'I never think anything.'

'No gut instinct?'

'Not even that.'

'Ignoring our assumption that he is emotionally involved and believes what he says, suppose Narvesen is sitting on the picture. Can we take any action? Can we search his house, for example?'

'*We* can't, but *Sørlie* can. Eco-Crime can whack a charge down on the table, alleging that the five million he withdrew in cash is being used for money-laundering. Then they can search his house and his office.'

'But will they find the painting?'

'Doubtful. He might have put it in a bloody safety-deposit box,' Gunnarstranda grinned.

'And he gets a solicitor who tears our arguments to shreds and says we've been taken in by some cock-and-bull story from Rognstad, who probably cooked something up to get a lighter sentence.'

'But if Eco-Crime and Sørlie take action, that side of things will never have to see the light of day. One of our people could be on the team.'

'Who?' Fristad asked immediately. 'Frank Frølich is out of the running.'

'I had Emil Yttergjerde in mind,' Gunnarstranda decided. 'I'll put a good word in for him with Sørlie.'

Fristad left. Gunnarstranda had just managed to get his legs behind his desk when Lena Stigersand arrived with a large pile of papers. 'Bull's eye,' she said and sat down so hard the chair rolled back more than a metre.

'Out with it.'

Lena Stigersand brandished the papers. 'Merethe Sandmo. She caught the plane from Oslo to Athens on 30 November. With Lufthansa via Munich.'

Gunnarstranda stood up. 'Ballo?' he asked.

Lena Stigersand shook her head. 'His name's not on the list.'

'So she travelled on her own?'

'That's not definite. He may have travelled under another name.'

'When did the chalet burn down?'

Lena Stigersand checked the papers. '28 November. During the night of 28/29 November. It was Sunday night, Monday morning.'

'On Sunday Merethe Sandmo has dinner with an unidentified man in Fagernes. The same evening the chalet burns down with

Elisabeth Faremo inside. The timing is perfect. End of November and the summer season, so no one else is around. And any weekenders in the area will have travelled back to Oslo on Sunday night. They strike at night. It ends with the murder of Elisabeth Faremo, which they try to disguise with a fire. On Monday they're back in Oslo. Tuesday, Merethe Sandmo – and in all probability Ballo – is sitting on a plane to Athens.'

Gunnarstranda stood lost in thought before continuing: 'Have you contacted the Greek police?'

'Usual procedure. Interpol office at Kripos. Photo and description of Merethe Sandmo are being faxed to Athens now, I understand. Didn't she get a job at a strip club?'

Gunnarstranda shrugged. 'A bar. That's the official reason she left at any rate – according to Frølich. Have you still got the passenger lists?' he asked.

'Yes.'

'Perhaps we can find Ballo under an alias. Check for Ilijaz Zupac.'

'Will do.'

38

Frank Frølich was searching for the note she had slipped into his hand. Finally he found it crumpled up in the back pocket of a pair of trousers in the dirty-linen basket in the bathroom. Her telephone number was written in large figures. The eight was two neatly drawn circles, one on top of the other. *What does handwriting tell you about personality?* He rang the number.

'Hello, this is Vibeke and I'm a bit busy. Leave your number and I'll ring you back in a moment.'

Now, at least, I know what your name is. He waited patiently for the tone. 'Hello, Vibeke, this is me, Frank. Thank you for everything. Hope you have some time for . . .'

He didn't get any further. She had picked up the receiver. 'Hello, Frank. Nice of you to ring.'

'I felt like talking to you,' he said.

'Are you all right?'

'Why wouldn't I be?' he said.

She left the question unanswered and he let the silence drag on.

'Are you there?'

'Shall we meet up?' he asked.

'Right now I'm a bit busy. But otherwise any time. I usually get up at about twelve.'

He looked at his watch. It was afternoon. 'What about one o'clock tomorrow?' he suggested. 'Lunch?'

'You can have lunch and I'll have breakfast. Where?'

Frølich racked his brains for names of cafés and chose the first one that occurred to him: 'At the Grand?'

'Cool. I haven't been to the Grand since I had a French vanilla slice with my grandmother there at least fifteen years ago.'

Lena Stigersand carried in a heavy pile of papers and asked: 'Where can I put these?'

Absentmindedly, Gunnarstranda glanced up.

'Where?' she repeated.

He nodded towards the table in the corner. She staggered across.

At that moment the phone rang. Gunnarstranda took it. It was Yttergjerde.

'Things are beginning to move, Gunnarstranda!'

'Oh yes?'

'Didn't find a painting.'

'You didn't expect to, did you?'

'Nope. I've just got back from searching the broker's offices, Inar A/S. The five million in cash. He claimed he'd put it in a filing cabinet drawer, didn't he?'

'You mean to say he didn't have the money in a drawer?'

'Right.'

'Well,' Gunnarstranda said, looking at his watch. 'He owes us an explanation.'

He put down the phone and rocked back on his chair.

Lena Stigersand, who had her back to him as she tidied the papers, glanced over her shoulder. 'You look happy. Indictment on the way?'

Gunnarstranda pulled his fingers until the joints cracked. 'Juicy grilled investor marinated in murder and seasoned with money-laundering!' He grinned. 'My goodness, there are times when I adore this job. It's going to be bloody awful being retired!'

Gunnarstranda sat working into the evening. One by one, the others went home. He had a dinner date at home with Tove. She had asked him to come at eight and he had nothing else to do to kill the intervening time. When he finally craned his neck to check the clock, he saw Frølich's jacket hanging over the back of a chair by the door. He stood up and opened the door.

'Frølich?'

Frølich turned round from the photocopier and said: 'Time to draw in my oars now. It's late.'

Gunnarstranda put on his coat and said: 'Thought you left ages ago.'

He observed his younger colleague as he went to collect his jacket and straightened the scarf round his neck. He said: 'How long have we been working together, Frølich?'

The latter shrugged. 'Ten years? Twelve? Thirteen? No, I can't remember. Why?'

It was Gunnarstranda's turn to shrug his shoulders.

Frølich said: 'I'm off then.'

'I'm off too.'

They stood looking at each other again. 'Something up?' Frølich enquired.

'In your view, should we have done anything differently?' Gunnarstranda asked.

'Why's that?'

'Do you think we've left anything undone – in this case?'

'Should have been more on our toes with regard to Narvesen maybe?

'We've had him under surveillance for several days,' Gunnarstranda said. 'He hasn't been for a leak without it being noted down. According to reports Narvesen does nothing in the evening. He stays at home. Sometimes goes into the cellar. That's all.'

'Carpentry?'

'Don't know.'

'What about Emilie?'

'Emilie?'

'His partner, Vietnamese-looking, attractive girl.'

'Her with the Porsche? She's a spinning instructor and is rarely at home.'

'What's a spinning instructor?'

'She drives to a fitness studio four nights a week, sits on an exercise bike in front of a load of other exercise bikes and then they pedal away to music while the floozy howls into the mike urging them on.'

'Oh.'

They left the building together. Neither of them said anything. They stopped outside and looked at each other again.

Gunnarstranda cleared his chest. 'Ri-ght,' he said. 'Have a good weekend.'

Frølich nodded in response. 'Have a good weekend.'

Tove had made lamb stew. It was his favourite. The food had the aromas of his childhood. Sunday lunches when he was a boy and the whole block could smell what was being cooked. The quarrels between him and his brother for the best bits of meat when the pot was passed around for seconds. But he didn't say that. He had said it before. Several times. The fact that she had cooked this meal was Tove's homage to precisely that nostalgia.

They had eaten, washed the meal down with a red wine she had chosen, a strong spicy Italian number of the Barolo variety, and they were now sharing the remainder. Louis Armstrong was singing 'Makin' Whoopee' on the stereo. Gunnarstranda observed Tove as she sat in the armchair deep in thought.

He said: 'What are you thinking about?'

She said: 'A patient. Vidar. He's crazy . . . no, he probably isn't out-and-out crazy, but he's one of our residents at the nursing home, poor boy. Barely thirty. He's so thin and his face is always twisted, staring diagonally up into the air, his mouth open, holding the lobe of his ear with one hand. His mother said he was listening to God's voice.'

'Terrible,' Gunnarstranda said and took a sip.

'If you close your eyes, does everything go black?' she asked.

He closed his eyes: 'No, there's a yellow flicker and I can see stars.'

'Not everyone sees stars, but many people can see a sort of yellow in the dark. However, if you concentrate, look straight ahead with closed eyes, the flicker you see focuses into a centre, a point of light somewhere between your eyes, and if you look harder, this point will be a part of a large black eye. That's your third eye looking at you.'

Gunnarstranda closed his eyes, raised his glass and drank. 'An eye? Who's looking at me inside my head?'

'It's God.'

'Who says it's God?'

'Vidar.'

'The crazy young man?'

'Mm.'

'Maybe he has a point. Would you like some more wine?'

'OK, if you tell me what you're thinking about.'

'Be bold, fair maiden, but not too bold.'

'Doesn't that come from a fairy tale?'

'Probably.'

'Come on, no wriggling out of it,' Tove said, getting up, fetching another bottle from the cabinet and opening it.

'Wriggling out of what?'

'Out of telling me what you're thinking.'

'I was thinking that I was looking for two people for murder.'

Tove filled both glasses and said: 'Don't you do that every day?'

Gunnarstranda pointed his forefinger at the stereo. It was Ella Fitzgerald singing the first lines of 'Autumn in New York'.

They both listened.

'This time it was you who interrupted me,' he said after a while.

'Me – and Ella.'

'The two people are under investigation for killing a security man, Arnfinn Haga, and for arson with murder.'

'What kind of people are they?'

'A lingerie model, twenty-nine years old, and a criminal on a disability allowance who has spent five-eighths of his life in the slammer.'

'But why are you thinking about them?'

'That's what I'm asking myself.'

They went quiet again. Ella handed over the microphone to Louis Armstrong.

Tove took a seat beside him on the sofa. She rested her head against his shoulder. They remained like that in the half-light. Car headlamps sent yellow rectangles across the ceiling as they rounded the bend outside. As Louis Armstrong blew his horn through the loudspeakers.

39

It was like a scene from a B-movie. It was evening. The slim, black-haired woman bounced on her high heels through the wrought-iron gate to the low-slung car. Her outline was silhouetted against the street lamp further away. She got in. The car door closed quietly and firmly. The engine growled like an unhurried, replete wild animal as the car drove away. Frølich watched the red rear lights. He had plenty of time. He was patient. Through the garden gate he went, off the shingle path, onto the lawn. A dog inside began to bark. He went on, undeterred. Crouched under an old apple tree, waiting. A shadow appeared in the window. Someone peeped out into the dark. The dog continued to yelp. Finally, the shadow moved away. Eventually, the dog quietened down. Frank Frølich wondered about the dog. The twitchy, lean setter.

What exactly is it I'm after? Why am I crouching here?

He blinked dry eyes in the dark. Blinked away his self-criticism, doubts, misgivings.

It was cold. The sky was black, no stars, no moon. The chill air augured snow. Frølich waited by his post as if hunting elk: stationary, eyes skinned for movement. After an hour the light went on in the cellar. Frølich glanced at his watch and made up his mind. Seven minutes. The light in the cellar window was still on. Another light went on in one of the basement windows. Four minutes passed. No more lights. Five minutes. The second hand crawled round. He was breathing faster. Six minutes. He straightened up. Had to control himself not to leap forward and knock down the door, not to hyperventilate. Seven minutes. He loped across the lawn, ran up the steps and rang three times. The dog began to bark. He ran down the steps again. Rounded the corner of the house, onto the veranda – without making a sound. He checked his watch again. *Relax! Breathe.* The dog had made its way to the veranda window. The bared red gums and white teeth drooled and yapped behind the transparent curtain. He could hear footsteps on the cellar stairs. A voice was scolding the dog, which continued barking madly. He waited for the front door to open. When the light from the door opening hit the opposite side of the lawn, he kicked in the glass door. As he kicked at the fragments of glass, he heard the man swear. The dog snapped at his foot. Frølich kicked it and sent it sprawling and whimpering. He was inside. The man came from the hall towards him. His face met Frølich's fist straight on. Frølich didn't say a word. Just lashed out. He got the man on the floor, rolled him onto his stomach, held his hands firmly in place with his knees and reached for the plastic strips in his belt. The dog was at him again. It barked and snarled ferociously, and snapped at his ribs. Frølich punched it and it flew across the floor. Then he tied the man's hands with the strips. He stood up. Now it was the dog's turn. It came bounding towards him. He grabbed it in mid-flight and squeezed its snout shut so firmly that it squealed; it was close to suffocating. The dog's hind legs gave way as it hit the floor. Then he let go. The dog crawled under the table with its tail between its legs.

He surveyed the surroundings: the man on his knees with his hands bound behind his back. He was abusive, but Frølich didn't listen. There was a fire in the hearth. A large glass chandelier hung from the ceiling. Otherwise the room was conspicuous for the heavy furniture and pictures on the wall.

Why am I doing this?

He strode to the front door. The man had left it open; he closed and locked it. He found the stairs leading to the first floor and ran up. Narvesen's yelling resounded behind him. He was sweating. Came out into a narrow corridor. Opened a door. A bathroom. Another door. Bedroom. Another door. Office. Desk drawers, papers. Slammed the drawers shut. Sneering laughter. From downstairs. *He hasn't run away. But he didn't follow me either. So I won't find anything here.*

He charged back down the stairs. Narvesen's laughter died in his mouth. Sitting on the floor. His eyes defiant, semi-triumphant, glared past him. He followed Narvesen's eyes. A door. He turned. Walked to the door. Narvesen screamed again, louder, uglier.

The door led to the cellar. He went down. It was a crude cellar. It smelt damp. Walls and floor of grey concrete. There was the hum of a freezer. He went on, past the freezer, through a door. The wine cellar. Small niches had been embedded in the wall, each containing a couple of hundred dark bottles on their sides. He walked through the next doorway. This was the boiler room. An enormous steel tank covered almost one wall. A modern boiler on the opposite wall. Pipes running off in every possible direction. He was sweating. Wiped his forehead. He could hear soft violins and followed the sound. The boiler began to roar. There was a click as the burner lit the flames. He went on, through the furthest low door, and entered a furnished room. It was small and dominated by an Italian designer chair, the reclining kind. A mini-stereo was playing something which reminded him of Mozart. A drinks bar. Half a bottle of Camus VSOP, a single glass. And in front of the chair a safe. The safe door was open. Inside the safe, a painting. Frank Frølich bent down.

'Don't touch.'

Frølich straightened up. Narvesen's voice was clear and razor-sharp. It felt like waking from a dream. He turned.

Inge Narvesen, his hands tied behind his back, stood in the doorway. His face was smeared with blood.

Frølich took the painting.

'Put it down.'

'Why?'

They glared at each other.

'You're a nobody,' Narvesen hissed. 'After this you're a nothing.'

'I've heard,' Frølich said, 'that you're vindictive. But you're too late. You ruined your chance when you set fire to my chalet. Now it's my turn.'

Narvesen supported himself on the wall. His face slid into shadow; his eyes became two narrow, moist slits.

Frølich studied the picture. It was bigger than he had imagined. A wide frame. 'Let's go upstairs,' he said, pointing to the steps. '*Après vous.*'

'Put back the picture first.'

'I make the decisions here.'

'Haven't you understood yet? You're nothing. Tomorrow you'll be out of the force. You, a policeman? That's just a joke . . .'

Frølich blinked.

Narvesen, his head jutting forward aggressively, came towards him with a rolling gait.

Frølich blinked again. He saw his own hand shoot forward. 'Up there!' Narvesen toppled against the wall. Frølich grabbed the bottle of cognac and held it up. Narvesen wasn't aggressive any longer.

'Careful with the picture!'

'Get upstairs!'

Narvesen staggered up the stairs with his hands behind his back. One shoulder hit the wall and he had to struggle to retain his balance.

'Keep moving!'

They stood on opposite sides of the fireplace. Frølich was having difficulty breathing normally. He blinked the haze out of his eyes. Between his hands: a piece of wood. An unusually wide gold picture frame surrounding a small motif. A woman with a headscarf holding a small fat child with curly hair. *So that's what it looks like.* He concentrated on breathing, in, out, in deep, out. Narvesen's eyes: wary, anxious. *He's not sure about me, my mental stability.* Frølich could hear his own voice, hollow, distant:

'Didn't think this would fit into a safety-deposit box.'

'The frame was taken off. But be careful, I have just had it reassembled.'

'It's a fine painting, but is it worth five million?'

'Five million is nothing for a picture like this. There are collectors who would give ten times that to own something similar.'

'Why's that?'

Narvesen hesitated. His gaze, first at the picture, then the ruined door, then the picture, then Frølich's face.

Breathe in, let it out, then in.

Narvesen said: 'All art . . .'

He pressed his lips together as Frølich raised the painting to the light.

'Carry on.'

'All art is cheap to acquire at some point. It's when art has communicated its value to the world that the price rises . . . but the way you're holding it is beginning to make me nervous. Will you put it down!'

'Explain what you mean.'

Narvesen's turn to concentrate on breathing, his eyes firmly fixed on Frølich. His hands bound tightly behind his back. 'For me as a collector, art and the experience of art are not simply two sides of the same coin, they are a part of my life, they're an indivisible part of me. My experience of art is as intellectual as it is emotional. You have to remember that art is the language of symbols that allows us to make sense of the world around us, which defines us as humans . . . '

'Etcetera, etcetera,' Frølich interrupted. 'But why precisely this painting? Bellini, the Madonna and Child?'

Narvesen's outline was sharper now. Frølich had him in focus. Narvesen was sweating from his brow. He cleared his throat. 'Something happened to art in 1420. An architect, Alberti, published a textbook on perspective. The Bellinis were among the first great . . . Giovanni Bellini was a master at capturing man's experience of worldly dimensions in paintings, in art. He was not only one of the first, but one of the best of his time, he interpreted the world with a completely new figurative language. So he contributed to laying the foundations, the base, for the aesthetics we pursue today. That is why this painting is the most outstanding example of art I can own as a collector. In this small painting the most vital elements are concentrated into one study: Life and the Divine, the son of man and the mother of God. I never tire of gazing at this painting. This is my *Mona Lisa*, Frølich.'

'It's not yours.'

'It's in my possession.'

Frølich lifted up the painting. 'It *was* in your possession.'

Narvesen fell quiet. His eyes were anxious now.

'How did you get hold of this painting?'

'You'll never find out.'

'Who sold you this painting?'

'Don't ask. You'll never know.'

'What are you going to do with a painting you can never show others? When you have to be on your own down there in your wank hole, gawping at it? You wait until your woman's out and then sneak down to your secret.'

'Don't you understand? Have you never been obsessed by anything?'

'Yes, I have,' Frølich said. *Long bones. The smell of smoke. Pain.* He raised the bottle of cognac and drank from it. Then he took the knife out of his pocket, cut the strips around Narvesen's wrists and folded back the blade.

Narvesen rubbed his wrists and said: 'Just say what you want. I have enough money.'

'I'm sure you do.'

'Just say the price.'

'I understand what you said about obsession,' Frølich said, grabbing Narvesen's hair and pulling his head back.

Narvesen sank to his knees with a groan.

'But I cannot accept that you tried to burn me alive.'

He let go of him.

Narvesen slumped down.

Frølich took the cognac bottle, poured the spirits onto the painting and threw it into the fire. The painting caught fire. An eruption of flames. Two seconds passed. Narvesen saw the fire. Another second. He comprehended what had happened. Then he screamed and ran towards it. Frank Frølich put out his foot and tripped him as he lunged. The man fell and crawled on all fours with his fingers in the flames. Frølich kicked him away. The painting was burning gaily. It blistered and cracked, the child's face disappeared in the flames. The wooden frame crackled. The fiery red-orange tongues of flame burned through the woman, licked at her face. Narvesen wailed, scrambled towards the fire. The picture was alight. The image was consumed. Only the carving distinguished the frame from a piece of wood. The dog, which had been lying under the table, became excited. It started barking once more. Bounded out and hit Narvesen's trousered legs. The man was squirming his way towards the fire. Frølich grinned, let him squirm, let him thrust his hand in the fire for the remains. The man blew on the charred residue like a young child trying to blow out the candles on a birthday cake. Frølich stood watching for a few seconds. As did the dog. It cocked its head in wonder.

'Now we're quits,' said Frank Frølich. 'You should be happy I didn't set you on fire.'

It was almost one o'clock when Gunnarstranda closed the door to Tove's flat and ran down the stairs and out into the night. It had begun to snow. A fine white carpet a few centimetres thick lay on the pavement. He padded his way towards Sandakerveien to find a taxi. There was chaos on the roads. Cars braked and skidded. A snow plough cast orange beams of light up the walls further along the street. He had set his mobile phone to mute, but felt it vibrate in his inside pocket.

It was Lystad from Kripos. He had a message. A body had been found. Name: Vidar Ballo. Cause of death: overdose. Place: Ballo's flat in Holmlia.

Gunnarstranda was unable to speak. What could he say, standing dumbstruck on a pavement in Sandakerveien in the cold of the night?

Lystad continued: 'A caretaker broke down the door because some neighbours had been complaining about the smell. That explains why he hadn't opened the door for several days.'

Gunnarstranda watched a Mercedes taxi with a lit roof sign glide past.

'You're so quiet,' Lystad said. 'Did I wake you?'

'No, no. I'm walking home. Anyone know how long he's been dead?'

'The forensic pathologists will be able to say in a few days. I only found out by chance. I called his mother in Kvenangen. The priest had notified her yesterday. His death has been registered as a clear case of an overdose, so it seems.'

'I may have been the last person to see him alive,' Gunnarstranda said gloomily.

'Will you investigate his death?'

'Strictly speaking, it's not me who decides that.'

'Nevertheless, some hypotheses will have to be reassessed,' Lystad said. 'For us and for you, I assume.'

'Absolutely right.'

Another taxi approached.

'Perhaps we should work together?'

Gunnarstranda hailed the taxi. The car stopped. The driver stretched an arm across the back of the seat and opened the rear door.

'Tomorrow, for instance,' Lystad said.

'Where are you now?' asked Gunnarstranda, getting in.

'Office.'

'I'll be there in ten minutes,' Gunnarstranda announced. He rang off and nodded to the driver. 'Kripos building in Bryn.'

40

The following morning Frank Frølich had a long lie-in. He didn't get up until eleven, then had a bit of muesli and prepared to go to the Grand Hotel.

It had snowed a lot in the course of the night. The cars along Havreveien were well packed in. Snowdrifts left thick layers on top of car roofs and bonnets, making them look like cream cakes. A few car owners had wriggled their way out of the drifts, leaving deep holes in the row of cars.

At the Metro station a tractor with rattling chains was clearing the snow. Frølich took the first train to arrive, got off at Stortinget and wandered down Karl Johans gate where the heater cables in the ground keeping the pavements snow-free had turned the snow on the road into a slushy, brown broth.

She was taking a seat at a vacant window table when he came through the heavy doors of the café in the Grand Hotel. She was wearing high-heeled boots, tight jeans and a woollen sweater. Her Afro locks seemed out of place with her regulation Norwegian outfit. The hat she was wearing looked too heavy for her.

He hardly recognized her. Perhaps because she had clothes on, he thought, as he went over to her table. She looked up.

'I've been keeping my eyes open for you,' she said.

'Where?'

'You know.'

He sat down. Met her eyes. They challenged him, but they didn't touch him. He couldn't penetrate her façade; he associated it with any one of the many uninspiring media celebs. *Heavily made-up face. Studied look rehearsed in front of the mirror. The smile, a practised muscle movement with lips and chin. Today she isn't wearing a mask.* The magic from an earlier evening was long gone.

She flashed her teeth in another fleeting smile. 'I've ordered a French vanilla slice and Coke.'

He looked at her askance. She wasn't joking.

The waitress was there. Frølich ordered coffee.

'You've done something to your face,' she said with downcast eyes.

'That was the key I was talking about.'

'You told me to pass on the message.' She was still studying the table.

'It's fine. Don't worry about it.'

'Don't ask me about him,' she said quickly. 'I don't know anything and if I did, I wouldn't say.'

'About whom?' he asked.

'Jim,' she said.

The waitress came with the coffee. Frølich stirred it. She had her vanilla slice and Coke. She tried to cut the cake with the spoon. The cream oozed out over the plate. She giggled and mumbled: 'Not so easy, this.'

'My boss says if you want to understand people's life strategies, you have to watch them eating millefeuilles.'

'I'm glad your boss isn't here now,' she said, squeezing more cream over her plate.

'I once saw an accountant eating a millefeuilles,' he said. 'The systematic approach. This guy removed the top layer with a spoon, neatly placed it on the plate, then he ate the cream, followed by the base and saved the top with the icing for last.'

She scooped up a pile of cream and icing onto her spoon, crammed it into her mouth and closed her eyes in ecstasy. 'The guy doesn't know what he's missing,' she mumbled.

'Vibeke,' he said.

She glanced up. 'Yes, Frank.'

They looked into each other's eyes.

She took another spoonful of cream and icing, swallowed and said: 'You don't know what you're missing, either.'

He averted his eyes. Not because of her lack of sophistication, more to avoid having to look through that worn expression of hers. 'I'm back at work,' he said slowly. 'I'm a policeman.'

She didn't answer.

'I'm working now.'

'Rotten excuse for not eating cake,' she said finally.

She giggled, but the smile went out when she saw his expression.

'Vibeke,' he repeated.

'Yes, Frank.' Her smile was wry and provocative again.

'I need to know something about Elisabeth.'

'I'm sure you know more about Elisabeth than I do.'

'But you knew her when she was with Ilijaz.'

'Are you jealous?'

'No, what Elisabeth and I had is gone.' He considered his words while scanning the room. Most of the people were hotel guests passing through. The rest were frail-looking ladies with blue-rinse hair and delicate wrinkles. The low winter sun pierced the tall windows. Outside, people in Karl Johan were hurrying past. A police car from the dog-patrol unit had pulled up in front of Stortinget. An elderly man was sitting on a bench playing blues on an electric guitar beneath one of the Storting lions; the music was just audible in the café. When he turned back to her, she had finished eating.

She said: 'Ilijaz is Elisabeth's great love. She would die for Ilijaz, however ill he is.'

He reflected on what she had said. For a second he saw a chalet burning in front of him. He cleared his throat, plucked up courage and asked: 'Was Elisabeth bisexual?'

'What makes you wonder that?'

'I believe she was.'

'Bisexual?' She sampled the word. 'That sounds very much like pigeon-holing.'

'Oh?'

'Sort of condescending.'

'I suspect Elisabeth was in a relationship with a woman.'

'I can imagine that,' she said, deep in thought. 'I think Elisabeth . . .' She pulled a face and said: 'Have you never played with the idea? Of probing the physical side of a relationship with a good friend?'

'No.'

She giggled. 'I believe you. But as far as Elisabeth is concerned – I can easily imagine her going to bed with women. That doesn't change anything about the totally all-consuming passion that existed between her and Ilijaz, though.'

'Tell me more,' he said.

'I don't know much more,' she continued.

'Was it stormy?'

'Did they quarrel? They probably did. You know what it's like for some – when the relationship is so intense that negative emotions are released with almost the same energy as positive emotions.'

For an instant he caught a flash of Elisabeth's naked foot. Her red varnished nails. His hand around her ankle with the thin gold chain.

'And some of that was because Ilijaz was not always good.'

'What do you mean by "not always good"?'

'He went with other women. Often.'

'So it wasn't a fixed, long-term relationship on his part?'

'Yes, it was. I'm sure he was just as hooked as she was. But he was also very macho at that time, a little childish, really. Always had to prove what a man he was, constantly on the pull. She got sick of it in the end and found someone else.'

Someone else. Frølich thought about what Gunnarstranda had said about a fourth man. 'Who?'

'Someone upfront.'

'Can you remember his name?'

'No.'

'Can you remember what his job was?'

'Haven't a clue.'

'When was this?'

'I don't remember.'

'Try. It must have been five to six years ago, or longer. Ilijaz was jailed six years ago.'

'Was he? Time passes. I can never tell one year from another. It's easier to pick out the school years but . . .'

'What work were you doing then?'

'Bar work. I've always worked in bars.'

'Which bar?'

'Six years ago? It was a bar in Bogstadveien. Closed down now.'

'And you knew Elisabeth at that time?'

'She was working in a shop. Ferner Jacobsen.' She motioned with her head towards Stortingsgata. 'In the basement. Elisabeth's the type who looks good in everything she wears. Anyone who sells clothes knows she's worth her weight in gold in a shop. I think she met the guy there. He was a customer. A guy with lots of money.'

'A criminal?'

'Either that or . . . it's just rich people who shop there. And this guy kept inviting her to dinner and wouldn't take no for an answer. That was how it was. And once when Ilijaz got in too deep with some woman, she accepted the invitation and they became a couple. Ilijaz must have been nabbed at about that time.'

'Did the relationship last long?'

'I don't know.'

'Did you meet the man?'

'Never. No one was allowed to meet the man.'

'Why not?'

'Elisabeth's like that. She likes secrets. You know that. She never takes you home, either, does she.'

He sat up straight in his chair. She talked about Elisabeth in the present tense. 'Elisabeth's dead,' he said. 'Didn't Jim tell you that?'

She looked down. Shook her head.

The silence lingered. *Why doesn't she ask about Elisabeth? How she died? What happened?* He pondered, formulated an answer for himself and said: 'Are you together with Jim?'

'Together with? No.' Her eyes were so fixed on the table they seemed to be closed.

'But you told Jim what I said about the key. You knew who I was when I came in and saw you dance.'

'I talk to Jim, yes, I do. But I'm unattached.'

'He'll probably be charged with murder.'

'Jim?' Her eyes still rooted to the table.

'Someone set fire to a chalet. Elisabeth was in the chalet.'

'When?'

'The night leading to 29 November. Sunday to Monday.'

'It wasn't Jim.' She finally looked up from the table, pensive, distant, and said: 'That night Jim was at my place.'

They didn't say anything for a long while. The noises in the café took over: the clatter of plates, cutlery, the buzz of muted voices.

'Are you sure?' he asked thickly, after clearing his throat.

She gave him a faint smile: 'Of course I'm sure.'

'I mean about the time.'

She nodded.

She broke the silence. And she did it after another wry, embarrassed smile: 'I'm sorry, but I don't want to lie to you.'

They walked down Karl Johans gate together, towards Oslo main station. He stopped at the Kirkegata crossing and pointed to the cathedral. 'I have to go that way.'

She stopped and looked at him for a few seconds. 'Sure?'

He nodded.

She stood on the tips of her toes and allowed her lips to brush his cheek before turning on her heel and continuing down Karl Johan. He watched her supple figure move towards the throng of people and disappear. Then he turned and strolled off – on the opposite side to Kirkeristen.

He hurried down to the Metro and caught a train home – impatient. Once there, he immediately went to his car. He cleared the snow off the boot lid and took out a brush and a shovel. Dug the bank of snow away from his car. He got in, started the engine and drove to Ring 3, which he followed to the end, then took Drammensveien out of Oslo and turned off at Sandvika heading for Steinshøgda. The beast was back in his stomach and he focused on the tarmac ahead, the snow between the tree trunks, the winter setting in. He drove up Begnadal towards Fagernes. However, this time there were no visions of flames, no images of long bones. There was just an indescribable gnawing at his guts. And he was beginning to reason in a fresh way. To re-examine every tiny detail, the words spoken, what they meant.

Per-Ole 'Cranberry' Ramstad was waiting for him, as he had promised, when he reversed in front of the police station.

'You're fired up, Frank. You look like you've just come from a week of training hell at Officers' School.'

'I have to know who saw this Sandmo woman in Fagernes a few weeks ago,' Frølich said.

'I believe you,' Cranberry said. 'I can see it in your face. But I don't know if I can help you there . . .'

'All right,' Frølich said quickly. 'I have no time to waste. Look at this,' he said, passing Per-Ole a photograph from the newspaper. 'Go to your witness and ask if Merethe Sandmo had dinner with this man.'

Cranberry took the picture and studied it. 'Bit of a limp fish,' he said in summary. 'What's his name?'

'Inge Narvesen.'

'What does he do?'

'Buys and sells shares at Oslo Stock Exchange. Billionaire.'

'That's good enough for me,' Cranberry said, passing back the newspaper cutting. 'The answer is yes.'

'Don't mess me about,' Frølich said. 'I want you to show me . . .'

'No need,' Cranberry said. 'The witness is me. I saw Merethe Sandmo having dinner at the hotel with this guy.'

'But why didn't you say so?'

Cranberry smiled a sad smile. 'It has nothing to do with you. It has something to do with my wife and the woman I was having dinner with at the hotel when I saw them.'

Frank Frølich took a deep breath. 'Thanks, Per-Ole,' he said gently. 'Next time we'll go fishing in Vællers. Thanks for this.'

He took his leave of Cranberry and drove back. Calmer. He put on some music. Johnny Cash sang a cover version of U2's 'One'. Acoustic guitar and a voice without any illusions. It struck a chord with what was going on inside him.

41

Once again Frank Frølich was sitting behind a two-way mirror. This time he was joined by Gunnarstranda. In the interview room, Lystad from Kripos was in mid-flow. Opposite the police inspector sat Inge Narvesen and his solicitor. The latter was a man in his fifties who was clearly more familiar with corporate than criminal law. He had a plump, moon-shaped face beneath a mound of unkempt curls. Neither the solicitor nor Narvesen seemed particularly happy to find themselves in this situation.

'Do you deny that?' Lystad asked.

'That I ate at the hotel? Not at all.'

'Alone?'

'No.'

'Who were you with?'

'No idea what her name was.'

'Have a try.'

'It's true. I have no idea. She called herself Tanja, but I doubt she was christened Tanja.'

'You're absolutely correct. Who was this "Tanja" for you?'

'A prostitute. She sold, I bought.'

'Bought what?'

'What do you buy from prostitutes?'

'Just answer the question.'

'I bought sex off her.'

'You went to Fagernes to buy sex off a woman working as a waitress in Oslo?'

'Obviously the term "waitress" does not completely cover this woman's activities.'

'OK, let's talk about something else. You started a relationship with a young woman in 1998, is that right?'

'It's possible. What do you mean by "young"?'

'Elisabeth Faremo. She was working as a sales assistant at Ferner Jacobsen where you were a customer. Did you start a relationship?'

Inge Narvesen shot a glance at his solicitor. He nodded. 'The term "relationship" is stretching it,' Narvesen drawled.

'Perhaps you would claim you confined yourself to buying sex off her, too?'

'No. We were a couple. But it wasn't a relationship of any duration.'

'I know,' Lystad said. 'It stopped when her real lover was arrested for breaking into your house.'

Narvesen said nothing. He flashed a raised eyebrow at his solicitor, who slowly shook his head.

Gunnarstranda and Frølich exchanged meaningful looks. Whatever sort of choreography this was, Frølich thought, there was no question it had been rehearsed.

Lystad got up and walked over to the window facing him. He stood surveying the street. 'You say you bought sex off this woman in Fagernes,' he said to the window. 'Where did you have intercourse?'

'At the hotel.'

'You didn't have a room at the hotel.'

'*She* did.'

'She *didn't*.'

'She must have been using an alias. We were in her room, in her bed.'

'What was the room number?'

'I really cannot remember.'

'Which floor?'

Narvesen smiled awkwardly. 'I'm sorry.'

Lystad gave him a stony look. 'Not so surprising that your memory plays tricks on you since neither the woman nor her alleged alias, Tanja, ever checked in at the hotel. But, for the time being, let us just say that your statement does not exactly tally with reality . . .' Lystad raised a hand when Narvesen made a move to intervene. He said: 'Where was her partner when you were having sex?'

'Don't know. She and I were alone.'

'But she was in Fagernes with her partner.'

'That's news to me. I didn't know she had a partner.'

'And you had sex before or after the meal in the restaurant?'

'Before.'

'I have a witness whose statement reads as follows: You came into the restaurant. A woman was sitting there already. First of all, this woman's name was not Tanja. She has been identified as Merethe Sandmo from Oslo. You sat down at Sandmo's table.'

'She called herself Tanja. I didn't know what her real name was and didn't want to know either. It's correct that we met in the restaurant . . . after having intercourse. We went down separately. She went first.'

'This woman has never been connected with this sort of activity before.'

'There always has to be a first time.'

'Do you believe this was the first time she had sold sex?'

'Don't know.'

'How did you set up this meeting?'

'Over the Internet. The usual procedure.'

'I'm not familiar with the so-called "usual procedure". How did you set up the meeting?'

'There's a website which arranges appointments for prostitutes and customers. Don't have the address in my head, but you can have it later.'

'Did you meet before you went to her room?'

'No.'

Frølich and Gunnarstranda exchanged looks again. Narvesen's solicitor reacted as well. He whispered into Narvesen's ear.

'You went to her room alone, but you can't remember which room it was or what floor it was on?'

'I apologize. I expressed myself clumsily.'

'Answer the question.'

'I made a mistake. She met me in reception and we went to her room together. She was an attractive woman. I was excited and don't remember which floor or . . .'

'That's enough,' Lystad said and turned. 'You're obviously lying,' he continued. 'You're showing contempt for everything I stand for and for the public prosecuting authority as an institution. I advise you to demonstrate greater prudence when we meet in court. However, we can come back to the trial later. As regards your meeting with Merethe Sandmo, I don't believe you were in any hotel room ever. I believe you paid her, yes, but she sold you information, not sex. I believe that afterwards you drove to a chalet in Vestre Slidre. There you met Elisabeth Faremo and killed her.'

The silence hung in the room. Narvesen had blanched. The solicitor sent him a concerned look, coughed and spoke up. 'Do you have any proof for that allegation?'

'I'm working on it,' Lystad said. 'You're the vindictive type, aren't you, Narvesen?'

'Inspector Lystad,' the solicitor interrupted. 'I have to ask you to be more specific and not to make unfounded allegations.'

'Of course I'll be more specific. Narvesen, can you tell us a little about your relationship with Halvor Bede?'

Narvesen sat looking at the policeman in silence. The solicitor leaned towards him. They whispered. The solicitor spoke for him.

'You can't just throw completely new information at us out of the blue, without giving us a chance to go through . . .'

'This is not a trial,' Lystad broke in. 'We're questioning Narvesen. However, you have the right to be informed. Narvesen, shall I or will you tell your solicitor about Halvor Bede?'

Narvesen didn't answer. He sat with his interlaced fingers resting on the table in front of him.

'Halvor Bede was a Norwegian ship's officer who once took the liberty of trying to blackmail your client,' Lystad said to the solicitor. He continued: 'He was convicted and served his sentence, but was unfortunately stabbed to death by an unknown assailant on the day he was released.'

'But what has that got to do with me?' Narvesen barked. 'Bede was killed in a bar fight. Some row about a woman or God knows what. I've never been near the bar and the case was shelved years ago.'

'Shelved, yes, but not closed. You are a vindictive type, aren't you?'

'What are you getting at?'

'We'll come to that. You like setting fire to chalets, don't you, Narvesen?'

'Don't answer that kind of allegation,' the solicitor exclaimed brusquely before turning to Lystad: 'Unless you have witnesses' testimonies or concrete evidence that connects my client to this alleged murder or any other alleged crimes, I would ask you to bring this session to a close right now.'

'We will continue for as long as I deem fit,' Lystad said, looking at his watch.

'Is my client charged?'

'No.'

'Is he under suspicion?'

'Very much so.'

'You have to be more open. You have to base your accusations on evidence.'

'It will be a pleasure,' Lystad said, opening his briefcase. 'This concerns a raid carried out by the Eco-Crime division on your business premises, Narvesen. There is also a minor matter regarding the specific withdrawal of a sum of cash you made: five million kroner. I can tell you that the numbers of the notes you were given in the bank were recorded. A selection of these notes has turned up in Fagernes, the same day you admit being in Fagernes with Merethe Sandmo. It is my belief that you handed over the five million to Merethe Sandmo.'

Narvesen observed him without uttering a word.

Lystad continued: 'What I am keen to find out is what she could offer you which would be worth five million. I don't even think your solicitor believes you paid her so much for a trick in a hotel room.'

The room had gone quiet.

The solicitor cleared his throat.

Lystad looked straight at him. 'At this juncture your client has only two options. Either he can make a statement or he can refuse to make a statement. The latter would not be wise. But you can discuss the matter for a minute or two. We'll take a break.'

He left the room.

Frølich and Gunnarstranda sat watching the interview room for a few seconds.

'Lystad is good,' Frank Frølich said. 'But the most important thing now is to talk to Merethe Sandmo.'

They stood up and went into the corridor.

'She's in Greece, as you know,' Gunnarstranda said.

'But we have to get hold of her.'

'Why?'

'Because she's the only one who can explain what actually happened when she met Narvesen. And another thing, as regards the fourth robber, in fact it could have been her – Merethe Sandmo.'

'Oh?'

'I've been pondering about that,' Frølich said. 'Everything has a logical explanation. Merethe doesn't have the experience so she panics. Or was she in the whole operation against her will? That would explain why she didn't make a run for it when security arrived on the scene. Her involvement and the consequent murder might explain why she agonized and tipped off the police. It also explains why she only tipped them off about three names and not four. Which, in turn, might explain why Elisabeth Faremo felt forced to give her brother and the two others an alibi. It could also explain why the gang broke up. It might also explain why Merethe Sandmo fled from Jonny Faremo into the arms of Vidar Ballo.'

'Naturally, that is a possibility. But there is one element which her potential involvement in the robbery does not explain.'

'And what's that?'

'Vidar Ballo's dead.'

Frølich was stunned. 'How long has he been dead?'

'A long time. A hell of a long time. His body was discovered when his neighbours reacted to the stench. Possibly he went home and died after talking to me.'

'So he was dead when the chalet went up in flames?'

'There is a large, very large possibility that he was, yes.'

'What did he die of?'

'He OD'd. Usual thing, heroin, standard user's kit, huge dose, etc, not an ounce of suspicion about the death.'

Frølich was silent.

Gunnarstranda coughed and motioned with his head towards Lystad, who was waiting for them by the table: 'Shall we have some coffee before the break is over? You and I have been invited to participate more actively in the next round.'

Frølich shook his head. 'Probably not a good idea for me to take part.'

Gunnarstranda raised both eyebrows.

'The second I show myself, Narvesen and his solicitor will start the mud-slinging.'

Gunnarstranda's eyes flashed. 'Tell me what you've done!' he demanded.

'I assume he will accuse me of criminal damage.'

'What have you done?'

Frank Frølich shrugged. 'Smashed a pane of glass in his veranda door.'

'You idiot!'

'Relax. It was just tit-for-tat – for my chalet which he set alight. He hasn't got the balls to do any more than sling mud. Whatever he says, it's just wild allegations. He'll bark a bit and that'll be it. That's why I'm going now. So I don't have to concentrate on that side of the case and I can be left to reflect in peace.'

Gunnarstranda took a seat beside Lystad, whose eyes were drearily following Frølich's disappearing figure.

Lystad said: 'What's got into him?'

Gunnarstranda shrugged. 'He's been like that for some time. It'll pass.'

Frank Frølich drove around aimlessly. When he turned into Hausmannsgate, he suddenly had a brainwave and continued into Mariboes gate. He found an empty parking space opposite the entrance to the Rockefeller music hall and walked down Torggata.

He was close to Badir's shop again and bought a frankfurter from one of the kiosks in Osterhaus gate – more out of habit than hunger. Continuing towards Torggata, he stopped in front of the steps leading up to the building which housed the Torggata baths. He stood there thinking about Narvesen, who would have to explain away a cash withdrawal of five million kroner, who was making a statement about the money at this very minute. Perhaps Frølich himself was in the process of losing his job at this very minute. He raised his head and sensed the idea forming in his mind. *It doesn't matter.*

He smiled to himself and chewed at his sausage, watching the flickering movements of dark figures on their way towards Storgata. *On the positive side: I don't care. On the negative: I don't care. What is important then? Finding out who killed Elisabeth and why.*

But is Narvesen likely to talk about the painting at all?

If he does, he'll also have to explain how he came into possession of the painting in the first place. So he's hardly likely to say anything – if he doesn't have to – to avert suspicion from something else: murder. And if I lose my job in the cause of truth, it's worth it.

He eyed Badir's shop and thought about Elisabeth and Narvesen. The shop was still shut – all of a sudden he had to jump out of the way of an irate cyclist who was unable to accept that he, a pedestrian, was standing in the cycle lane in Torggata. He took another bite, watched the woman on the bike and almost choked on the sausage. He had seen her before. No, not her – someone else. The image returned. The day they staked out Badir's shop: he was walking down the steps to the former Torggata baths to await the signal. Then he had seen her – not this woman – but the image of a woman on a bike with her head down over the handlebars pedalling along Torggata. He had had one foot in the cycle lane, heard a bicycle bell ring and was forced to take a step back, out of the cycle lane. The radio crackled and he had taken up a position further along the street opposite Badir's shop. *That was where she had come from.* She had passed Badir's shop, kept cycling, so she was going somewhere else. Then she had passed him on his way down the steps. But could that have been Elisabeth?

Frank Frølich was objective now: it could have been her. He had been focused on the action; he hadn't taken any notice of her face. But she might have noticed his. She could have seen him: a face she knew from Ilijaz Zupac's trial. She might even have got off her bike without him seeing, she might have doubled back, stood looking at him for a moment, made up her mind and cycled back, pushed her bike through the cordon they were setting up. Afterwards she might have shoved her bike into his field of vision, outside Badir's shop. And then everything came back: the shriek of the cycle stand. Her entering the shop and his running across the road after her.

But what did this sudden inspiration mean?

He knew what it meant.

Gunnarstranda's words were still resounding between his ears: *Frølich! Stop being so bloody naïve! There's something not quite kosher about this bit of skirt. It doesn't matter which way you look at every single bit of what you've told me, it all boils down to a con!'*

The old fox had been right the whole time, as always – and now suddenly Frank Frølich was in a hurry.

He rang Gunnarstranda on his mobile.

'I thought you wanted to get out and reflect,' Gunnarstranda drawled.

Frølich said: 'That's why I'm ringing. Has Narvesen confessed?'

'Not yet, but we've reached an interesting phase of the questioning. Let's put it like that. It concerns Narvesen's private house, a destroyed veranda door and a certain policeman on leave.'

'Has he talked about art?'

'Art? No. Why would he?'

Frølich's brain raced.

'Why would he?' repeated Gunnarstranda impatiently.

'. . . it was just something that occurred to me – but now to something important. The bank manager in Askim said Ilijaz Zupac had been in to pick up something from the safety-deposit box, didn't he?'

'You know that.'

'It just occurred to me that Ilijaz is quite an exotic name,' Frank Frølich said slowly.

'We're not working on that case any more, Frølich. Not until our investigations have come up with a result.'

'Are you happy with that?'

'This isn't about whether I'm happy or not.'

'If Lystad wants to arrest Inge Narvesen for Elisabeth's murder, he needs a motive. Such a motive has to have some connection with the 1998 break-in. And that case is linked to the safety-deposit box. So it wouldn't hurt to ring the bank, would it?'

'One snag – what would I say to the bank staff?'

'Ask which gender the person pretending to be Ilijaz was.'

Silence at the other end.

'Gunnarstranda,' Frølich said, condescendingly. 'Please be brief.'

'I reckon you've got a point, Frølich, about gender. What put you onto that?'

'Couple of things. One of which was what you told me about Ballo's death. And it wouldn't be much hassle for you, would it? To ring the bank and ask for a description of the person using Ilijaz's name?'

Gunnarstranda considered it. 'I could check that, as a favour,' he conceded finally. 'The question is: what could you give me in return?

'Evidence.'

'What sort of evidence?'

'Evidence which would rule out all the suspicion against Narvesen. And then no one will bother about a smashed veranda door.'

'Come on, what sort of evidence?'

'A strand of hair,' said Frank Frølich.

42

The heat hit him the moment he got off the plane.

The policeman who met him in the arrivals hall was called Manuel Komnenos.

'After the emperor,' he explained with a little smile. He stood outside the customs queue with a white cardboard sign in his hand. The man had spelt his name wrong. The sign read: F-Ö-R-L-I-C-H.

Frølich shook hands and had to confess he had no idea which emperor he was talking about.

'Good,' Manuel said with a grin. He was wearing a creased grey suit and a white T-shirt. There was a big gap between his front teeth. He continued: 'Every time you hear the name Manuel you'll think: Which emperor?'

Frølich took to him from the very first second. They walked out of the arrivals hall together towards the car park. The wheels of Frølich's suitcase rumbled over the tarmac. Manuel stood behind a sloppily parked Toyota Corolla and opened the boot. Frølich put the suitcase in and said he had the same car at home. 'Well, almost – an Avensis.'

They waited behind the car. An aeroplane was hurtling down the runway in a crescendo of noise. Manuel lit a cigarette and waited for the din to subside. The aeroplane took off and rose like a hungry shark moving towards the light.

Manuel told him that Merethe Sandmo had hired a car from Hertz on 1 December. 'A Toyota.' He closed the boot lid. 'At least she knows a thing or two about cars.'

They both grinned.

Frølich looked north. An aeroplane was coming in to land. Far up in the blue he could glimpse aeroplane number two, also on its way down.

'She drove north and handed in the car at an office in Patras,' Manuel went on to say.

'She didn't hire another car?'

'No.'

'Just disappeared?'

Manuel nodded. 'Didn't check in at a hotel.'

'But what about the other woman?'

Manuel grinned again and took a deep breath. 'She appeared.'

'Where?'

'On the ferry quay. Bought a ticket to Bari.'

'Bari? That's Italy.'

Manuel waved the car keys. 'Still interested in the car?'

Frølich nodded and took the keys. 'Don't worry,' he said. 'I know where I'm going.'

The beach wound round the blue-green bay like a golden-white new moon. Heavy, leisurely waves unfurled onto the shore, stretched out, washed inland, lapped their way up the sand before retreating into a rolling wall to smash the next wave to pieces. There was a rhythm to it, first a lapping surge, then the next wave is shattered by the previous one, over and over again. Frank Frølich observed the spectacle, musing that if you stood there long enough you could eventually believe it would never end.

No one had ventured into the water. Bodies lay scattered across the sandy beach on sunbeds. Some sat up and looked around through sunglasses or rubbed sun cream over their sunburned arms. Some fat men in shorts with sun visors shading their eyes strolled along the water's edge where the sand was firmer and cooled by the sea. A woman was walking. She was wearing a sky-blue, baggy, sleeveless dress which flapped in the wind. Also an alice band in matching blue. He realized he had never told her – blue suited her.

He stood still and waited for her to discover his presence. It pleased him that she didn't falter, but continued at the same sedate pace as the waves washed over her feet and ankles.

When she was one and a half metres away, she stopped. They looked into each other's eyes.

'I'm actually on my way for a swim,' she said. 'Would you like to join me?'

An appraising gaze. Calm. He shook his head. 'I've got something for you,' he said, passing her the folded piece of paper – Reidun Vestli's suicide note.

She took the letter. Her head dropped as she read. In the end she folded the paper and tore it into small pieces while focusing on a point in the distance. The white scraps of paper fluttered in the wind and disappeared in the froth of the waves.

'How touching to see the impression it made.'

'I'm unable to concentrate.'

Frank Frølich followed her gaze, to the two uniformed men looking down on them, each with a foot on the stone wall by the road.

'Are they with you?' she asked.

'Yes.'

Her eyes, scrutinizing. 'Why?'

He didn't answer. The wind caught hold of her hair. She had to stroke it away with her hand. 'I found her,' he said eventually. 'She had taken tablets. Sent me the letter through the post. She asks you for forgiveness, but why?'

'No idea. Now and then Reidun was difficult to fathom.'

'You need to be able to concentrate to love,' he said.

She looked at him side-on. 'I'm sorry,' she said.

'What for?'

'For how you feel. It doesn't have to be like this between us.'

He had to examine her more closely before he answered. 'What there was between us was ground to dust a long time ago.'

'I don't believe that. You've come here, to me.'

'The Elisabeth I knew is dead,' he said gently. 'She was burned, but I have recovered.'

'Don't talk like that.'

'I apologize,' he answered. 'I know it was Merethe Sandmo who physically died in the fire, and the knowledge of that is only one of the many things I cannot ignore with regard to us.'

'I've found out a little about you since I saw you last,' he continued, his mind focused. 'I know, for example, that you met Inge Narvesen when you were working at Ferner Jacobsen six years ago. I know you started a relationship and went with him on a romantic holiday to Mauritius. That was more than you and I managed in the time we had together. But then I have less money to splash around.'

'Keep Inge Narvesen out of our relationship. Inge and I – it was just stupid. It was nothing.'

'Ilijaz wasn't very happy either, was he?'

She clammed up. Her blue eyes were inscrutable.

'I visited Ilijaz at Ullersmo.'

'He wasn't like that before.'

'How was he before?'

'Strong, amusing, a man who took the world for granted.' She searched for words. He waited. She faced into the wind and added: 'Who took me for granted.' She was lost in thought for a few moments. 'But Ilijaz needed to be reminded that I could be hurt, that I had feelings.'

They began to walk along the beach. The waves washed over their feet. Frank Frølich stopped and rolled up his trousers. Her feet and legs were bronzed by the sun. She had painted her nails red-brown. For a fraction of a second he imagined the scene: she was sitting in the sun with her knees raised, concentrating on varnishing her toe nails.

Her flapping dress stuck to her body, her legs clearly outlined with every step she took. She walked with her head erect, the wind tossing her black hair.

He said: 'Perhaps you went with Inge Narvesen to punish Ilijaz, but I don't think Narvesen realized. Not even when you told Ilijaz about the safe with the painting in it.'

'Ilijaz is one of God's lost sheep,' she said. 'Completely lost.'

'At that time Ilijaz was in total possession of his faculties and had to take responsibility for his actions. He shot a man dead – he didn't have to do that.'

'He's destroyed. You've met him and you know he has completely snapped. How does it feel to work for a system which does something like that to people?'

'There's only one person to blame for Ilijaz being sent to prison – and that's Ilijaz. He didn't need to steal the safe. He didn't need to shoot anyone.'

'Prison is there to deprive people of their freedom, not to cause them to rot from the inside.'

'I know you feel a need to vent your feelings of guilt, but elevating your status to a kind of avenging angel is sick.'

'What are you talking about?'

'I'm talking about you.'

'Are you accusing me of converting emotions into actions?'

'Actions *are* your problem, Elisabeth, because people die.'

'I can't take responsibility for anyone except myself.'

He stopped and laughed.

'What's so funny?'

'Your pompous nonsense.' He imitated her: '"I can't take responsibility for anyone except myself." *You*, the person who asked Ilijaz and your brother to steal the painting so that you could sell it back to Narvesen afterwards. *You*, who started off all this business, *you* cannot take responsibility for anyone except yourself?'

She didn't answer; she just glanced at him out of the corner of her eye. They resumed their walk in silence, side by side. Frank Frølich broke the silence: 'I know you postponed selling the painting back when Ilijaz was imprisoned, but for some reason you planned to sell it back without the others knowing. Why?'

Again she didn't answer.

'I've understood that you joined forces with Merethe Sandmo – against the men – that night in November when she went with the gang as a driver, when your brother and she were witnesses to murder.'

She stopped.

He said: 'I woke up when you were talking to Merethe. And I realize she must have been very depressed when she told you about the guard who was knocked to the ground, but how did you get her to tip off the police?'

'You're wrong,' she snapped. 'What must you think of me?' Her blue eyes flashed. 'Merethe was a stupid cow. Why would I ask her to squeal on my own brother? When Merethe rang, she'd already talked to the police. She rang me to talk about it, to be comforted. That just tells you how downright simple-minded this woman was. She had begged again and again to take part in one of the jobs; she wanted the kicks. When she finally got her way she came face to face with reality. And then the daft bitch chose to ring the cops and tell them what had happened!'

'Perhaps she wanted someone to help the man who was dying?' Frank Frølich objected meekly. 'He was lying in a pool of blood.'

'If that was the idea, she wouldn't have needed to give names, but she told the cops who was on the job – she named everyone except herself. So I was forced to stand up for my brother. You know that – don't you?'

The sapphire eyes were soft again. Three shades of blue, he thought. The sky, the dress and her eyes.

They suddenly came closer. 'When I left you that night,' she whispered, 'it was because I had to help Jonny. But I didn't want to get you involved, do you understand? I couldn't know you were going to work on that very case, could I?'

Frølich was staring at her hand. Her long, slim fingers were stroking his forearm.

'I see it a little differently,' he answered in a whisper.

Her fingers stopped caressing him.

'You left the key to the safety-deposit box at my place.'

'It was secure there.'

'Very practical as well. When the men were banged up, you got hold of the second key. When they were released, you were on your way to Askim with one key in your pocket and the other in safekeeping at my flat. You drove to Askim after giving your testimony at the hearing. You identified yourself as Ilijaz Zupac at the bank. You took the painting from the vault.'

She was gazing at the horizon, silent.

'Didn't Jonny know what you were planning?' he asked.

She didn't answer.

'So he did know,' he concluded.

'Have you ever thought that when a plane is moving down the runway to take off,' she said, 'it's something absolute, final. Acceleration increases, it goes faster and faster. But the runway is so short that when it has reached sufficient speed it would be impossible for it to stop. Putting on the brakes would cause a disaster. There's only one solution, to keep going, to get the plane off the ground.'

'Jonny met you there, in the bank, didn't he?'

'What do you actually want?' she said, irritated. 'Have you come here to tell me how smart you are?'

'For me personally, it's important to have the facts out in the open.'

'Why?'

'Because, basically, this is about you, about me, about us.'

They looked into each other's eyes again. 'Are you sure?' she asked softly.

'I know Jonny drove to Askim while you were there. I know he was seen with another person on a tractor track leading down to the Glomma. I know your brother either slipped and fell into the river or he was pushed by the person he was with. Would you help me to complete the picture?'

'What do you mean, this is about us?' she asked again.

'Jonny was in Askim,' he persisted. 'You were there too.'

She turned to him. Her blue eyes observed him from a distance, dreamily. 'I don't believe you. For you, this is not about us. It's just about you.'

'Was his drowning an accident?'

'Of course! What did you think?'

'Who suggested going for a walk by the river?'

'I did.'

'Why?'

'To calm him down.'

'I'm not sure if I believe you.'

'You can believe what you like. No one will ever come between me and my brother.'

'But you didn't ring emergency services when he fell in – although the river has a strong current and the water was damned cold. Jonny would have had hypothermia, but he could still have been rescued. The air ambulance would have been there in minutes.'

'You don't know what you're talking about. You just focus on yourself and your own self-pity.'

'Maybe I don't know what happened on the river bank, but I know you went back to his car alone, drove off, contacted Reidun Vestli and asked for help. You met her after getting rid of Jonny's car, you hid in her chalet. I know you got in touch with Narvesen, made him go to Fagernes and meet Merethe Sandmo. I know he paid her five million in cash to get the painting back. The thing I'm curious about is what triggered the whole process. Was it me?'

She smiled with disdain at the last word. The wind played with her long hair and the waves lapped over her feet.

'You always have to be the centre of attention, don't you?' she said. 'I'm not like that. I did what I did because I never think about myself. It's all Merethe's fault. She started everything. She blew the whistle. I had no option but to stand firm behind Jonny . . .'

'You never think about yourself? Merethe Sandmo did what *you* told her to. She took the picture to Narvesen, got the money and then went to Reidun Vestli's chalet. There, you took the money before killing her and setting fire to the chalet. You appropriated her identity and used her ticket to Athens. To plan this and execute it, you must have been absolutely furious with her. Anyone who is that furious with another person does not focus on anyone except themselves.'

'I haven't killed anyone. And you don't know what you're talking about.'

'On the contrary, I know very well what I'm talking about. I've been round the whole circuit. Starting the night I had to go down and look at the murdered security man, a young man, a student doing a part-time job. Clubbed to death.'

'Jim Rognstad killed the man. He's got nothing to do with me.'

'But you gave Rognstad an alibi for the murder. Isn't that playing on the same team as him?'

She didn't answer; she looked across the sea. On the horizon there were two enormous tankers sailing in a line.

'You didn't have to give the men an alibi for that night,' Frank Frølich said.

'Frank,' she said gently. 'Why don't you believe me?'

'I'm not saying what I believe; I'm saying what I know. For example, I know you recognized me in Torggata before the stake-out on Badir's shop. You doubled back, placed yourself in my field of vision, you wanted my attention.'

'I had no idea what was going to happen. I just wanted you to see me. But it was you who threw yourself on me.' She snatched a sidelong glance and smiled wanly. 'Do you remember?'

'What I remember best is that you sat beside me in bed that night, waiting for me to go back to sleep so that you could sneak out and start the whole nightmare.'

They stood still, without speaking. The wind was pulling at her clothes. The waves crashed onto the shore.

He was startled by the touch of her fingers on the back of his hand.

'Do you sometimes think that the earth looks blue?' she whispered. 'Seen from afar?'

'What makes you say that?'

'Everything that has happened between you and me depends on where you're standing, Frank. I know you're bitter because I didn't say anything to you that night, but I'd been told Jonny was going to be arrested for killing a man he hadn't even touched. You were a policeman. I kept you out of it and I did what I thought was right.'

He looked down at her hand. It was the first thing he had noticed: her hands. Her black gloved fingers putting packs of cigarettes into her rucksack. The same fingers which were stroking him now closed around his hand. The warmth from her hand shot up his forearm. He closed his eyes for a second, feeling her touch. Then he put his hand in his pocket and said: 'Did you do what you thought was right when you went back to your flat and cleaned it thoroughly? When you planted Merethe's hairbrush on your bed for the police to find? So that they would use Merethe's DNA profile to identify the bones in Reidun Vestli's chalet? When you made Merethe spread rumours about her having a job in Athens? When you made her buy a plane ticket?'

She didn't answer.

'Was it right to kill her?'

'If anyone killed Merethe it must have been Vidar Ballo. I don't know anything about Merethe or what happened to her.'

'Jim Rognstad may have killed the guard in Loenga. Your brother may have slipped into the river by accident. Reidun Vestli did take her own life. But Vidar Ballo cannot have killed Merethe. He was dead from an overdose when the chalet burned down.'

Frølich put his hand in his inside pocket and passed her a sheet of paper. 'Another copy.'

She read the copy of Reidun Vestli's suicide note and began to tear up this letter into small pieces too.

'I read through the letter again on the plane coming here,' Frølich said. 'And I wondered for the umpteenth time what it was that Reidun was asking forgiveness for. Were you supposed to forgive her for leading some nasty brutes to your bolthole? Who were these brutes? When her chalet was on fire, Jim Rognstad was with a woman in Oslo and Vidar Ballo was dead, so if those two didn't set fire to the chalet, who beat up Reidun Vestli? And why was she only beaten up *after* the fire? The answer to that was difficult to unearth, precisely because no one beat her up. She faked the attack. She wanted the police to believe that *someone* beat the information out of her to track you down. If necessary she would *claim* the assault was carried out by Rognstad and Ballo. She would be believed because she was a respected academic. But while she was simulating the attack she must have known about parts of your plan. She must have sacrificed the chalet. But if there weren't any attackers, the one single, large, in fact the real, issue remains unresolved: Why is she asking for forgiveness?'

'A few minutes ago you said this was about us, Frank. Why did you say that?'

'If you won't answer, let me do it for you. Reidun is asking for forgiveness because she's dropping out. She couldn't stand being part of your blood-stained steeplechase. She didn't have your motivation. All she had was love for you. But that only went as far as an appeal for forgiveness. *You* were the one who planned the fake attack. *You* wanted the police to believe someone had beaten her up and she'd betrayed where *you* were hiding. To suggest that *someone* wanted to find you and take your life. In this way you would be able to divert the blame for the fire and your murder. But Reidun Vestli didn't want to be an accessory to murder. She therefore opted out of your insanity – and begs your forgiveness.'

She shook her head. 'That's the craziest story I've ever heard.'

He smiled; his lips were dry. 'It's not over yet. You were enraged by Merethe, I know that. And perhaps you blamed her for Jonny's death. Wherever you stand on this, whatever fantasies you have, the fact is that you overlooked a couple of tiny details when you planned your revenge. You forgot, for example, that you should have worn a hairnet when you slept in my bed. You left one long hair on my pillow the night you left me. The DNA profile did *not* tally with the hair on Merethe Sandmo's hairbrush and it did *not* tally with the bones in the ashes of the chalet. Your story, Elisabeth, hung on a hair. I have an irritating terrier of a boss and when I brought in your hair and forensics found there was a mismatch, he had to go to Merethe Sandmo's flat and get further samples there. Guess what? The samples matched.'

She stood still, looking at the hotel. The wind was still ruffling her dress.

'Merethe Sandmo was on a plane to Athens. Although, according to the evidence, she was dead,' he said. 'The same woman who called herself Merethe Sandmo got off the plane and hired a car which she drove to Patras where the car and the keys were handed over to the Hertz agent. And this is where Merethe Sandmo vanishes. Into thin air. At the ferry quay, though, in the same town another woman turns up: Elisabeth Faremo. She buys a ferry ticket to Bari, on the Italian side of the Adriatic Sea. Elisabeth Faremo disappears here, but a woman by the name of Merethe Sandmo turns up two days later in Ancona on the coast. She buys a ticket to Zadar in Croatia. The woman who bought the hotel there is unknown. It was a long detour, but your problem is that the woman who owns the hotel paid her bills with Norwegian currency, the numbers of which are recorded with Eco-Crime. Elisabeth, there is a whole team of policemen who know that Narvesen's money is financing your stay here.'

'Have you come all the way here, have you tracked me down, just to tell me these things?'

He stood looking at her. Suddenly the situation seemed unimportant. He thought about the collection of poems he had found. The conversation in bed when she had told him the name of this island.

'I've been waiting for you,' she continued. 'But I wanted you to be driven here by longing, not negative emotions.' She placed her hand on his arm, stretched up on her toes and brushed his cheek with her lips. He remembered her touch.

'I knew,' she whispered, 'that you would come here and find me.'

He tore himself free. 'It's too late.'

'No,' she said. 'Nothing is too late.'

'Why did you do it?' he whispered, despising his own wretchedness. 'At least you can give me this. You can tell me what the sense of it all was.'

'I have nothing without Jonny.'

He thought about what she said. 'Do you mean that nothing would have happened, that life would have been normal if Jonny . . .'

'Now I have only you,' she interrupted.

'That's not true, Elisabeth. You left me behind.'

'I've been waiting for you,' she repeated.

'But we can never belong to each other.'

A minor eternity passed. Only the sound of waves murmuring. Two metres between them. When they finally looked into each other's eyes, he could read that something had happened. She was in a different place.

'You've forgotten one thing,' she said roughly.

'Remind me.'

'Inge Narvesen will keep his mouth shut. He will never say anything in public about having a stolen painting in his possession. You have nothing on me. Without the painting your story is so much thin air. Without the painting, there would have been nothing to collect from the bank vault. Without the painting, there was nothing to sell to Inge. You were quite right, I used Merethe's name and ticket to get away, but I had to, I feared for my life. Someone had killed my brother and then Merethe.'

'The painting?' Frank Frølich asked in surprise. 'What sort of painting are you talking about?'

'You know very well which painting I'm talking about.'

'If you mean the study of the mother and child which disappeared from an Italian church in 1993, the painting has disappeared, just as it did in 1993. No one has seen it since. If anyone claims they have seen it in Norway, they must be having delusions. The painting is not there, you see. Sorry, Elisabeth. What is important in this case is the human remains in the ashes of the chalet. Back home in Norway, the police have proof that the woman received five million kroner in cash from Inge Narvesen. He has finished making a statement about this. At first he tried to make Kripos believe that Merethe was selling him sex. But five million for sex is a bit on the steep side, so they didn't believe him. In the end, he admitted that Merethe Sandmo had told him some cock-and-bull story about a Renaissance painting he could have for five million. He was foolish enough to believe her and stumped up. The painting never showed up. He paid her and received nothing. He was swindled. And attractive women who dupe idiots with pots of money are the sort of thing to make Norwegian judges yawn. Unless the painting turns up, that part of the story is of no interest. What will interest judges are the cleverly worked-out plans behind your new life down here. You used Reidun Vestli to underpin the enactment of your own death. You used Merethe Sandmo as a go-between to barter for the money. It is proved that you took the money from Merethe – since you've been spending it every day – and killed her – since you have assumed her identity and escaped using her name.'

When he finished she was standing as before with her gaze directed towards the sea.

He gestured with his head towards the hotel. 'Shall we go?'

'Are you in such a hurry?' Different intonation yet again. Almost cheerful.

They looked into each other's eyes. He attempted to see inside and interpret what was going on in the black wells surrounded by the blue lustre, but he gave up.

'Surely you won't deny me a last wish,' she continued with a mocking smile.

'It will have to be a modest wish then.'

'I said I was going to go swimming. If you like, you can join me.'

He stared at the water and hesitated.

She began to undress. Soon she stood in front of him wearing a bikini. The wind caressed her black hair. Once again she brushed her lips against his cheek. 'Do you dare to be so decent?'

He sat on the sand as she walked to the water's edge. He watched her attractive form wading in, her bronzed legs ploughing through the foaming sea, her swaying hips. The water must have been cold – no one else had ventured out. Yet she went on undeterred. When she started swimming, he stood up to see her better. He scanned the sea for her dark hair which was hidden by the waves until it bobbed up again. Disappeared. Bobbed up. Disappeared.

He thought about what she had said.

He scanned the sea in vain.

He felt a paralysis spreading across his body.

When he finally managed to turn away and ran to the hotel the two policemen were already on their way across the sand.

43

'And that was fine with you? Her going into the sea?'

Frølich didn't answer.

'Go on,' Gunnarstranda said in a monotone.

'She undressed . . .'

'Concentrate on the essentials.'

Frølich scratched his cheek. 'She waded into the sea without looking back.'

'And?'

'When the water was up to her waist she started swimming into the open sea.'

'Was anyone else swimming?'

'No one.'

Gunnarstranda gave him a stern look.

'There was nothing to hide behind, no mountain, no rock, no boat, not even a beach ball, nothing but sand and sea.'

'You could have refused.'

'Perhaps I could have said it was not permitted, but what then? I didn't have the authority to arrest her. That was up to the Croatian police.'

'But you shouldn't have been on your own with her.'

'Listen . . .'

'No,' Gunnarstranda interrupted him angrily. 'It's you who should listen. You were entrusted with bringing her back to Norway. But she's gone. Disappeared! *Your* ex-lover goes swimming and disappears.'

'The local police explained about the currents in the sea. She drowned.'

'And you accept that? That she simply disappeared?'

'We've got the money, her things, passport, bank card, all her personal items. Believe me, Elisabeth Faremo is dead.'

'That woman has been dead once before, Frølich!' Gunnarstranda stood up and went to the door. He turned before leaving. They faced each other. 'The case is closed,' Gunnarstranda announced. 'Are you happy?'

Frank Frølich didn't answer. He absentmindedly watched the door closing. In his mind he had one single image: the figure of a sun-tanned woman in a blue bikini leisurely wading further and further out into the sea without looking back. He raised his hand to scratch his cheek again. It wouldn't stop itching. He continued scratching. It began to smart. He put his hand on his thigh. His cheek still smarted. He couldn't get the idea out of his head. It smarted and burned precisely where she had touched his cheek with her lips before turning to wade into the sea.